Sam's Crossing

Sam's Crossing

Tommy Hays

Atheneum
New York 1992

Maxwell Macmillan Canada
Toronto

Maxwell Macmillan International
New York   Oxford   Singapore   Sydney

Atheneum   Maxwell Macmillan Canada, Inc.
Macmillan Publishing Company   1200 Eglinton Avenue East
866 Third Avenue   Suite 200
New York, NY 10022   Don Mills, Ontario M3C 3N1

Macmillan Publishing Company is part of the Maxwell Communication Group of Companies.

Library of Congress Cataloging-in-Publication Data
Hays, Tommy.
        Sam's crossing / by Tommy Hays.
            p. cm.
        ISBN 0-689-12169-5
        I. Title.
        PS3558.A875S26   1991
        813'.54—dc20   92-13294

Macmillan Books are available at special discounts for bulk purchases for sales promotions, premiums, fund-raising, or educational use. For details, contact:

                    Special Sales Director
                    Macmillan Publishing Company
                    866 Third Avenue
                    New York, NY 10022

10 9 8 7 6 5 4 3 2 1

Printed in the United States of America

For Connie

Sam's Crossing

Chapter One

In the twilight, Stone Mountain rose above Highway 78 like a dark wedge of premature night—a monadnock, Willy had once called it, something formed when everything wears down around it—making Sam think, as he sat in the backseat listening to Kate and Willy, that hearts should be made of granite.

Willy threaded the VW bus through light outbound traffic, sipping from the last can of Stroh's. Kate traced "Wash Me" on the inside of her window and ate French fries from an Arby's bag on her lap.

"Couldn't they've chosen a little safer place to camp?" Kate asked.

"Like the backyard?" Willy squinted into the rearview mirror.

"But the Okefenokee?"

Sam rolled down his window. He smelled the acrid diesel of tractor-trailers and behind it the warm, spongy oncoming of spring. It was only March. Winter had been so mild, more of a lull than a season. Willy said it was the greenhouse effect, that cold was something our grandchildren would ask us about.

Kate reached for Willy's beer and took a sip. Sam watched her. Sometimes it took the distance of disagreement to remind him she was pretty—not in a conventional way, with her thin face and the sweeping curve of her cheekbones. She always looked older than she was, but she never looked old. Hers was a face you might find in a fourteenth-

1

century religious painting. That she wore Sam's old clothes softened her face—a Madonna in a flannel shirt.

A tractor-trailer rumbled up right behind them, flashing its brights for Willy to move over.

Willy lifted a finger in the rearview. He had to floor it, slipping into a gap in the next lane just as the truck seemed about to mow them down. It brushed past, rocking the bus.

Even with his leather jacket, hair down to his shoulders, and scruffy beard, there was no mistaking Willy's resemblance to his older sister. He had the same thin face, the same cheekbones. The only difference was that if Kate had an almost beatific presence, Willy had the wasted, hollow-eyed look youth can afford.

Another tractor-trailer swept past them, rocking the bus again.

Sam watched brother and sister from the backseat. In the presence of such delicate good looks, he felt clunky. His eyebrows were too thick, his nose too broad, his forehead too high, his mouth too wide. His features were unsubtle and overstated. People expected things from a face like his—strong opinions, swift action, immediate resolution—which from childhood had made him self-conscious and shy. From the time he was a little boy, he hunched his shoulders and often stared at the ground, assuming the posture of a walking question mark.

Willy shifted down as the traffic slowed for a lane closed for construction.

"Aren't you the least bit worried that at this very moment our mother is canoeing among several hundred pairs of hungry alligator eyes?" Kate asked.

"They've taken alligators off the endangered-species list," Willy said.

Kate sighed. "Several *thousand* alligator eyes."

Maggie, who was Kate and Willy's mother, had gone on a camping trip with a friend to the Okefenokee. She had rafted the Colorado last year, hiked the Himalayas the year before; she'd rappelled the Rockies, gone caving in the Smokies. Sam didn't understand why Kate worried about her now. Canoeing the Okefenokee was the safest thing she'd done in years.

They passed men in hard hats raking gravel and smoothing tar behind a row of orange barrels while dump trucks and bulldozers growled in the shadows, stirring up dust and rock. Roads were always widening in Atlanta, like rivers spilling over their banks.

Sam turned to look behind them, seeing downtown Atlanta, a distant cluster of skyscrapers, most of which were so new that they made downtown look contrived.

Kate tapped her window, pointing at a Corvette that had pulled even with them. "What do people with tinted windows have to hide?"

Sam looked across at the black windows. "That's what they want you to wonder."

"He's still with us." Kate handed the fries back to Sam.

"I thought he'd astral-projected to the Gobi Desert." Willy smiled at him in the rearview mirror.

Sam ate a couple of French fries. "If I astral-project anywhere, it'll be to the beach."

"The beach," Kate said wistfully. "Oh, to feel heat again." She took another sip of beer and passed it back to Sam. "The rest is yours."

Kate's face was half-hidden by her long black hair, so he couldn't see her expression, but Sam took the beer as a sign of forgiveness since this afternoon's argument, which was more of a standoff, the latest in a series.

"She wants a baby," he'd whispered to Willy when they'd stopped earlier at Arby's. Kate had gone to the rest room.

"So?" Willy shrugged.

"How can I even think about being a father when I'm not sure I have what it takes to be a husband?" Sam kept his eye on the rest-room door. "I don't think anybody should have kids till they've got love, happiness, and a sizable savings account."

"You're talking extinction." Willy flicked his hair back over his shoulder.

They were almost to the Stone Mountain exit when Kate asked Willy to pull over. She wanted to drive.

"You don't know how to drive a stick shift," Willy said.

"Sam's been giving me lessons." She held a barrette in her mouth as she gathered her hair and clipped it back.

"I don't know if you're ready for traffic." Sam had taken her out to an empty Kmart parking lot a couple of times and let her drive his old Tempest. "The shift on my car is on the steering column, and this one's on the floor."

"Pull over." She tugged on Willy's sleeve.

"In the middle of the highway?"

Sam recognized a calculated recklessness in her tone. Usually she got like this at parties after she'd had a little too much to drink. She'd dance close to the men and wildly with the women.

"Come on, pull over."

Willy gave her a long look, then pulled into a brightly lit used-car lot that had a big blinking sign that said Nice Cars. Sam thought if he were going to buy a car, he'd buy it here. One time, when he and Kate were driving in the mountains, they'd stopped at a place called Good Food. It was the best meal he'd ever had in his life.

Kate climbed into the driver's seat, sliding it forward so that her feet reached the brakes. She adjusted the rear-view mirror, glancing at Sam. "Prepare to meet your maker."

"This is first, that's second, this up here is third. . . ." As Willy guided her hand through the gears, Sam snapped on his seat belt. In the few years they'd lived together Kate had been in more car accidents than he could count. None serious, but he didn't understand how someone so vigilant about life in general could overlook stop signs and traffic lights.

Kate drove the last couple of miles, grinding from one gear to another. Cars and trucks whizzed around them at seventy-five and eighty miles an hour, while they crawled along at thirty-five. Sam stopped turning around, certain that he was about to become a hood ornament for some sixteen-wheeler.

Willy reached over and put on the warning flashers.

Even Kate breathed a sigh of relief when she exited at the Stone Mountain ramp. A long line of slow-moving cars led to the park's front gate.

"Surely all these people haven't come to climb the mountain." Kate jammed the shift into second.

"The laser show." Willy hit his forehead. "God, I forgot they'd started those back up."

Every time the traffic moved, Kate let up on the clutch too fast, and the car cut off. She'd crank it and inch the car forward a few more feet. "Practice makes perfect."

It was dark by the time they reached the parking lot. Orange-vested men, frowning with responsibility, brandished their red-coned flashlights.

Kate pulled into a space between two cars. She forgot to turn off the engine before she let up on the clutch. The bus lurched forward and then stalled.

"We're here." She hopped down out of the bus.

"Thank God," Willy whispered over the seat to Sam.

"I heard that," Kate said.

A stream of people walked past, carrying blankets, coolers, and lawn chairs. They were headed in the direction of the music—"I Heard It Through the Grapevine." Light shone through the trees from the field beyond, where a muddled announcer's voice was lost in the loud applause.

As they joined the line of people, an old black woman carrying a quilt misstepped ahead of them and crumpled onto the gravel.

Kate ran up to the woman, who sat in the middle of the parking lot, her legs splayed. Her pocketbook still hung on her arm.

"Are you all right?" Kate bent down beside her.

The woman blinked, looking around her, disoriented.

Willy and Sam hurried over.

The woman started to pick herself up.

"Let us help." Kate took her arm as Sam and Willy got on either side and gently lifted her.

"Are you hurt?" Kate asked.

"Can you stand?" Sam still held her.

"I'm fine." She waved Willy and Sam away.

Kate dusted off the woman's skirt.

"If I'd watched where I was walking . . ."

"Nana! Nana!" A little girl in pigtails ran up to them from between some parked cars. "Are you okay, Nana? What did they do to you?" She sneered at Kate, Willy, and Sam.

"Hush, Letitia." The woman pulled the little girl back into her skirt. "These nice people helped me up."

A short, young black man, wearing glasses, pushed through the people, hefting a cooler and a couple of lawn chairs. When he saw the old woman holding on to the little girl and Kate, Willy, and Sam standing across from them, he dropped the cooler onto the gravel and rolled up his sleeves. "What's going on here, Aunt Myrtle?" His tone was weary, yet irked.

"I tripped over myself, and this nice lady helped me up, Horace." The woman shook her head.

"I hope you didn't sprain anything." Kate dusted off the woman's quilt, handing it back to her.

The man squinted at Kate in the dark. "Kate? Kate Sterling? Is that you?"

"Dr. Franklin?"

"Y'all know each other?" Sam asked.

"Dr. Franklin," she said, "this is my friend Sam Marshbanks."

"Horace Franklin." The doctor clasped Sam's hand. "Didn't we meet at the staff Christmas party last year?"

Kate introduced Willy, who leaned against the trunk of a car, his hands in his pockets.

"This is my great-aunt Myrtle Franklin." The doctor put his arm around the old woman and rested his hand on the little girl's head. "And my daughter, Letitia."

"Letitia Mae," the little girl corrected.

"She was born with the big head." Myrtle pulled the little girl back into her skirts. "Inherited it." She nodded at the doctor, who bent down on one knee to Letitia.

"This lady works at the hospital. She's the social worker."

"Do you look after the babies, too?" the little girl asked Kate.

"She looks after the parents," the doctor said.

They stood there a minute longer, having run out of niceties. More people still passed by on their way to the field. Sam noticed that Kate seemed at a loss for words, which was a rarity.

Finally, she did say something. "Can we help y'all carry some stuff?" She grabbed one side of the cooler.

"Let me give you a hand." Sam picked up the end Kate had started to pick up. The doctor and Sam lifted the cooler between them.

Kate took the old woman by the arm as they fell in line behind Sam and the doctor and joined the crowd moving toward the music.

Letitia and Willy walked ahead. Willy carried the lawn chairs.

"Are you her boyfriend?" Letitia asked Willy, nodding back at Kate.

"Her brother."

"Is he her boyfriend?" She nodded back toward Sam.

"Why? Are you in the market for one?" Willy asked.

The little girl shook her head. "Don't want to be tied down."

The six of them melted into the long line of people that snaked through the dark pines. The music stopped. Sam could hear voices and the sound of hundreds of people walking through the woods. A thousand twigs snapped underfoot.

There was a loud crackle, then a pop and a flash through the trees, like thunder and lightning. Then another and another, as if a storm were suddenly right on top of them. Soft strains of "Dixie" began to play, followed by the "Battle Hymn of the Republic."

"And I thought we'd settled all that," the doctor said.

Sam realized that what they were hearing was the sounds of battle.

"It's starting." The little girl ran ahead.

"Letitia," Myrtle called after her. "Letitia Mae Franklin."

The little girl froze in her tracks.

"You get back here and hold somebody's hand."

The woods opened onto a row of trailer stands, where black men and women wearing little white hats sold soft drinks, beer, and hot dogs. The smoke from a barbecue stand stung Sam's eyes. People came away from it holding their dripping sandwiches out in front of them, their faces smeared with sauce.

Past the concession stands was a field filled with picnickers stretching all the way to the mountainside. Blankets and quilts carpeted the field, and parents slumped against coolers or sat up in lawn chairs as they ate sandwiches and drank beer while keeping an eye on their children, who had already found other children to run between the blankets with. Vendors worked the crowd, their necks and hands on fire with fluorescent necklaces and wands. Everyone seemed oblivious to the ghostly Confederate dream that hovered over them, an immense carving of Robert E. Lee, Stonewall Jackson, and Jefferson Davis on horseback.

After they found a place and helped the doctor and his aunt spread out the quilt, they said good-bye and picked their way back across the field, past the concession stands, toward the trail up the mountain.

"It's a giant party." Kate sipped from her beer. Horace had insisted they each take one.

They had to step over a lot of couples kissing, some of them pretty passionately. "Tacky" was the word that came to Sam—the same "tacky" his mother used in reference to toothpick sucking in public. But he wouldn't mind pulling Kate down with him right now, right here, with these thousand other people in the semidark. It'd be a whole different kind of solitude.

Willy stopped at one of the stands to get a hot pretzel. It didn't matter that they'd just eaten. Willy ate constantly, always nibbling on something—a candy bar, crackers, cookies, a banana, or just a piece of toast.

While Willy was in line for the pretzel, Kate went to the bathrooms behind the concession stands, leaving Sam alone, underneath a streetlight. A red-haired woman in a miniskirt and black fishnet stockings came over to him.

"Jack? Are you Jack?" She had to shout over the blasting music.

"No," Sam said.

"What?" The music was very loud.

"I said no!" He talked into her ear.

Her face fell. "Are you sure? You look just like he described himself."

"I'm sure!" He smelled beer on her breath.

She squinted at him through her mascara. "What if you are him? You might've seen me and decided you didn't want to go through with it."

"I swear," Sam said. "I'm not me!" He paused. "I mean I'm not him, Jack, the guy you're looking for!"

She frowned.

"You want to see my license?" He started to take out his wallet.

"Maybe Jack's not your real name. Maybe you made it up so that if you saw me and didn't like me, you could be Sam. Maybe Sam is your real name!"

"Sam is my real name!" He was losing patience.

"So you are Jack!"

They both laughed.

Looking around the crowd, she bit her finger. "I don't want to face the fact that I've been stood up." She moved back out of the light. "Sorry to have bothered you." Then she turned around, cocking her head at him. "Could I interest you in being Jack for the night?"

"I'm with someone." Sam looked off in the direction of the bathrooms. No sign of Kate. He could see Willy still standing in line at the concession stand.

"What?" She leaned her ear toward him.

"I'm with someone!"

She waited for the applause to subside. "Too bad," she said. "Funny, you're just how I pictured him—medium height, slight build, and a little on the wan side. . . ."

"You mean hollow-chested."

She traced her finger above his eyes. "I didn't imagine such bushy eyebrows. They grow together."

"My mother used to pluck them with tweezers."

"Grace?" A man's voice called from the other side of the concession stands.

"That must be him." Grace squeezed Sam's hand. "Some other time." She moved off into the crowd. He touched his eyebrows.

A hand slipped around his waist, startling him. It was Kate's. "Who was that?"

"Never seen her before in my life," he said.

"You talked to her long enough." She turned her face up to his.

"Okay. She's an old flame I ran into."

"You didn't talk to her long enough for that." Kate turned down the collar on Sam's jacket.

"She's a new flame I arranged to meet here."

"You wouldn't have talked to her at all, then."

Sam tapped her chest. "Why don't you tell me who she was."

Willy loped back from the concession stand, carrying three soft pretzels in wax paper. They stood at the edge of the field and washed down the warm, salty dough with their beers. Laser lights spun and exploded across the mountainside.

"Is it called an affair even if you aren't married?" Kate licked her fingers.

"That's just 'cheating.'" Willy crumpled up the wax paper and tossed it ten feet into a garbage can.

"Come on, Kate," Sam said. "You don't seriously believe—"

She took him by the arm as they headed around the edge of the field into the dark, where the trail began. "I can't picture you coming on to anybody."

"I can think of a more straightforward compliment."

Willy walked ahead of them, shining his pocket flashlight.

She fell in behind Willy as the three of them walked single file up the trail, the flashlight cutting a tunnel of light through the trees.

Halfway up, the trail steepened, and the pines thinned, giving way to shrubs and patches of granite whose flecks of mica glittered in the moonlight. Willy turned off his flashlight. They saw better without it.

Sam sat down on a rock to tie his shoe.

"Race you to the top," Kate said to Willy.

Sam watched them streak up the last part of the trail, which was mostly bald rock. Kate and Willy were in such good shape, especially considering that neither of them exercised. They'd both been star track runners in high school, although Sam would've never found out if he and Kate hadn't been rummaging through Maggie's basement one afternoon and found a box of old trophies—all first-place finishes. He wondered if there were other dusty secrets.

When he reached the top, Willy and Kate were perched on the ledge, catching their breath and dangling their legs over the thousand-foot drop.

The wind was pretty stiff. It was always ten degrees cooler up here.

Kate pointed to the Atlanta skyline, which blazed with city lights.

Sam sat between them and folded his legs in his lap. He could never bring himself to dangle them over the edge. Cautiously, he leaned out. The drop was precipitous. The field below was a crazy quilt of blankets.

"A few folks down there." Kate pulled Sam's old shirt closer around her.

"A couple of thousand," Willy said.

"What're they all talking about?"

"Oat bran," Sam said.

Red, green, and blue blades of laser light cut through the air and wheeled across the mountainside. "Born to Be Wild" echoed up to them.

"Daddy used to bring us up here at night sometimes," Kate said, "before they ever had these laser shows."

"I don't remember that," Willy said.

"You were too young. We all came. Me, you, and Maggie and Daddy. We sat right here and looked at the lights. I remember one night the moon was full and we could see the carving clearly." She nodded at the memorial of the three Confederate heroes. "Maggie said that instead of the generals, they should've carved the generals' wives sitting at home, waiting for bad news."

Willy lit a joint. They passed it around. Sam was surprised to see Kate smoke. She'd sworn off marijuana ever since she'd read, in a study in *Reader's Digest*, that women who smoked marijuana were more likely to have retarded children.

Kate pinched the joint between her fingers, took a long, deep drag, then threw her head back to look up at the sky. "I always forget about stars." She passed the joint to Sam.

He waved it away. "Horace is married?".

She handed it to Willy. "Divorced. He has partial custody of Letitia. The mother lives in D.C. Letitia shuttles back and forth."

"That'd be enough to make a child schizo." Willy took a drag.

Kate waved her hand toward the sky. "Think how long it takes starlight to travel."

"All those stars could be dead now." Willy lay down on the wall and looked up.

"How do we know we aren't stars to each other?" Kate asked.

"Come again?"

"Couldn't we all be dead, too? We see each other. We hear each other. We can even touch each other. But how do we know our senses don't deceive us? How do we know that the person we see isn't already history?" Kate threw her head back and laughed. "This is the trouble with marijuana."

Laser lights shot across the mountainside in different patterns, spun in and out of each other, changed colors, throbbed in time to the music. The lights were projected from a small building at the back of the field. The beams knifed the air, solid enough to walk on.

Kate took another drag, then leaned way out over the edge. "Do y'all ever get the urge to throw yourself off?"

Willy rolled over on his side and looked down. "You'd die of fright before you hit."

"That's comforting." Sam sat back. "Be careful. What if a strong wind comes?"

Kate leaned out a little farther. "Sometimes when I'm like this, I feel something tug on me."

"Otherwise known as gravity," Willy said.

Sam leaned over a little bit. "High places always remind me of *The Bridge of San Luis Rey*."

Kate laughed, then leaned back and rested her head against his shoulder. "I haven't thought about that book since eighth grade."

Willy lit another joint, took a drag, and handed it to Sam, who handed it to Kate.

"There goes fifty points off your kids' SATs," he said.

"What do you care?" She took a long drag. "You don't want kids." She passed the joint back to Willy.

"I said I wasn't ready."

"I'm thirty-two years old," she said. "Thirty-three in a couple of months."

"Some women have children when they're forty."

"I want to be a parent, not a grandparent."

"You're being overly dramatic."

"You're being overly you."

The music changed to an old Stones song. Kate picked herself up and danced around the ledge. The first time Sam had glimpsed Kate was at the bookstore Halloween party. She'd come as a Gypsy and danced most of the night in a corner by herself.

"This is excellent music." She unclipped her hair and let it fall around her shoulders. "Nobody's better than the Stones." She pulled Willy up to dance with her.

Sam wished they wouldn't dance so close to the edge, but he knew it wouldn't do any good to say anything. The mood Kate was in, if he did say anything, she'd probably jump. Still, it made him nervous to watch. He walked back down the trail a little way, then crossed around to the far side of the mountain, where signs posted on a chainlink fence said No Trespassing. He crawled over the fence and walked around until he was out of hearing distance of the music. He sat on a rock and listened to the wind rustle the stunted pines that grew from the rock.

He felt lousy. The tension between him and Kate was getting worse every day. He knew what she wanted. She wanted a lifetime commitment, a love that was thorough and expansive, that included children and their children's children. She wanted a home, and he wanted to give her that. He honestly did. He just didn't believe he was capable. In fact, the only thing he was confident about was his uncanny ability to make a mess of things.

He thought he heard somebody call his name. He hurried back around the mountain, crawled back over the fence, and walked out onto the ledge, where Kate danced by herself.

"Where's Willy?" Down below, the crowd cheered and applauded a new pattern of lights on the mountainside.

"Gone looking for you. Come dance." She waved him over to her.

"Maybe I ought to go look for him?"

"Maybe we ought to spend the whole night looking for each other." She grabbed his hands. "Come."

"Not so close to the edge."

She pulled him up onto the stone wall. Looking down at the immense open field, he felt dizzy. He thought of *The Bridge of San Luis Rey*, those people falling into the gorge. "Gesticulating ants"—that's how Wilder had described them.

"Isn't the view incredible?" she asked.

He had to step back down off the wall. "Come on down, Kate." He reached for her hand.

She pulled away from him, lost her balance for a moment, holding her arms out, then slipped.

To the crowd below, her scream, if they heard it at all, probably sounded like another sound effect, part of the show.

Sam dove for her and caught her by the waist, but the momentum of his dive pushed them to the very edge of the wall, and they both seemed about to go over. Her hair whipped against his face as he found himself looking out over the valley, and something in him resigned itself to the fall.

That's when he felt a hand on his belt. There was a moment when the force of their motion outward and the strength of the hand tugging on his belt achieved a perfect and frightening balance. Then, slowly, they were dragged back across the wall.

Kate and Sam collapsed onto the ground, gasping.

"Jesus Christ." Kate's voice trembled. "I feel like Charlie Chaplin or Buster Keaton." She laughed hysterically. "Jesus Christ!" She hugged Sam.

He was so shaken he couldn't speak. He still felt an immense emptiness under him.

"Y'all all right?" Willy bent down beside them. He was feeling his hand. He'd strained it pulling them back over.

Kate lowered her head into her hands. "Tell me that didn't just happen! I'm stoned. I was hallucinating, right?" She shuddered. "It was a scene out of a bad movie." She shuddered again. Her arms bled a little where they'd been scraped along the rock wall. She clung to Sam.

His stomach hurt where he'd dove onto the rock. He saw that his shirt was ripped in a perfect horizontal line.

Colored shafts of light shot over their heads, filling the air. Bruce Springsteen echoed up to them. Then there was a loud blast and an explosion of fireworks, which ended the laser show. The crowd below applauded and cheered.

"And you were worried about Maggie," Willy said to Kate. Then he turned to Sam. "Who needs the Okefenokee when you've got my sister?"

They didn't start back down the mountain until well after the show was over, the lights extinguished and the field below emptied. Although the moonlight was waning, they could still make out the carving, which looked ghostly now—three beleaguered men on horseback, their hats held over their hearts as they stared ahead of them.

When Kate stood, she realized that one of her shoes was missing. She looked around the rock. "I wonder . . ." She put her hand over her mouth. "It must've fallen off while I was . . ."

"Somebody got a Birkenstock in their potato salad." Willy leaned over the edge.

"A lot of good one does me." She slipped out of the other shoe and tossed it over the edge. "Maybe they can be a couple in paradise."

They walked down the trail slowly. The wind had picked up, and the trees rustled all around them. As solid as the rock underneath them was, Sam couldn't shake the feeling that at any moment an abyss could open.

"You know what flashed through my mind when I thought we were falling?" Kate held Willy's flashlight at her feet, picking her way down the mountain barefoot. "A meeting I'd scheduled with some parents tomorrow morning."

The three of them hooted, their laughter echoing down the mountain.

"I'm sorry, Miss Sterling won't be in today." Willy held his nose, imitating a secretary's voice. "She fell off Stone Mountain. Would you care to reschedule?"

"Anything flash through your mind?" Kate asked Sam.

"Peach cobbler," Sam said. "A blue bowl of steaming peach cobbler."

"I didn't know you liked peach cobbler," Kate said.

Sam shrugged. "I've never given it much thought."

He didn't mention the other thing that had gone through his mind in that millisecond when he was sure they were going over—earrings, the way the red-haired woman's earrings caught the light.

Chapter Two

Sam left Kate in the garden taming the rototiller while he went back into the house for a couple of Cokes. Through the kitchen window he watched her rein in the machine. Under her steady grip it didn't buck or lurch but slowly churned up the soil in neat, even rows. He had tried. He tried every year, and every year the claw-footed contraption dragged him back and forth across the backyard in whatever direction it decided. Kate showed him how to lean back and let it dig in, but he could never quite get the hang of it.

On his way back outside he detoured through the den and turned on the TV. Sunday morning evangelists crowded the channels. Sincere men with tacky souls. Sometimes he liked to watch with the sound turned down as they flailed their arms and pounded the air in a demonstration of spiritual calisthenics. But this morning he couldn't bear to watch these wide-eyed men who believed too much. He changed it to CBS's *Sunday Morning* with Charles Kuralt, whose voice reminded him of wheat fields. Last Sunday, Kate and he had made love on the sofa while in the background Kuralt narrated a film clip about the long, lonely flight of Canadian geese.

He went out on the front porch. Up and down Elmira Street, his neighbors—armed with Weed Eaters, leaf blowers, and electric hedge clippers—fought back spring's generous onslaught. He had to admit he hardly knew his neighbors, black or white. It sometimes surprised him that he

18

lived in an integrated neighborhood. As a child, he'd imagined that blacks rode the evening bus home to a country of shadows.

The Siamese from next door crossed the yard, intent on a sparrow, reminding him of a cat he used to have named Onion. One day he'd found Onion lying on his back, crying. He rushed the cat to the vet, who diagnosed the ailment as FUS (feline urinary syndrome). Sam asked if it could be fixed. For $300, said the vet. The operation was a success. Three weeks later, Onion ran away. Whenever Sam saw a cat, he'd think, Somewhere in this neighborhood there's a cat running around with a $300 urinary tract.

A small black boy rode past on his bike. He was in a white dress shirt, brown pants, and polished loafers—his Sunday clothes. "Hey, Sam, look." He lifted his hands off the handlebars.

"How's it going, Raymond?"

"Mama wants me to pick up some milk at the 7-Eleven." He nodded that he needed to keep going. Raymond, the youngest of three children, lived two houses up. Sam didn't know the older children, Charles and Deborah, who were afflicted with the nonchalance of teenagers. Raymond's mother, Virginia Brennan, was the head pediatrics nurse at Grady Hospital. She often caught a ride to work with Kate, or she'd walk past Sam's house on the way to the MARTA station. The only time he saw the family together was when he happened to see them pull up in their driveway on their way back from church.

Kate turned off the rototiller when Sam brought the Cokes. She wore overalls over an old T-shirt of his and had tied her hair back with his old Boy Scout kerchief. Her face was smudged and streaked with dust and sweat. She reminded him of a gleaner in a Millet painting. Sam wasn't sure why she always reminded him of paintings except that there was a stillness about her even when she moved.

She was frowning. She'd been frowning all morning.

"Still thinking about that baby?"

They sat on the old picnic table where they sometimes ate supper when the weather was nice.

Last night a baby had died in the neonatal unit, and she'd been called to the hospital to console the parents. He'd felt her crawl back into bed about two in the morning.

This particular baby, Melissa, had been one of Kate's recent favorites. She'd been born with severe respiratory problems. The doctors had said she didn't have a chance, but she lived, and after a month they became hopeful. Her parents visited every day. Her mother was a teacher; her father, a motorcycle cop.

"I thought she was supposed to be out of the woods." Sam sipped his Coke.

Kate wiped her forehead with a handkerchief. "That's what they thought."

"How did the parents take it?"

"She got there before he did. He was out directing traffic and had to be radioed." She drank her Coke. "I sat with the mother until she broke down. I led her back to my office, and when we came back, the father was in the nursery. He was wearing a gown over his uniform, and his gun bulged underneath." She dug dirt from her fingernails. "It was so strange to see this policeman in the middle of these babies, like some law had been violated."

Sam didn't know what to say. He never knew what to say when a baby died. He had grown fond of Melissa, as he had all the babies Kate told him about. She talked about them over supper—babies with seizures, heart murmurs, undeveloped lungs, deformities. Some were even missing vital organs. Sometimes the house felt crowded with sad stories. Kate kidnapped pain.

Sam was relieved to see Willy's VW pull into the driveway.

"The second string is here," Kate said.

Willy got out, sauntered over to the picnic table, and slid in next to Kate. He had on torn jeans and wore a sweatband around his head.

"Your field hand is here." Yawning, he plopped a greasy bag filled with Krispy Kreme doughnuts onto the table. His hair was uncombed, and he had bits of sleep in the corner of his eyes. He seemed in a perpetual state of waking up.

They sat there for half an hour eating warm, sticky doughnuts, sipping Coke, and talking. Willy, at the age of twenty-six, lived at home with Maggie and delivered newspapers for a living. He often came over in the afternoon to help with the garden or other chores or just to hang around.

"You're in time to help with the rototiller." Kate finished a last bite of doughnut and wiped her fingers on her pants. "But it needs gas."

"Keep your seat." Sam waved Willy to sit back down. He walked to the very back of the yard, where they'd put up a small aluminum toolshed. Kate had needed it for her garden tools, so last year, on her birthday, after he'd taken her to a good restaurant, he took her to Kmart, where, in a low-cut, black satin dress, she walked in and out of toolsheds, deciding on the one she wanted.

When he came back with the gas can, Willy and Kate were talking in low voices. Once, when he'd overheard her tell Willy they hadn't been having very good sex, he waited until Willy left and then asked her what right she had to tell Willy about their sex life. "He's my brother," she said, as if that explained everything. At first, he'd been jealous that she'd confided in Willy so much. But over the years, not only had he accepted their intimacy, he even became grateful to Willy. Willy was like rain; he cooled things off.

Through the back screen door they heard the phone ring. Kate ran across the yard and inside the house. Whenever she was on call, the phone rang off the hook.

Sam poured the gas into the rototiller. "Another baby died last night," he said to Willy, keeping his voice low. "It takes its toll on her."

Willy checked the rototiller's oil stick, wiping it on his shirt.

"I'm not sure how good this job is for her," Sam said.

"She needs it." Willy shrugged. "She's always needed to be at the heart of matters." He started up the rototiller and began to plow more ground, finishing the row Kate had started.

Then why in the hell was Kate ever attracted to a guy who'd drifted to the periphery? Sam wondered. He'd arrived in Atlanta ten years ago, a couple of years out of college, ablaze with the English major's dream to write the great American novel, but that quickly cooled when he found that writing required writing. He started a novel but became bored a hundred pages into it. He started another, but this time he lost interest after fifty pages. He started another but only wrote twenty pages. His ambitions dwindled with his output until he found himself alone in Atlanta writing the great American sentence.

By the time Kate came along Sam had given up writing altogether and taken a job in a bookstore, deciding that if he couldn't write books at least he could work in their proximity. He liked to hold them.

Perhaps Kate was attracted to the failure in him, taking him on as another one of her projects. But he did not take advantage of what she offered, and now he believed his failing was wearing thin.

He found himself staring at the back of his house. It needed so much work—new window frames, new gutters, a new roof. He had bought the house when he realized he couldn't write and needed something to do with his time. He thought he would fix it up himself. He decided to take it room by room: He tore out the crumbling plaster walls and the ceilings, put up new Sheetrock, and painted. He stripped the old hardwood floors, then sanded and rewaxed them. But he'd only finished half the downstairs rooms, so that the house had a schizophrenic feel. Now it stood as a daily reminder of something else he hadn't finished.

Fifteen minutes later, Kate came back out, a glass of ice water in her hand. She sat down beside Sam, watching Willy steer the rototiller through the garden. She smelled of sweat and dirt.

"What'd the hospital want?" He had to talk over the roar of the rototiller.

"A mother was upset because her baby had to go back on the ventilator."

"That's not unusual, is it?" For preemies, ventilators were a way of life.

"Something about the way the doctor told her scared her."

He never understood how these doctors could perform the most delicate, most sensitive surgery on minuscule organs of infants and yet were all thumbs when it came to handling parents.

As Willy plowed up the garden, Kate spread the morning paper out on the grass and lay on her stomach, reading it, holding her long legs up in the air. Sam leaned his head on her bottom and closed his eyes. The sun was so warm on his arms and legs. He saw a beach curving outward for miles in either direction. All along it were dots, some together, some alone; some moved, some stood still. As he walked toward the dots, they gradually became people—families, women by themselves, boys walking along the surf, girls lying in the sand. He walked out into the water, and when the tide receded, he looked for crab holes. He dug his toe under one and flipped out a tiny crab. The crab didn't waste any time tunneling down again. Sam stood in the water a long time. He looked along the beach; everybody was gone.

Sam opened his eyes. Rows of pale young women, their heads covered in white, smiled at him over Kate's shoulder. She was reading the wedding announcements.

Willy had finished plowing the garden and was wheeling the rototiller back to the toolshed when a large black woman in a loose white dress charged around the corner of the house. Sam didn't recognize Virginia Brennan at first because she wasn't in her nurse's uniform.

"Have y'all seen Raymond? He hasn't come back from the store." She tried to catch her breath, her hand on her heaving chest. "I thought y'all might've seen him."

"He rode by about an hour ago," Sam said. "He was on his way to get milk."

"He never came back. I've been up and down this street, and nobody's seen him." She folded her arms across her chest, mad at the neighborhood for not keeping an eye on her son.

"He couldn't have gone far," Kate said. "Where are Charles and Deborah?"

"There was a teen picnic after church." Virginia threw up her arms.

Sam only spoke to Virginia in the mornings or the late afternoons when she walked back from the MARTA station, looking competent and stiff in her uniform, her eyes cast downward at her white hospital shoes. Now he was confronted with a different Virginia Brennan. Her hair, usually clipped under the nurse's cap, sprang up from her head. Her big body moved powerfully under the loose dress.

She sighed, and her face softened. She closed her eyes and rubbed her forehead. "You don't think . . . ?"

"Let's not jump to conclusions." Kate held Virginia's hand.

He knew what Virginia must think—what every black mother in Atlanta thought whenever her child was a little late getting home. Even though Wayne Williams was locked away, cruel rumors still circulated that they'd convicted the wrong man.

"Did you try over by the railroad yard?" Sam had seen Raymond there with some kids the other day, playing around the tracks.

"He knows better than that. He'd have to cross DeKalb Avenue, and that's out of bounds."

Sam wasn't sure if she was angry at the thought of Raymond's playing where he wasn't supposed to or if she was mad at Sam for suggesting he'd disobey her. "I saw him there just the other day." He regretted betraying Raymond to prove his point.

"I saw some kids playing down by the railroad yard when I passed half an hour ago." Willy said, coming back from the toolshed.

Virginia clapped her hands. "I've told him to stay away from those trains. I've told him and told him and told him." Her booming voice carried next door, where old Mrs. Smeak, who was out in her bonnet snipping ivy off her backyard fence, waved at the four of them.

"Fine, thank you," she said.

Virginia stamped the ground. "I will not have it!" Her head rocked. "Playing around trains is a good way to lose an arm or a leg." As a pediatrics nurse, she spoke not just from the hypothetical fears of a mother but as one who had changed the bloodied dressings of children's mangled limbs.

"He's in his Sunday clothes!" She marched down the driveway, toward the railroad yard.

"Let's give her a ride," Kate said.

The four of them piled into Willy's bus. The floor was a yellowed crust of old newspapers. He delivered the morning *Atlanta Constitution*. The bus smelled of the inky acridness of newsprint. Willy said there was a direct relationship between the pungency of the print and the severity of the news. He claimed he could actually smell bad news.

Virginia sat up front with Willy. "Hold on," she said just as he was pulling out of the driveway. She went over to the pile of hedge trimmings in front of Mrs. Smeak and came back to the bus with a two-foot green stick, stripping the leaves off. She climbed back into the bus. "Okay." She looked straight ahead and patted the stick in her hand.

Sam and Kate sat in the backseat, watching her. Sam brushed some dirt off Kate's nose. "You've got half the garden on your face."

She covered his hand with hers but hadn't taken her eyes off Virginia's stick. "That switch ought to really scare him."

Virginia didn't say anything.

Willy glanced at Sam and Kate in his rearview mirror.

"I hope he's there," Sam said.

"He's there." Virginia slapped the switch against the dashboard.

All three of them flinched.

Willy turned right onto DeKalb Avenue—a long street that divided Little Five Points and Candler Park from Reynoldstown and other black neighborhoods. To Sam, DeKalb Avenue always seemed tensed for robbery, with its burglar-barred liquor stores, 7-Elevens hidden behind green-tinted glass, and auto-parts stores barricaded with high chain-link fences tipped with barbed wire. The street itself was dangerous, with its "reversible" middle lane, which, depending on whether the green arrows or red X's were blinking, changed directions constantly. DeKalb was notorious for head-on collisions. Sam understood why Virginia didn't want Raymond playing down here.

They rode down the street in uneasy silence.

Virginia began to recite Raymond's offenses to herself: "He missed lunch. He rode across DeKalb, which he knows is out-of-bounds. And he's playing around trains, which I've told him and told him about. . . . Good God!"

Willy turned left through an underpass that cut through to the railroad yard. Rows of trailers without trucks waited for a crane to swing them onto waiting railroad cars. They called it piggybacking. It was a strange sight to be stopped at a railroad crossing by a trainload of these amputated trucks perched on top of railroad cars. The two forms of transportation had hatched an ungainly mutant.

Since it was Sunday, the crane was still, and the yard was empty except for a cluster of little boys who climbed all over an empty railroad car. Sam didn't see Raymond among them. He felt relieved that the boy might escape Virginia's switch. Kate gave a little sigh, too. But then she squeezed his hand. The same thought that had occurred to him had come to her: If Raymond wasn't here, where was he?

Virginia had no trouble picking Raymond out of the pack. Before Willy could even pull into the parking lot, she flung open her door and hit the pavement running. She covered ground, sprinting on her toes, the switch in her fist.

"She won't hurt him," Kate said as Willy screeched into a parking place. The three of them jumped out of the bus and hurried over to where Virginia stood on the edge of the tracks, her hands on her hips, her white dress fluttering against the black railroad bed.

All Sam knew about Virginia was what Kate had told him—that her husband had died while she was pregnant with Raymond. A tree limb had fallen on him. Gene Brennan had been a tree surgeon.

Fifty yards away, the boys swarmed over the railroad car, shook thick chains, swung from handholds, and chased each other between the heavy wheels. Their shouts and laughter, which drifted across the tracks, already sounded over to Sam, who stood with Kate and Willy, just behind Virginia.

"Ray-mond Brennan!" Virginia's voice exploded across the railroad yard, paralyzing every child on that car. Sam imagined her voice echoing through the neighborhoods, with children all over northeast Atlanta snapping to attention. Sam found himself standing a little straighter.

A small boy in a white shirt dropped off the railroad car, landing on all fours. Slowly, he picked himself up, wiped his hands on his pants, and with his eyes on the ground, began the slow walk toward his mother.

Kate slipped her arms around Sam's waist, giving him a sad half smile.

"I can't watch this." She walked back toward the VW with Willy.

The children on the railroad car hadn't moved, but watched Raymond pick his way over the rails toward his mother, who tapped the switch against her side.

Raymond's steps shortened the nearer he came. He glanced up at his mother once, then down at his scuffed shoes, his mud-caked pants, and his filthy shirt. Sam had never seen such a sober face on a child. He was fully aware of what he'd done and even more aware of the consequences. His bright eyes had turned ashen. His frown extended to the ground. He stopped just a few feet from her.

"What do you have to say for yourself?" Her voice made Sam shiver.

Raymond lifted his eyes to his mother, and for a moment Sam thought the boy might actually say something, that he might have a perfectly good explanation for missing lunch, for crossing a road he shouldn't have, for playing around the trains. Sam pulled for Raymond. He racked his mind for a loophole, a technicality that might get the boy off. But as Virginia smacked the switch in her hand, he knew that justice would not be impeded.

"Bend over." There was a tenderness in her tone.

Raymond, who was ready to get it over with, seemed almost happy to bend his small, square bottom toward his mother.

Virginia raised the switch, then, just as she was about to bring it down, hesitated, spun on her heels, and pointed the switch at the children paralyzed on the railroad car.

They scattered across the railroad yard, their feet crunching the rocks of the railroad bed. Some picked their bikes up out of the grass, vaulting on them in mid-run. Others just ran, pumping their arms harder when they heard the pop of the switch against Raymond's rear end.

The way Raymond bent over, he faced Sam as his mother raised the switch, not too high, and smacked his bottom. The pop made Sam flinch, but Raymond's face remained impassive. His round eyes stared in Sam's direction but went right through him. His mouth hung slightly open. The lines in his face had relaxed into an emptied-out expression. Behind Raymond, Virginia's stormy face had calmed to a tranquil reflection of her son's. Her arm, which switched him, moved mechanically, without vehemence.

Out of the corner of his eye, Sam saw Kate off to the side, watching with her arms folded. She squinted the way she did when she made up her mind about something. Every time Virginia raised the switch again, Kate looked away and then looked back.

Sam moved toward Kate.

"Virginia?" She walked toward Virginia and Raymond. "Don't you think that's enough?"

Virginia didn't lift her head. Her arm didn't hesitate in its path toward Raymond's bottom. She hit him a little harder. Not that this showed on Raymond's face, but he rocked on his heels.

"I think that's enough!" Kate stood behind her, her hands on her hips.

Virginia hit him again.

"Please," Kate said. As Virginia brought the switch back, Kate grabbed hold.

Virginia didn't turn around, but stood there with the switch behind her head. Raymond turned around, a confused look on his face.

"Let go, Kate." Sam came up behind her.

She'd braced her feet and wound the switch around her fist. Her teeth were clenched.

"Let go." One by one, he pried her red fingers from around the stick until only Virginia held it again. "This is none of our business."

She struggled against him, even kicked his shin, but he held her wrists.

"Kate, it is none of our business."

"Goddamn you." She tried to jerk her hands out of his grip.

"Calm down."

"Like hell I will!" She jerked her right hand free and slapped him.

He was so stunned he let her other hand go.

She held her hand over her mouth. "Oh, my God, I'm sorry." She touched the red imprint on his face. "I didn't mean to . . ." She held her hands out to him and let them drop. She shook her head slowly. "You're not going to even try, are you?" Her question echoed across the empty railroad yard. A large crow lifted from the middle of the tracks, circled over their heads, and flew in the direction of Reynoldstown.

Sam touched his face, which stung. He'd never been slapped.

Virginia had dropped her switch and hugged Raymond against her dress.

"What'd he do, Mama?"

Embarrassed, Kate turned and half-walked, half-ran across the parking lot and out the gate.

Virginia patted Raymond's shoulder. "Get your bike."

Sam ran after Kate, catching up with her at the gate. He reached for her arm, but she pulled it away. "I'm sorry," he said. "It just wasn't any of our business."

She wheeled around. Her lip curled in anger; her eyes reddened. "What are your plans for us?"

He looked at her, not knowing what to say. "To be together," he said lamely.

Raymond and Virginia came up to them. Raymond guided his bike with one hand and rubbed his bottom with the other.

"We're going to walk back," Virginia said coolly.

"You don't want a ride?" Sam asked. "His bike will fit in the bus."

Virginia glanced at Kate. "We'll walk."

Kate took Virginia's hand. "I'm sorry. I got carried away, Virginia. That was none of my business."

"Damned straight!"

Raymond's eyes widened at hearing his mother curse.

"Come on, Raymond." She grabbed the handlebars and led the boy away. Then she turned around and walked back up to Kate. For a brief second Sam thought she might slap her.

"There are things you don't know about." She paused. "Thank you for helping me find my boy." She walked back to Raymond, who'd decided it was more comfortable to walk his bike.

"We can give you a ride," Kate called to her.

Virginia raised her hand. The two of them trotted across DeKalb Avenue, making it to the other side just as two long-ladder green fire trucks howled past, helmeted firemen swinging casually from the rear. Raymond stared after them, envious, worshipful.

Willy, Kate, and Sam marched back to the bus. Willy walked on ahead of them and started the VW, clouding the parking lot with exhaust.

"I am an idiot," Kate said. "A white idiot." Then she stopped, holding Sam by the arm. "What's going on with us?"

"I wish I knew." But didn't he know? Hadn't he known from the beginning that he would fail her? He put his hand over her head, tracing her part with his finger—a pale, innocent line. She let him hug her. Behind them he was conscious of the empty railroad yard where a few moments ago Raymond had slowly crossed the tracks toward his mother, knowing what was coming and how much it would hurt.

Lamar stooped over the grill, with a hair dryer trained on the coals, while Joey, his hands opened toward the fire, whispered to Kate, who held him on her hip, "Hot!"

"That's right," Kate said.

"Hot!" Joey warned Sam.

"Very." Sam held his hand out toward the coals. "Oww!" He shook it and blew on it, pretending he'd burned it.

Joey laughed.

"Sam hurt his hand," Lamar said to Joey. "He needs some loving."

Joey reached both his hands out and brought Sam's hand to his lips.

"That feels better." Sam noticed Kate smile for the first time since the scene at the railroad yard. She'd hardly talked to him the rest of the afternoon, but her mood had lightened as soon as they'd gotten here.

It was almost dark as they stood in a semicircle around the grill, facing the back of Rose and Lamar's house—a brick ranch-style like a lot of the houses in Winona Park, like the house Sam had grown up in, in South Carolina, except his neighborhood wasn't integrated. The only black people he saw were the uniformed maids who rode the bus into his neighborhood every morning to take charge of households.

Winona Park had more trees than Little Five Points, and the houses were spaced farther apart. Lamar and Rose had moved to Winona Park when Joey was born. Before then they'd lived on Battlefield Avenue in Kirkwood, a mostly black neighborhood, the only one in Atlanta where they'd been able to afford a house. Sam had felt self-conscious whenever he and Kate pulled up in front of Rose and Lamar's Kirkwood house, the indulgent eyes of the neighborhood upon them.

"How long before they're ready?" Rose stuck her head out the back door, shouting across the backyard.

"Five minutes!" Lamar flicked the setting higher on the blow-dryer, causing the coals to glow. "It's ingenious, isn't it?" He waved the blow-dryer, which was plugged into an orange extension cord that trailed back to the house. "This way you have a steady stream of air on the charcoals. . . ." He flicked the hair dryer to the highest setting; the coals glowed even brighter. "Voilà, instant coals." Lamar spent most of his spare time saving time.

He leaned over and gave Joey a loud kiss.

"Daddy," Joey said.

Lamar handed Sam the hair dryer, taking Joey from Kate. He threw him way up into the air. Since Lamar was tall, anyway, about six feet five, in his arms Joey was already in another stratosphere.

Joey squealed. "More, more."

Lamar threw him even higher, so that Joey's head nearly scraped a low branch of a dogwood. It made Sam nervous the way Lamar played so wildly with him. He'd flip him onto the couch, bounce him on his leg, fling him into a somersault in midair.

"That's enough." Lamar handed Joey back to Kate. "If your mother catches us . . ." He wrapped his hands around his throat, made choking noises, and stuck out his tongue.

Joey laughed.

"I'd say those coals have arrived." Lamar took the hair dryer back. He leaned over and whispered into Joey's ear, "Say Daddy's a fucking genius."

Joey put his hands out toward the fire. Kate set him on the ground. He bent his head straight back and looked up at her.

"I'm going to get you." She stooped beside him.

He squealed, rocked forward on his toes, almost lost his balance, then ran stiff-legged. Kate stayed right behind him, taking quick baby steps.

They ran to the back of the yard, circling the big pecan tree. Sam started to run after them, but something about the way Kate and Joey's bodies blurred in the dusk kept him still. They looked like enough, running around the tree trunk, intent on each other.

He was glad they'd come over tonight, especially after what had happened with Virginia today. Lamar and Rose were good for them as a couple. They were restorative. If he and Kate had had a fight or just felt depressed, they could count on feeling better after a visit with them— especially if Rose and Lamar had had a rough day, too, had fought, or the baby had been cranky. Misery didn't just love company; it craved it.

"Would somebody tell Rose the coals are ready?" Lamar asked.

"We'll go tell her." She swung Joey onto her hip. "Let's go tell Mama."

Joey coughed. "Tell Mama."

"It'd be good to get him out of this night air," Lamar said.

She carried Joey back toward the house, where Rose moved in front of the lighted kitchen window.

"Mama." Joey pointed to Rose in the window, but

she didn't see him. Her head was bent over the sink, her eyes cast downward.

Sam watched her carry Joey inside. Joey was the first baby Sam had known personally. He and Kate baby-sat Joey sometimes. Kate fed him and changed his diapers, and Sam trailed him around the house, making sure he didn't lick a light socket or chew a dead moth. The last time they'd baby-sat, he became intrigued with their staircase. (Since Rose and Lamar's house was a single-story, there were no steps.) He'd crawl up the stairs, glance over his shoulder, and laugh at Sam, who'd crawled right behind him in case he slipped.

Lamar spread the pile of coals across the bottom of the grill with a stick.

Two bats flitted back and forth across an open space between the trees. In the bushes, crickets sang, emboldened by the cover of night. Sam felt awkward, wanting to talk to Lamar about Kate.

Lamar put his arm around Sam's shoulder. "Let's go camping." Lamar's dark face looked almost black in the waning light. "We can go up to the Smokies. I've got some vacation coming to me." Lamar was the head chef of an executive dining room in a bank building downtown. He was so bulky and so loud that it was hard for Sam to imagine him working in such a hushed, elegant setting. "We could spend a week. Could you get that much time off from the bookstore?"

"Maybe." They'd talked about this camping trip ever since they'd known each other.

"What am I thinking? Rose would never stand for that, having to take care of Joey that long by herself." He sighed and poked the coals with the stick. "Kids change everything."

"Do they?"

"Just to go to the movies is a pain. Even if you get a baby-sitter, you spend half the movie worrying whether you should call to make sure everything's all right." He sighed. "I've about decided it's not worth it."

"Kids?"

"Movies, which is why I've been pricing VCRs."

Woodsmoke lifted from the chimney of the house next door. An elderly black couple lived there. They heated with a wood stove, and smoke poured from their chimney even in summer. On the other side of Lamar and Rose lived an actress, a young white woman who was dying of cancer. Sam had never met her, but Lamar and Rose had had her to dinner with her boyfriend. Rose said they were a happy couple, determined to make the most of the time they had left.

"What's it like to be a father?" Sam asked Lamar.

Lamar poked at a coal with the stick. "One thing having children teaches you—in the scheme of things, you're not as important as you thought you were."

"But I'd think being a father would make you feel very important. You have all that responsibility—a wife and a child, a whole family counting on you."

"I guess what I'm talking about is self-importance. You forfeit that as soon as you become a father because now you're part of something bigger than just you." He lifted his chin. "But don't get me wrong, it does make you feel necessary in a new way."

Sam dropped a dry leaf on the coals, watching it hiss, then flame, its skeleton curling up. "Kate wants a baby."

"It's the rage." Lamar looked up at him, then back at the coals. "What do you want?"

"I don't know." He let his hands flop against his sides. "I want to want what she wants. I want to make her happy."

"But?"

"But how do you know when you're ready for a baby?"

"Sam, there is no way to get ready. Babies come, and you deal with them."

"I have a hard enough time taking care of myself."
He paced around the grill.

"Is it the baby that scares you"—Lamar poked at the coals—"or what having a baby means?"

Sam sighed and looked toward the house, where he could see, through the kitchen window, Kate talking to Rose. "It seems to me that if you agree to have a baby with someone, you commit yourself in a very permanent way. You—"

"You get married."

Sam held up his hands. "That's the word I was looking for."

"Marriage isn't easy, but it makes everything less tentative. It gives you something to fall back on. It keeps small things from meaning too much so that every time you have an argument, you don't feel the whole relationship is at stake."

"I just don't know if I can handle it."

"Before Joey came I felt the same way," Lamar said.

"You did?"

"I was scared to death when Rose showed me the little pink dot on the pregnancy test."

"You were?"

"I don't know one father who hasn't had the prebaby, disembodied blues. Mothers walk around all buoyant, feeling the weight of the baby, feeling it kick and squirm and even hiccup. But we fathers skulk around without a clue."

Sam stared at the coals. "The thing about all this is that Kate believes in me more than I do."

"It all changes when the baby actually comes." Lamar unplugged the hair dryer and wound the extension cord around his arm. "When you have something to hold."

The back screen slammed, and Rose came out, across the backyard, carrying a plateful of amberjack steaks in one hand and a couple of beers in the other. She handed the beers to Sam and Lamar.

She was a small woman with coppery skin and dark eyes. Her father, a doctor from Colombia, had come to the United States forty years ago to attend medical school and had met her mother, who was from the mountains of Tennessee. The result was Rose, an exotic-looking woman with a thick southern accent. Sam had always had a crush on her. She was a special-education teacher and taught autistic children. Sam used to visit her classroom sometimes or go with them on field trips. He could never get over how pretty the children were, how content they seemed locked in their own little worlds. Their vacant eyes had a sweet anonymity.

"Y'all got quiet all of a sudden," she said.

"We were talking babies." The steaks hissed as Lamar set them on the grill. Lamar pulled her next to him, nuzzling the top of her head. Rose was small, but next to Lamar she looked dwarfish. Despite their difference in size, something about them fit.

"Why were y'all talking about babies?" Rose asked. "Are you ready for another one?" Rose had had a difficult time getting pregnant. Scar tissue had blocked one of her tubes.

Lamar flipped the steaks. The flames jumped from the grease. "Sam brought it up."

"Sam brought up babies?" She slid her arm around Sam's waist, too, so that the three of them stood there watching the fish cook. "Has being around Joey made you think you might want one of your own?"

"He's cute, but not that cute." Sam rubbed his eyebrows.

"It's different when they're your own. Isn't it, Lamar?"

"I remember the first time I held Joey at the hospital," Lamar said. "I couldn't believe anything that small could work."

An old black man came out of the house next door

and picked up a couple of pieces of wood from the pile against his house.

"How's it going, John?" Lamar called out.

The old man looked up, surprised to see them there. "Fair to middlin'."

"Nice night, isn't it?" Rose said.

"I reckon it is that," the old man said. He paused and looked up at the sky, then back at them. He went back into his house.

They stared at the coals, listening to the fish sizzle and hiss on the grill.

"The hardest thing about having a baby—" Rose said. "You realize that all the terrible things that happen in the world could happen to your child. It brings all the sadnesses home."

"The hardest thing for me is that life can't be improvised anymore," Lamar said. "We can't just do things on a lark. Everything's always prefaced with 'Can we get a sitter?'"

Rose patted Sam's shoulder. "You and Kate have been great to baby-sit as much as you have."

"They'll cash in on it one day," Lamar said.

Sam smiled into the coals, which flamed as the grease dripped onto them. The wind picked up, bending limbs overhead. The fire fluttered, blowing smoke in Sam's direction, stinging his eyes. How was it that others were surer of him than he was of himself?

"Where is Kate?" Sam asked.

"Reading Joey a *Winnie-the-Pooh* story," Rose said.

He imagined her sitting by Joey's bed, reading, stopping now and then to show Joey the pictures. She might even sing to him in that dreamy tone she sang in whenever they were on a long car trip. Sometimes she'd just start singing, often a song he'd never heard.

Chapter Three

Since business was slow, Sam kept an eye on the register and shelved a cart of romance novels, turning the covers face out. He'd worked at Brilliant's Bookstore so long that shelving had become an involuntary action. At parties where he didn't know people, he'd often find himself in the corner rearranging a stranger's books. Kate would whisper to him to stop embarrassing her. She'd take him by the hand and lead him across the room to some guy she'd been having a conversation with.

"She's the limit." A dumpy, bald man with a handlebar mustache came out of the back of the store, shaking an invoice in his hand. "Our queen of the skinheads received Knopf and Farrar Straus and left me three boxes of Schaum's Outlines, two boxes of maps, and four boxes of *children's* books." The latter he said with particular disdain. "She leaves me the dregs."

"Have you talked to Paula?" Sam continued shelving. "Maybe she just didn't think."

Carl grunted. "I know it seems petty, but when you sit back there and open boxes all day, now and then you want to open something that's halfway interesting." He shrugged. "No use getting bent out of shape about it, I guess. Want anything from next door?"

"No, thanks," Sam said.

"That girl will put me in an early grave." Carl walked out the front door, headed for Gorin's. Carl had worked at Brilliant's even longer than Sam. He opened the store every morning, brought in the morning paper, made up a drawer for the cash register, and vacuumed the store. With his shiny bald head, his handlebar mustache, and his deep voice, Carl could've passed as the bass in a barbershop quartet. Actually, he'd been a funeral-home director before he'd come to Brilliant's. He still free-lanced occasionally and took a day off now and then to "prepare" a deceased friend or relative. Every year they held the staff Christmas party at Carl's house, which was remarkable for Carl's paperweight collection. Paperweights of all shapes and sizes glistened from every available surface.

Sam finished the cart of romances and rang up newspapers for businessmen, who'd rush in, snatch a paper, slap a quarter on the register, and sprint out. Except for the usual early-morning flurry, business had been slow. The only people in the store were a couple of bums who'd come in to get warm. There was a soup kitchen three blocks down at the Presbyterian church. Street people were given a free breakfast on condition they listen to a sermon—variations on a general theme: Jesus' bread is enough for the hungriest of souls. However, not all bums were believers. Sam once overheard one bum ask another, "If Jesus is so hot, how come he don't feed the masses New York strip?" So they'd slip out in the middle of the sermon and panhandle their way up to the bookstore. On chilly mornings they'd wander in and look at magazines. They'd ask Sam to keep an eye on their bundles, as if a Kroger sack stuffed with dirty socks and half-eaten sandwiches were a briefcase filled with important papers.

"Into the bosom books again?" Jessie Brilliant pushed her bicycle into the store. Short and sturdily built, she had long brown hair tinged with gray and wore thick-lensed glasses, making her look owlish. "Does Kate know how much time you spend fondling Rosemary Rogers and Danielle Steel?" She unsnapped her helmet. Sam liked the idea of an employer riding her bike to work—not that a bookstore owner could afford much else.

"How's business?" She set her helmet on the counter, then came around and opened the cash register.

"Slow."

"Nonexistent." She fingered the few bills. "Where's Carl?"

"Next door getting coffee."

"He's got a crush on the new guy they hired." She raised her thick eyebrows. "Let's hope Gerald doesn't find out." Gerald was the man Carl lived with, whom Sam only knew as the sullen figure who shut himself away in his bedroom at the staff Christmas parties, emerging just long enough to fix himself a drink.

"I know Paula's not in yet." She patted Sam's back. "I'm glad somebody minds the store." She picked up her helmet and started to roll her bike back toward the office. "Could you set up an Easter display? Maybe on the table with the best-sellers."

He rolled the empty book cart out of the aisle. "Do you have a theme in mind?"

She shrugged. "Bunnies and/or Jesus." She pushed her bike toward the back.

As he went through the store gathering books for a display, he thought about his conversation with Kate that morning. He'd cooked breakfast, as usual, while she ironed her clothes for work. He liked to cook breakfast, and being chronically rumpled, he seldom ironed anything. Kate ironed everything down to her underwear. She'd come to breakfast in her robe while her newly pressed clothes hung on the back of the closet door. She waited until after breakfast to dress, risking as few wrinkles as possible.

She frowned as she cut into her eggs.

"Too runny?" He came over from the stove.

She shook her head, which was wrapped in a towel, her hair still wet from showering.

He slid an egg from the frying pan onto his plate, spooned up some grits, and came over and sat down.

She took a bite of egg. "How long have we lived together?"

He looked up at her. "Breakfast is no time to take stock of a relationship."

"How long?" Her robe had fallen open, and a single bead of water ran down between her small breasts.

He held up his hands. "About four years."

She buttered her toast. "And in these four years have I made unreasonable demands upon you?"

He shook his head, wondering where she was going with this.

"Have I said or done anything to make you feel that you are somehow inadequate or not right for me?" She bit into her toast.

"No."

"So when I say I want us to have a baby, do you interpret that as your not being enough for me?"

Sam put his napkin beside his plate.

"I do want a baby, but I want *us* to have it. I want a family, but I want you to be part of it." She peppered her eggs and grits. "Is it wrong for me to want us to be more than we are?" Her voice shook a little. "Is it wrong for me to be ambitious for us?"

Sam stared at his plate. "I'm afraid."

"Of what?"

"That I'll let you down, except that I won't just be letting you down. I'll be letting the baby down, I'll be letting our family down, I'll be letting our parents down, I'll be letting our friends down, I'll be letting the whole world down."

"I'm not asking you to populate the solar system." She took another bite of egg. "I'm just talking about you and me. You make everything so big, so impossibly important, that you scare yourself out of making a move." She wiped her plate with a piece of toast, then ate it.

"When you have a baby, you open yourself up for all kinds of things going wrong," Sam said.

"Have you considered the possibility that something might go right?" She glanced up at the kitchen clock. "I'm late." She took one last sip of coffee, then hurried upstairs to get dressed for work.

Disappointed with himself, he crumpled his napkin and dropped it into the middle of his untouched food. Time, he was sure, was running out.

"I want a book about training cats." An old woman in a fur coat stood in front of Sam as he arranged the Easter display. Her breath smelled of peppermint and something else—scotch. She wore another coat under her fur coat, and there was probably another coat under that one. He imagined her as a body of coats.

"We have books about training dogs." He led her back to the pet section, pulling out a couple of books.

"Dogs aren't cats." She eyed the books contemptuously.

"I didn't realize you could train cats."

"You wouldn't," she said. "You're a man. All men hate cats. My husband did." Her voice quaked. "My Alfred used to say, 'What good are they if they can't fetch my slippers?' " The woman's face was flushed, and Sam worried that the situation was getting out of hand. "And I'd say, 'Alfred' "—she tapped her bony finger on Sam's chest— " 'not everyone was put on this earth to serve you!' "

Jessie stepped out of nowhere and took the woman by the arm. She must've heard her all the way in the back. "I'm sure we can find you a suitable book about cats."

The old woman's tone changed immediately. "Do you have cats? Only we women understand cats. Cats are too subtle for the male intelligence."

Jessie led her back toward the books, winking at Sam over her shoulder.

The old woman turned to Sam. "Any idiot can pick up slippers with his teeth."

Sam went back to the office to make coffee and collect himself. They were out of filters, so he used a paper towel instead, a trick Jessie had taught him. Jessie coped. He saw her guide the old woman around the store. Jessie hadn't had an easy life, not that she talked about it, but in three years Sam had pieced together a life let down by men. She'd been divorced three times. Now she lived with a woman, Sylvia, whom she'd been living with for eight years. She said her only regret was how long it had taken her to realize she was gay. She wasn't bitter toward men.

"I have nobody to blame but myself," she'd say. "Men expect to be loved, not counted on."

Kate didn't answer her office phone, so he had the hospital page her. He imagined her name being called down the long white hospital halls. She'd be outside the intensive-care nursery, calming distraught parents, or in her office, catching up on paperwork.

Finally, she answered. "What's wrong?"

"Nothing." He didn't call her often at work. It was so hard to get through to her. He worried he might interrupt something important. "You're with someone?"

"What is it, Sam?" It surprised him to hear her say his name, as if he were somebody else.

"An old lady came in a minute ago asking if we had any books on training cats." He glanced out the office window at Jessie showing the woman a book in the pet section.

"I didn't know you could train cats."

There was a pause; neither of them spoke. Sam worried that their relationship had lost its sense of humor.

"I'm with a family," she said.

"I'm sorry to have bothered you." He twisted the telephone wire in his fingers.

"You didn't bother me."

"Now you sound mad."

"I'm not mad." She sighed. "I wish I could get my hands on Alexander Graham Bell."

"Why?"

"For inventing the phone."

He heard a doctor being paged in the background.

"They're about to take a baby off life support."

"God." When doctors decided there was no hope, they'd take the baby off the ventilator, unfasten all the wires and tubes, and let the mother hold the baby while it died.

"I need to go," she said.

"About this morning . . . I didn't like the way we left it. I wanted to tell you that I . . ." His heart pounded.

"Sam, I have to go."

"That I want to try to work things out." There was a long pause. "Kate?"

"What do you mean?"

There was a pause; he couldn't think of anything to say.

"We'll have to talk tonight," she said. "I have to go."

What had he meant? he asked himself after they hung up. He shouldn't have called. He'd raised her expectations. He'd raised his own. But then, if he didn't come around, he'd leave her no choice but to leave him. She'd as much as said that this morning. And if there was anything that frightened him more than having a baby, it was the thought of being without Kate.

Carl emerged from the receiving room with suspiciously perfect timing. "How's Kate doing these days?"

"A baby is dying." Sam poured himself some coffee.

"I don't envy her her job," Carl said. "Bereaved children were hard, but bereaved parents were the hardest." Carl appreciated the difficulty of Kate's work, having had so much experience with death.

About midmorning Sam finished the Easter display and was rearranging the best-sellers when a young woman in tails and a top hat hurried in. She could've been an urchin out of *Oliver Twist*. Her head was shaved except for a blond tuft of hair with blue and pink streaks that fell down over her forehead. Her eyes were puffy.

"Late night, Paula?" Sam asked.

"Four o'clock." She yawned. "At least that's when people started leaving."

"Another party? I thought you just had one night before last."

"Last night was the sequel." Paula lived with Macon, her husband, in an apartment in a big house that was more of a punk commune. Sometimes Sam gave Paula a ride home after work, and there was always a steady stream of men and women in their late teens or early twenties wandering in and out of the building or hanging out on the fire escape, drinking beer. Sad-eyed and uncommunicative, Macon would sometimes drop by Brilliant's to borrow money from Paula. He had trouble finding a steady job, probably because he couldn't string enough words together to ask for one. As far as Sam could see, they lived off what little Paula made. It was hard enough to support oneself on a book clerk's salary. He didn't see how two people could even breathe at $5.50 an hour.

"Carl's gunning for you this morning," Sam said. "He's pissed that you received all the good boxes."

She rolled her eyes. "He's too much. I received what needed to be received. If I waited for him to do it, we'd be buried in books." She smiled at her pun. It was true that Paula could receive a whole roomful of boxes in the time it took Carl to finish one. Not only did she receive faster than anyone; she shelved like a demon. She knew the inventory better than the computer.

Paula started back toward the office, caught sight of Carl through the window, did a U-turn around the hardback fiction, and passed by Sam.

"I'm going next door for some espresso." She was out the door just as Carl came up front.

"That's funny," Carl said. "She turned around as soon as she saw me. Like she knew what I was going to talk to her about." He frowned at Sam.

"What do you think of my Easter display?" Sam rearranged a couple of books.

Carl studied it critically, tapping his long fingers against his chin. "Needs to be more Eastery." He had a weakness for arrangements and began to move the books around.

Close to noon a bum wandered into the store, approached the register nervously, reached into his oversized coat, and took out a dollar bill.

"Four quarters okay, Ronnie?" Sam opened the register.

Ronnie tapped his fingers on the counter.

"Four quarters." Sam counted them into Ronnie's hand.

Ronnie put the quarters back into his pocket, smiling with relief. He came in every day for change for the bus. He wore clothes that were a couple of sizes too big, hiding himself. His hair was long and matted, and he hadn't shaved. Even so, something about him was different from the other listless men who roamed the streets. Jessie said it was his eyes.

Ronnie stood at the register, seeming to want to make conversation. Finally, he said, "Is that James Taylor on the radio?"

Sam reached behind him and turned up the radio on the counter. "It sure is. 'Carolina in My Mind.' "

Ronnie nodded and still stood there. He'd come to the bookstore and gotten change for the bus as long as Sam had been there. Sam didn't know where he went on the bus. Maybe he had a relative he visited, or maybe he went to a soup kitchen downtown, or maybe he just rode somewhere and rode back to pass the time.

"I used to have a radio. It played James Taylor all the time." He put his hands in his pants pockets. "My girl-friend took it when she left."

Sam had never heard Ronnie mention anyone connected with him. It was so easy to think of street people as having no family, no history, no series of sad events that led them here.

Ronnie drummed his fingers on the counter. "It had AM *and* FM." He turned and walked out of the store.

The needle edged toward the red danger zone as the Tempest threatened to overheat in the crawling lunch-hour traffic. Sam put his head out the window to get a better look at a wreck at an intersection two blocks away. He noticed the sky—how blue it was. It was one of those rare days in Atlanta, which was warm enough to be pleasant, yet cool enough to be clear. It wouldn't be long before summer's humidity suffocated the city.

The line of traffic moved but then stopped again. Sam had pulled even with a Tempest like his, except in much better condition. Two middle-aged men jogged up the sidewalk, their barrel-chested bodies listing from side to side on pale, bony legs. They shouted conversation over the traffic, making better headway than the idling cars. On the corner, an old, very thin man held out bunches of flowers to passing cars. Jessie said he'd worked that corner for ten years. A sign propped against his bucket of flowers declared: I Am *Not* a Moonie! Every morning he stopped in the bookstore to buy a *Wall Street Journal*.

Traffic inched forward. Off to the right, downtown skyscrapers rose up over the trees. He hardly ever went downtown but was always aware of it, even miles out on the expressway. All he had to do was glance in his rearview mirror and there it was—a vain city waiting to be noticed.

He'd come to Atlanta from Greenville, South Carolina, having just broken up with a woman who cared more about plants and Jesus than about him. They'd dated throughout college, but because of her religious convictions and her rubber tree, which required a certain kind of indirect light, she wouldn't move in with him. When they finally broke up (one of the few decisions they ever reached together), he tossed his clothes, some books, and an old Underwood typewriter into the backseat of the Tempest and fled South Carolina. He would always remember that drive, although he'd made the trip many times before, in college and afterward, to hear Richie Havens at the Great Southeastern Music Hall or Judy Collins at the Fox, to drink beer from hurricane glasses in the ghostly light of Underground Atlanta or to shop in Lenox Square, the mecca of malls. Even as a child he'd visited Atlanta with his parents to watch Hank Aaron drill another one over the center-field fence, to ride the sky lift over Stone Mountain's carved faces, or just to stay in the motel downtown, whose pool and Coke machine were probably not much different from those in any other motel, but to Sam it was a thrill just to know he was in the middle of Atlanta, the South's rendition of a big city.

The day he left South Carolina, he felt some of that same childhood thrill as he drove the rolling hills of I-85, a 140-mile stretch of grazing cows and Stuckey's billboards. He'd left behind a strange girlfriend, a lousy job, and a dark apartment; still, they had been his, and as the Tempest closed in on Atlanta, he knew, maybe for the first time, that a loss is a loss, no matter how much one needs to lose it.

Sam pulled up next to the flower man and was about to ask him how much a bouquet was when the window of the Tempest next to him lowered, revealing a black man wearing a white coat. It was Dr. Franklin, the pediatrician Kate had introduced him to at Stone Mountain. He held out two dollars to the flower man and took the daisies.

"Dr. Franklin," Sam called out.

The doctor didn't see him and rolled up his window.

Swamped with lunchtime traffic, waitresses one-handed immense trays of food, poured coffee, bused tables, sorted silverware, and still took time for small talk with the customers. In their frenzied efficiency, they never lost sight of the tip.

The lunch crowd at the Rainbow Cafe was more disparate than breakfast or dinner. Business people ate next to workmen, men next to women, old next to young. At the takeout line at the cash register, a black woman in a business suit laughed with an older white man wearing a construction helmet and mud-caked boots.

Sam sat in a corner booth, finishing his BLT. He popped the last bite into his mouth, washed it down with a swallow of iced tea, and wiped his fingers with his napkin. The food at the Rainbow was greasy but sincere.

He'd thought about going back to the pay phone in back of the diner and calling Kate. But they'd been through that before—calling each other every five minutes, back and forth, trying to get things right. The phone was deceptive that way; it gave the impression that something was actually being accomplished.

He kept hearing his phone conversation with her, telling her he wanted to work things out and she asking what he meant. He'd better figure out what he meant if they were going to talk about it tonight.

Marriage. That's what he'd meant. Why was he being coy with himself? The more he thought about it—the possibility of Kate's leaving him—the more he'd realized that marriage was the only way to keep her. Maybe he could do it. Maybe he had more emotional stamina than he gave himself credit for. The thought of being a husband and a father still gave him butterflies, but maybe there was no way to get ready; maybe he just needed to stop thinking and do it.

A waitress refilled his tea, jiggling the big silver pitcher so that chunks of ice slid into his glass. She yawned.

"Long day?" he asked.

"Long life." She yawned again. "My daughter had me up half the night, helping her cram for a biology test." She picked up his empty plate and dropped it in the busing tray behind his table. "I dreamed parameciums." She wrinkled her nose. "The night before, I stayed up helping my son hinge plywood together for his science project." She tapped the bottom of the tea pitcher with her ring. "Kids may get the diploma, but it's parents who get the education." She scratched her head. "Do you have kids?"

"No." He shrugged. "Not yet, anyway."

"I tell mine that when they grow up and get good jobs, Mom's coming around for a cut." She raised her eyebrows. "I'm not waiting tables in my dotage." Her face was dark and full. Although pretty, she had the hardened features of women who've had to raise their children alone. He guessed she must be new, because he hadn't noticed her before.

"Miss?" A black man in a blue plumber's uniform held up his empty glass.

"On my way." She leaned over to Sam. "When you have kids, don't get too attached." She pushed a loose strand of hair out of her eyes. "They grow up faster than you think. In three years both of mine will be off at college." She sighed. "Parenthood is the only job whose point is to become obsolete." She hurried over to the man's table and filled his glass, saying something to him that made him throw back his head and laugh. She moved easily between the tables and booths, refilling glasses and making small talk.

Sam leaned back in the booth and ate the pickle off

his plate. If this woman could raise a family alone, surely he and Kate together could pull it off. That's what he had to remind himself—that he would not be in this alone.

He began to feel better. Things lost their edge in the smoky warmth of the Rainbow, a dingy red-brick building whose grimy outside had all the charm of a car-parts store. He had lunch at the cafe almost every day, and since it wasn't far from his house, he and Kate ate breakfast here sometimes. On Saturday mornings Kate liked to get up early and go to yard sales, so on their way they'd stop and have breakfast at the Rainbow.

He'd read the sports section while she underlined yard sales in the classifieds. He liked their being the only ones in the Rainbow, the only couple awake in the neighborhood. They'd sit together in a booth, sipping coffee. Sometimes a few workmen would wander in. They were carpenters, plumbers, delivery men—men so used to early hours that even on their days off they couldn't sleep late. Sam found peace during this hour with Kate. Sometimes he would look up from his paper and notice the sign over the counter: Be Nice to People. While Kate underlined yard sales, the waitress filled their cups, and a couple of men at the counter talked in low, scratchy voices. He would think, This is where I want to be—alone with Kate in the Rainbow Cafe.

"Anything else?" The waitress stopped by his table, holding an empty tray at her side. "Dessert? How about some strawberry pie? I had a piece this morning. Lord knows, I might as well apply it directly to my hips." She patted her hip with the tray.

"I need to get back." He looked at his watch.

"What do you do?" She pulled a pad out of her apron and a pencil from behind her ear and filled out his check.

"I'm a book clerk at Brilliant's."

"I've always thought that'd be the perfect job. To sit around and read all day."

"It would be if that's what book clerks did."

She nodded. "The grass is always greener, I guess." She tore the check off her pad and put it facedown on the table. "Come back." She hurried off to take orders from a table of women who'd just sat down.

It wasn't until he'd walked up to the register that he noticed her note on the back of the check. She'd drawn a smiley face, but instead of "Thank you" or "Have a nice day," she'd written, "Good Luck." And it was signed: "Leila."

On his way back to the bookstore, he felt the gearshift stick in second gear. "Shit." The Tempest crawled along, backing up traffic until he could pull over in a parking lot. He opened the hood and jostled a metal rod Willy had shown him to fiddle with whenever the gear stuck. It wouldn't move.

He felt a little giddy with this new hope. He was becoming more accustomed to the idea of something permanent with Kate. He might not have entirely reconciled himself to all the complications of family life, but he would take it one step at a time. Tonight he'd ask her to marry him. Under his hand, he felt something click into place.

Carl came up to the front as Sam wrestled a Julia Child cookbook display that had come with a life-size cardboard likeness of the author. Sam couldn't get her to stand up.

"She's been hitting the sauce." Carl stood on his tiptoes, going over the back of the books with his fingers. "Have you seen a hardback copy of *Tortilla Flat?*" he whispered.

Sam picked up the cardboard Julia Child again, trying to fold the flap on the back to make it stand.

"The computer says we have one in stock." Carl

stroked his mustache. "I spent the whole morning looking for it. I think we sold it."

"I haven't seen it." Julia slowly tipped backward. "Ask Paula."

Carl put his fingers to his lips. "I don't want to give her the satisfaction."

Paula's head poked up from behind the fiction bookshelf, where she'd been stooped, checking inventory. She walked up to the shelf where Carl had been looking and pulled off a hardback copy of *Tortilla Flat*. "If it'd been a snake . . ."

He rolled his eyes, then actually smiled at his foolishness. Jessie had already derailed his anger toward Paula by asking him to organize a book signing for Bill Gullard, a local newspaper columnist who'd just published his eighth or ninth book. (The books seemed pretty interchangeable to Sam.) The rest of the afternoon Carl bustled around the store, composing lists and making calls. It was an ingenious move on Jessie's part. If there was anything Carl loved to handle more than books, it was the writers themselves.

That afternoon, Raymond came by the store, as he often did after school. His knapsack slung over his shoulder, he'd make for the children's section, pick out a book, and disappear into the miniature log cabin Jessie had had a friend of hers build for kids to read in. Raymond was getting a little too big for the cabin. He had to draw his knees up to his chin to fit. He'd stay in there reading for hours. Sometimes Sam would forget he was in there until he went back to the children's section to shelve or find a book for a customer and he'd see Raymond's elbows jutting out of the windows.

For a week after Virginia had whipped him down by the railroad tracks, Raymond didn't come in. Sam saw him ride his bike on Elmira, but always up the street, away from Sam's house. Sam thought he might be mad that he'd told Virginia he was down at the railroad yard. Kate said he was probably just embarrassed. A week later, he was relieved to see Raymond walk through the door, but he barely nodded to Sam.

He waited on a couple of people, then, when the store was empty, wandered back to the children's section and asked Raymond what he was reading.

"*Charlotte's Web*." Raymond's voice echoed in the cabin.

"That's a good book." Sam stooped down beside the cabin.

"It's okay." Raymond had drawn himself up, the book resting on his knees. He turned a page, still reading. "But somebody ought to tell this E. B. White that spiders can't spell."

"How's your mother?"

Raymond turned another page, betraying the fact that he really wasn't reading. "Fine."

Kate had gone up to their house the day after the scene at the railroad yard to apologize to Virginia. Virginia invited her in for coffee. She told her how hard it had been raising three children without their father. She said she missed her husband. The thing she missed most about him was that when the kids were on the verge of driving her out of her mind, she'd go into the bedroom with her husband, shut the door, and lie there on the bed, talking about trips they'd take when the kids were grown and out of the house. They'd even started a small savings account for a Winnebago. She said she missed her husband's soothing voice, going on and on about places he'd always wanted to see—Niagara Falls, the Grand Canyon, and the Redwood National Park, where he planned to drive that Winnebago right through one of those tunnel trees.

"You aren't mad at me, are you, Raymond?" Sam asked.

Raymond turned another page. "About what?"

"That I told your mother you were at the railroad yard."

He turned another page. "You're a grown-up; you didn't know any better."

By late afternoon, it had clouded over outside, and with the front door propped open, he heard the distant rumble of an approaching storm, the first thunderstorm of the season. Sudden breezes lifted the covers on the rack of paperback best-sellers. The newspapers rattled in their stand. The cardboard Julia Child, which (with Carl's help) Sam had finally gotten to stand, teetered but didn't fall.

Sam asked Paula to watch the register while he went over to Mr. Berkowitz's to buy some wine for tonight. All afternoon he'd been planning the evening, trying to contain the quiet elation that had been building in him. He'd been tempted but had decided not to tell anyone until he'd asked her. He didn't want to jinx it.

Mr. Berkowitz chewed a cigar stub, leaning his aged bald head close to a yellow legal pad, which he wrote on furiously. An avowed pacifist, he was famous for his letters to the editor, confronting the atrocities of mankind, from SDI to the gassing of kittens in the county animal shelter.

Mr. Berkowitz put down his pen. "The usual, Sam?" He took a bottle of wine from a sale bin next to the register.

"Something better tonight," Sam said. "Something to go with fish."

"Something better?" He peered at Sam over his glasses. "The book business flourishes?" He nodded to himself. "Thanks to the Ayatollah." Then he shrugged. "At least Rushdie knows he's getting read."

The old man shuffled back through his store. Whenever Sam asked Mr. Berkowitz how long he'd had his liquor store, he'd reply, "Since creation." Sam pictured the old man shuffling around the Garden of Eden, a cigar stub in his mouth.

"You're celebrating something?" Mr. Berkowitz took a bottle off the shelf.

"I hope." He felt the flutter of butterflies in his stomach.

"Either one celebrates, or one doesn't." He held the bottle out to Sam. "She'll like this." He shuffled back behind the register. "Your anniversary, maybe?"

Somehow Mr. Berkowitz had gotten the idea that Sam was married. Sam had never had the heart to correct him. For years he'd gone along with the charade. The old man was a bachelor and considered marriage a perfect state that he himself could never attain.

Back outside, Sam glanced through the store window at Mr. Berkowitz, who'd taken up his pen again. The old man used his whole body to restrain the pen's fury. Sam reached into the bag, feeling the cold neck of the bottle. What if Kate said no? What if she refused him? He watched Mr. Berkowitz, wondering if he himself might not wind up a lonely old bachelor scribbling letters of misdirected passion.

Sam bumped into Carl, who was on his way out of the bookstore.

"I have to get home and close my living-room windows before it rains on my new rug." Carl hurried on down the sidewalk, his briefcase bumping against his leg. The only thing he'd ever seen Carl take out of that briefcase was a brown paper sack containing his lunch.

When Sam walked back inside, his heart skipped a beat when he saw that no one was watching the register. "Paula?"

"I'm keeping my eye on it, Sam." She stood around the corner of a bookshelf. Macon, her husband, was with her. He was a thin, slump-shouldered boy with very fine blond hair and weary eyes. They talked in low, quick snips. Rather, Paula talked, and Macon mumbled.

"You'd only been there two weeks," Sam heard her say. "You can't tell anything about a job in two weeks." She came up to the register and wrote out a check for twenty-five dollars. "Would you cash this for me, Sam?" Embarrassed, she didn't look at him.

He slipped the check into the register and counted out two tens and a five, which she handed to Macon, who mumbled something and walked off.

"That's for groceries," she called out to him. "Don't spend it on records."

Macon had already turned the corner.

Paula stood there by the register with Sam, looking out at the approaching storm. Her face had gone pale. "He'll spend it on records."

"Then why'd you give it to him?"

"He's depressed. We'll manage. It just means another week of macaroni and cheese." She headed back toward the receiving room.

A young woman who'd been browsing in the fiction section asked Sam if he could suggest a good book. "Something funny. Not hilarious," she said. "Funny, but a little sad, too." She cocked her head. "Maybe even a little sexy." She laughed. "A recipe for a good book." She patted the life-size Julia Child. "Am I making it impossible?"

"Not at all." He recognized her voice, but why would he know her voice and not her face? He picked out several books he thought might fit her description. He was surprised when, without even glancing at them, she said she'd take them and wrote a check.

"Maybe you should at least read the dust jackets."

"I trust you."

He almost asked, "Don't I know you?" Maybe she'd been in the store before and he just hadn't noticed her. Although it would've been hard not to notice her long red hair and her face, which was distinctive and open. She wore a simple black cotton dress and sandals. Everything about her felt unencumbered.

"What kind of ID do you need?" She unzipped her pocketbook.

"I trust you." He slipped the check into the drawer without looking at it.

There was a loud crackle of thunder. Sam was grateful for the distraction. The wind picked up, rifled through the books, and knocked the cardboard Julia flat on her face.

He came around the register to close the door.

"I think it's really going to storm," the woman said.

They stood looking out at the wind bending the trees. There was another loud crackle of thunder.

"I've missed that sound," she said. "I've been living in California. They don't have lightning and thunder out there."

"I didn't know there was anyplace it didn't thunder."

She checked her watch. "I'm late for my geology class." She started to push open the door. She brushed his wrist.

"Maybe you ought to wait for it to blow over. You could be a little late." Was that a line? Attractive women always did this to him—turned him into a walking innuendo.

"I can't be late. I'm the teacher." She pushed open the door.

"Let me know what you think of the books." He held the door open for her as she ran up the sidewalk, her long hair blown back by the wind.

He went back to the register, opened the drawer, and took out her check. He looked at the name. It didn't ring a bell. He held the check up to his nose. It smelled of patchouli. She was the woman who'd come up to him at Stone Mountain, the woman in the shadows. The name printed on the check was Grace Smith.

He raced back outside, hoping to see her in the distance, her hair like a red flag. The sidewalk was empty as the first drops of rain popped against the pavement.

Someone put a hand on his shoulder. It was Ronnie. "Looking for James Taylor?"

Chapter Four

The first thing he did when he got home was to clean the house. Kate didn't come home until eight o'clock, sometimes later on Fridays, so he knew he had at least an hour or two to get ready. He made the bed, washed the dishes in the sink, swept, vacuumed, and mopped.

Clutter made Kate tense, and Sam wanted conditions to be as favorable as possible. Not that he thought she'd say yes just because he'd taken out the trash, but it might be a little harder for her to deny him in straightened rooms.

He even tried to bring some order to his study, a little room in the back of the house crammed with sagging bookshelves and more books piled on the floor. (As an employee of the bookstore, he got a 30 percent discount, so that he had half his paycheck spent before he even left the store.) In the middle of the room was a small desk with his Underwood typewriter, surrounded by dusty mounds of paper, a yellowed sheet still in its carriage. Dust had all but obscured framed photographs of Eudora Welty and William Saroyan that hung on the wall. As he picked up the books and organized the papers, he felt inertia creep over him. This room always sucked him into a malaise. He began to doubt his whole plan about Kate. He slumped down at his desk, stared at the unfinished sentence in the typewriter, and for a moment gave up. But then he took a deep breath, pushed himself up, rushed out, and shut the door behind him.

In the backyard, he dragged out the rusted old grill,

61

which, propped against the back of the house, had weathered the winter. He knocked out the leaves, spiderwebs, and slugs and spread a layer of aluminum foil across the bottom, covering a big rusted hole—the result of years of standing in the rain. One of its legs had broken off. He had to prop it up, a little precariously, on a board he found in the basement. It wobbled but seemed sturdy enough. He built a small pyramid of charcoals in the center, soaked them with lighter fluid until they shined, threw a match onto them, and standing on the edge of plowed garden, watched the flames shoot up.

The grill had been one of the first things Kate brought over from her apartment. There had never been any official moving in. One night she just didn't go home. The rest was a kind of osmosis. At first, she just brought clothes over from her apartment, then more clothes, then the ironing board, then her stereo and her grill, then more substantial things, like rugs, her kitchen table, her desk. She kept her apartment for a couple of months after she was sleeping at his place. It wasn't until three months into their relationship that one day, when they were trying to maneuver a very heavy dresser through her apartment door, Sam asked if she thought it might be a good idea to move in.

Sam marinated salmon steaks in a pan of Mr. Berkowitz's wine, adding olive oil and basil. Through the kitchen screen he saw the glow of the charcoals in the grill as he brought the rice to a boil, then lowered the flame and covered the pot. He snapped some green beans, washed them, and left them in a colander in the sink. He sliced up a loaf of French bread, buttered between the slices, and slid it into the oven, ready to be heated. He covered the dining-room table with the good tablecloth, setting out candles. He cut off most of the lights in the house and put on Jean-Pierre Rampal.

He went out back again to check the charcoals. "Almost ready." He clapped his hands as the flute music floated through the house, out into the backyard. "The food is ready. The house is ready." He laid his hand on his chest. "*I* am ready." He couldn't refrain from sighing. "Maybe I *will* pull this off."

A twig snapped behind him, and the Siamese slunk up, rubbing against his leg. "What's this?" Sam bent down to stroke the cat's back. "A change of heart?"

It sniffed the salmon on his fingers, licking them with its sandy tongue.

"I should've known you had an ulterior motive." He petted the cat.

He was spooning the marinade over the salmon, thinking he'd call Kate at the hospital to see if she'd be much later, when he heard footsteps cross the front porch. Quickly, he poured a glass of wine and hurried out to the foyer, stopping in the dining room to light the candles.

"Anybody home?" Rose's head poked around the door, with Sam standing there holding out a glass of wine.

The door pushed open. Joey charged in, wearing his *Sesame Street* pajamas and dragging a wooden fire engine behind him; its bell clanged. The needle skipped, then tore across the Jean-Pierre Rampal record as Joey ran up the hall and disappeared into the bathroom.

"Joey!" She ran after him in a black sequined dress that hugged her hips. Her high heels tapped across the floor. She carried a canvas bag over her shoulder that Sam recognized as containing baby supplies.

There was a silence; then the toilet flushed. They found Joey pointing down into the swirling water. He made a low gurgling noise, imitating the whirling water.

"He's discovered the aesthetics of the commode." She carried him back into the living room. She had her hair pinned back, wore eyeliner and lipstick, and had her dress pulled down around her shoulders.

"You look devastating." Not sure what else to do with it, he held the glass of wine out to her. Why was she here?

"No, thanks." She glanced at her watch. "I have to go back and pick up Lamar. You know he can't hurry when he gets dressed or he starts sweating; has to take another shower and start all over." She nodded at Joey, who tore across the living-room floor, dragging his fire engine. "I hope you don't mind."

"Mind what?"

"Kate didn't call you? I called her late this afternoon and asked if y'all wouldn't mind baby-sitting. Our usual baby-sitter is sick, and this is a big dinner with Lamar's boss."

"Kate must've gotten busy." He had a sinking feeling.

"She said y'all didn't have any plans for tonight." She saw the candles burning over the dining-room table, which was set with the tablecloth and the good wineglasses. "But *you* had plans. Oh, Sam, we've ruined something."

"We eat like this every night." He waved his hand toward the candles.

"Yeah, right." She tugged at her dress. "And this is an old thing I knock around the house in. We'll just take Joey to the restaurant with us."

"No, no, no. Isn't it almost his bedtime, anyway? We'll just put him down and then go on with our evening." If worse comes to worse, he could ask Kate tomorrow.

A wineglass shattered in the dining room. Having climbed up onto a chair, the baby reached for the burning candle, knocking off knives and forks. "Light."

Rose snatched him off the table as he was about to touch the flame. "No," she said. "Hot!"

"Hot?" Joey frowned at the candle.

She stooped down, picking up pieces of the broken wineglass.

"Don't worry about it." He straightened the table. He got a broom and swept up the glass.

"Now that he's a little bigger," she said, "he gets into everything. He can even reach doorknobs. Lamar says it's like rising floodwaters; no shelf is high enough." She shook her head at the dustpan of broken glass.

Sam took Joey out of her arms, lifted his shirt, and blew on his stomach, making him squeal. "We'll be fine, won't we, buddy?"

Joey pointed to the doorway that led to upstairs.

"I see he's still into stairs." She closed the door to the stairway and locked it. She held the baby up to her face and kissed him. "You be good while Mama's gone and don't shit more than you have to." She handed Sam the canvas bag that he knew from experience contained Pampers, wipes, a bottle, some toys, a couple of books, and his blanket. She kissed Sam's cheek. "Good luck with your plans." She nodded toward the set table.

Joey wriggled out of her arms and headed back to the bathroom. "Joey!"

She started after him, but Sam held her back.

"I'll watch him. You run on before Lamar starts sweating."

"One day we'll do the same for y'all." She called down the hall. "Good-bye, Joey."

The toilet flushed.

Joey crashed two lids together like cymbals, playing with pots on the kitchen floor, while Sam checked the rice, put the beans on, and got the salmon ready to grill. He could see the coals glow in the dark as the Siamese pressed his nose against the screen and sniffed.

Yes, Sam told himself, looking around, everything's

under control. He'd be able to manage with Joey. It might even be good luck to propose with a baby in the house.

The phone rang. It was Kate calling from work. "We're supposed to baby-sit Joey tonight."

"Really?"

Joey sat on the kitchen floor with several different-sized pots turned upside down, beating them with a wooden spoon.

"I tried to call you at work, but I guessed y'all had already closed. I've been tied up with a patient ever since." She paused. "What's that noise?"

"It's not Ringo."

"I'm sorry," she said. "I didn't think you'd mind." She sounded tired.

"Rose was really decked out."

"It's some big deal with Lamar's boss. I'll be home soon. Can you survive?"

"Everything's under control."

After he hung up, he and Joey spent the next half hour playing Joey's favorite game, which was to climb the staircase on his stomach. Joey crawled up the steps, occasionally stopping to look back at Sam, who crawled right behind him in case he slipped. Joey laughed when he saw Sam on his hands and knees, as if he looked absolutely ridiculous. When he got to the top, he walked down with one hand on the rail and one hand in Sam's hand. He took it one step at a time, giving a little grunt every time he touched the next step. They'd gone up and down twice when Sam decided he'd better put the salmon on before the coals burned out. He carried Joey back to the kitchen, closing the door that led to the stairs.

"In case you get any bright ideas." He poked Joey in the stomach.

"Up." Joey pointed at the closed door.

With Joey in one arm and the pan of salmon in the other, Sam went out back to the grill. He set Joey down while he spread the coals, then laid the salmon on the grill. The steaks sizzled, dripping their juices onto the coals. The phone began to ring inside. Gathering up Joey, he hurried back in. It was Kate. She'd been held up again but was on her way.

"Should I pick up something for dinner? I'm sick of Arby's. What about Wendy's?"

"That's okay. I've thrown a little something together."

"Tell Joey not to do anything too cute till I get there."

As Sam hung up, he heard a loud crash in the backyard. He ran outside and saw the grill turned over on its side; charcoals spilled across the ground, glowing in the grass. The board he'd propped it up with had slipped.

"Shit." He'd have to rinse the steaks off and cook them in the oven. He picked up one of the steaks, which was covered with sand and grass, but he couldn't find the other. He saw the Siamese drag a salmon steak through the hedge. "Son of a bitch!"

The cat ran when he saw Sam coming, leaving the steak hanging in the shrub.

"Fuck." Sam tried to pull the steak loose, but it tore apart in his hands. "Fuck." He threw the pieces across the yard. "Fuck, fuck, fuck!"

A small fire smoldered in the leaves and dry grass around the grill. He hauled Kate's garden hose out of the toolshed and soaked the grass and the coals. "Unbelievable." He kicked the grill. He tried to think how he might salvage the meal. They did have some Stouffer's chicken pies. It wasn't grilled salmon, but it would suffice. It might even be kind of quaint. Something he could tell their grandchildren. I proposed to her over chicken pot pie.

When he walked back into the kitchen, his heart lurched. Joey. He wasn't there. "Joey?" Cabinet doors were flung open, pots and pans strewn all over the floor, as if there'd been some kind of struggle. Joey had been playing with them, he reminded himself.

"Joey?" Sam bent down, looking inside the cabinets, thinking he might be hiding. He checked behind the stove, behind the refrigerator. He thought he heard a noise in another part of the house. The bathroom, of course; he breathed a sigh of relief. He ran up the hall and turned on the bathroom light. No Joey.

"Joey?" Out of the corner of his eye he noticed that the door leading upstairs was cracked. A chill ran through him. He heard Rose's voice: "He can even reach doorknobs." He'd forgotten to lock the door. He heard Joey's voice. "Up." He flung the door open and froze at the bottom of the stairs.

The stairway was dark, but in the light at the top of the stairs he saw Joey grip the rail as he extended his foot out over air, reaching down for the next step.

"Joey, no!" He held his hands out. "No!"

Joey grinned at Sam. He thought it was a game. He dangled his foot out over the step again. "Up."

Sam took a step up.

Joey stepped down, wobbled, then lost his grip. His scream stopped suddenly, as if someone had clapped a hand over his mouth, and his head bounced against step after step—a sound Sam would never forget.

Sam was halfway up the stairs when he caught Joey, whose limp body rolled into his arms. "Joey?"

Joey's eyes stayed closed, his mouth hung open slightly, and his arms fell down by his sides. He looked exactly the way he did when he fell asleep on the couch in Rose's lap. As Sam carried him out to the couch, he would later remember that he tiptoed.

"Joey?" It wasn't until he laid him down that he felt the growing knot on the back of Joey's head. Then he noticed a stillness about the baby. His face had drained to a frightening paleness. Sam put his hand on the baby's forehead. This isn't right, he told himself; the baby wouldn't have a fever. Sam felt tears of panic well in his eyes. "Fuck," he cried, looking around the room. "What the fuck should I do?"

He leaned his ear down to the child's mouth. Joey wasn't breathing! For a second he had the dizzy feeling that this wasn't happening. The next thing he knew he was running down the front steps with Joey in his arms. He ran across the yard and up the sidewalk, keeping his hand under Joey's head. Wasn't that what people always said about holding babies? Support the head.

It was a dark, cool night, really a beautiful night—some part of him noticed, the part that watched. There was even a bird singing. What kind of bird sang in the dark?

Raymond was riding his bike in circles under the streetlight. He stopped when he saw Sam.

"Go get your mother." He realized why he'd been running in this direction—Virginia, of course. "There's an injured baby here."

Without a word, Raymond wheeled his bike around, jumped the curb, and pumping the pedals fast, rode up into his yard, threw his bike down, and ran up the steps, yelling, "Mama, Mama, come quick!"

Sam hurried up the sidewalk, kicking at the beagle that barked around his feet. He felt a wash of relief when Virginia stepped out on the porch, wiping her hands on her apron. Raymond was right behind her, followed by Charles and Deborah, Virginia's two older children.

Sam held the baby out to her. "He fell. Hit his head on the steps. He's not breathing."

She took the baby into her big arms. She felt under the baby's neck. Without a word, she carried the baby back inside, Raymond holding the screen door open.

"Charles, call an ambulance." Virginia commanded as they passed through the den where the TV was on.

"What's the number?" he asked.

"Don't you know anything?" Deborah said. "It's 911."

Sam and Raymond followed Virginia into the bright

yellow kitchen, which was warm with the smell of cooking vegetables and a heavier, richer smell—chicken. Pots boiled on every eye of the stove, their lids jittering with steam. In the middle of the kitchen, a rectangular white metal table was set for supper. On the counter, four glasses were filled with ice, ready for tea, which brewed in a big pitcher with tea bags tied to its handle.

"Clear the table," Virginia said.

Raymond picked up the silverware. Sam moved a big bowl of artificial fruit to the counter.

She laid the baby down; his head lolled back too far, and his mouth opened. His skin was ashen against the white table. Sam had never seen eyes so closed.

Virginia felt under the baby's neck again. "No pulse." She ripped off his *Sesame Street* pajamas; the buttons popped across the kitchen. She held the baby's neck up with her hand, then put her mouth over the baby's nose and mouth. She breathed into the baby once, then again, then, with her two fingers on the baby's chest, pumped. She breathed into the baby again. His tiny chest rose and fell. She pumped his chest. She repeated this twice more, then stopped and felt under the baby's neck. She shook her head and sighed.

Grease popped in the oven, the TV blared in the other room, and they heard Charles on the phone. "We need an ambulance at 23 Elmira Street, pronto."

She bent over the baby again, held his neck up as she breathed into him, and pumped his little chest. Her forehead glistened with sweat.

"Ambulance on the way, Mama." Charles came into the kitchen, with Deborah behind him.

He prayed to God or anybody who could tilt things in Joey's favor. He thought of all the babies that had died in Kate's neonatal unit. But death was not confined to the hospital. He found himself playing that old game with himself of expecting the worst to prevent it from happening.

Virginia's breathing seemed to fill the kitchen. She'd

turn her head, listen for a breath as she pressed the baby's chest with her two fingers, and whisper, ". . . three, four, five." The children and Sam pressed against the kitchen wall.

One of the pots on the stove bubbled over; the blue flame hissed underneath and flickered yellow, threatening to go out. The grease sizzled inside the oven.

Joey seemed to have drifted beyond even Virginia's powerful reach. Sam felt numb. His attention wandered to the cheery yellow wallpaper with pale blue stripes that made the kitchen seem bigger than it was; the windowsill above the sink, where carrot tops sprouted a crown of leaves in the tops of peanut-butter jars; the refrigerator door, which was draped with a large watercolor of brown not-quite-stick figures standing in front of a lopsided house. The faceless figures, two tall ones and three small, had their arms around each other, posed for a picture. Printed in large purple letters across the bottom of the page were the words WE ARE FAMILY, and squeezed in the very bottom of the right-hand corner was an apologetic signature, "Raymond Brennan."

"Come on, darling." Virginia put her mouth over the baby's again.

Raymond stepped closer to get a better look. "Come on, baby," he whispered. "Breathe, man."

The children's eyes were wide, their faces solemn with renewed respect, seeing their mother in action. She'd told Kate she'd been there when her husband fell from the tree. Sam could picture her on the ground, bent over her husband, trying to breathe life back into him.

He felt a part of himself walk out of the room, wander through Virginia's house, through the pine-paneled den, where a cluster of photographs hung over a long white couch, then back into the children's bedroom, then into Virginia's room—the same room, the same bed where she'd retreat with her husband to contemplate the ceiling and plan trips.

"A pulse." Virginia had her hand on the baby's neck. She leaned her ear over the baby's mouth. "This darling is breathing again."

The children jabbed each other in the ribs, smiling at the miracle their mother had just performed.

Sam watched the color come back into the baby's face. "Jesus Christ," he whispered. He slumped down into one of the straight-backed chairs. His body felt wrung out. His shirt was soaked with sweat. "Is he going to be okay?"

She pulled his pajamas back over him.

Raymond reappeared with a comforter he'd taken off one of the chairs in the den. "He looks cold." He watched her wrap the baby in the comforter. "Why doesn't he open his eyes?"

"He might not open them for a while. He has a concussion."

"You get those when you hit your head." Raymond turned to Sam. "I got one when I fell off my bike. Couldn't see straight. I had to walk my bike home, and everything looked fuzzy." He lightly patted the baby. "Sleep is the best thing for it."

Sam studied the baby's closed eyes and thought of all those maudlin TV news features of children in bad accidents who fell into deep comas: Parents kept vigil by their bedsides, read them stories, sang to them, brought in their favorite toys—to bribe them back into consciousness. "When will we know for sure?"

"Whenever he comes to." She felt his neck. "His pulse is strong."

"Helloooo? Anyone home?" Sam recognized Kate's voice.

Deborah went out to the den and opened the door. "Is Sam here?" he heard her ask.

"He's here," Deborah said. "He's back in the kitchen."

"Is anything the matter?" He heard them walk back

through the den. "Mrs. Smeak said she saw Sam run up here carrying something. . . ."

"We called an ambulance," Deborah said.

"An ambulance?" Kate hurried into the kitchen, still wearing the white lab coat she wore at the hospital. She went right over to where Sam sat. "Are you all right?" She pushed the hair back on his forehead, looking for an injury. "Who's hurt?"

"You better sit down." Sam got up and offered her his chair.

"Who's hurt?" That's when she noticed Virginia cradling the baby in her arms. "What's wrong with Joey?" She took a step toward Virginia. "He's not—"

"His heart stopped," Virginia said. "But we got it going again. His pulse is real strong now."

"I hit his head," Sam began. "I mean he fell down the stairs and hit his head. I forgot to lock the door."

Virginia unwrapped the comforter from the back of Joey's head, revealing an immense bruise.

Kate gasped. "Oh, my God."

"His breathing is steady," Virginia said. "His pulse is very strong. This is one tough little life." She guided Kate's fingers under the baby's neck. "Everything looks good."

As the two women bent over Joey, a siren moaned in the distance.

The three children looked at each other, then ran out on the porch.

"Did you see Mama bring that baby back?" Charles's voice drifted back through the house. His tone was respectful.

Kate pulled a chair up next to Virginia and Joey. "How long was his breathing stopped?"

"Three or four minutes from the time Sam brought him in," Virginia said.

Was that all it was? Sam asked himself. It had been a century to him.

"How long was it from when he actually hit his head?" Kate turned to Sam.

"I'm not sure. A couple of minutes." Sam knew she was talking about brain damage, how long Joey's brain had gone without oxygen.

"I'm not blaming you." Kate's voice was even and calm now. She covered his hand with hers. "It's something the doctor will want to know."

"Two or three minutes. It might've been longer." He felt the two women look at each other, the silent communication of professionals.

"Coming up the street, Mama," Deborah said from the front porch.

Outside, the siren wailed louder as the ambulance made its way up the street. Kate and Sam followed behind Virginia as she carried the baby outside.

Sam glanced back at the empty kitchen. Ice had melted in the glasses. Pots still simmered on the stove, their contents limp and tasteless by now. In the middle of the room stood the empty white enamel table where the family had been about to sit down to supper.

I couldn't remember how you take it." Sam handed Lamar one of the covered Styrofoam cups out of the cardboard tray he'd brought up from the hospital coffee shop. He dropped a handful of sugar packets, creamers, and plastic stirrers onto the table. He offered a cup to the middle-aged couple who'd come in a couple of hours ago. Their daughter, a heavy-faced little girl who must've been around Raymond's age, slept with her head in her mother's lap, a sheet of her shiny blond hair hanging over the chair. They were the only other people in the waiting room.

"Thanks," the man said. He wore a light blue shirt,

navy pants, and the heavy black shoes of a bus driver. Often Sam had found himself staring at the sturdy polished shoes. There was something reassuring about them. "What do we owe you?"

"It's on me," Sam said.

"Appreciate it."

The mother nodded at Sam, her hair rolled in curlers. When they'd first come in, she'd kept saying, "How? How could Leon do this to us?" Finally, the man, who'd been reading a magazine, turned to her. "He didn't do it to us. He did it to himself." Kate found out from one of the nurses that when the husband came home from work in the middle of the night, he found their thirteen-year-old son passed out on the bathroom floor, his wrists slashed. He'd lost a lot of blood but would live.

Lamar's hand trembled as he tried to take the lid off the coffee. He set it on the table, then peeled back the white plastic lid. He was still in his suit, although he'd loosened his tie and unbuttoned his vest. He tore open a sugar packet, spilling it all over the table.

"Here." Sam stooped down beside him, emptying a sugar packet into Lamar's coffee. "Cream, too?" He'd never seen Lamar like this.

"Yeah." Lamar's voice was scratchy from staying up all night.

Sam stirred the cream into his coffee. Coagulated white lumps floated to the top. "It's a little curdled."

Lamar held the cup with both hands, didn't drink it, but stared up the long hall—the pediatrics floor. At the far end, Kate and Dr. Franklin, who'd been the pediatrician on duty tonight, talked outside Joey's room. Rose was in there, sitting with him. Every few minutes a nurse disappeared into Joey's room. Kate said they checked the heart monitor, making sure he was still breathing.

The doctor had been very good with Lamar and Rose, telling them that it wasn't unusual that Joey hadn't responded yet. He said they should all go home and get some sleep. "That's what Joey's doing." But when Rose said she was staying no matter what, the doctor said that one of them could sit with the baby. Rose had been in there almost all night, watching the still baby through the crib bars. Lamar had watched him for an hour while she'd tried to sleep scrunched up in a waiting-room chair.

"How's the baby?" the bus driver asked Lamar, but Lamar didn't seem to hear him.

"I think he's about the same," Sam said.

The woman in curlers stroked her sleeping daughter's hair. "Kids are resilient."

The bus driver put his hand over hers.

Through the waiting-room window Sam noticed the surfaces of buildings—brick, concrete, glass—as they emerged from the vague silhouettes he'd stared at all night. The Atlanta skyline assembled under the pink backdrop of dawn. Although Virginia had offered, Kate insisted on riding with Joey in the ambulance. Sam followed in Kate's car, keeping right behind the ambulance as it careened through intersections, ran red lights, and weaved through halted traffic. The way the cars pulled over to let them pass made Sam feel in sync with the city.

Kate had stayed with the baby in the emergency room. Sam found a pay phone in the lobby and called the restaurant Rose said they were going to. He had Rose and Lamar paged. When Rose answered, she already sounded worried. "What's wrong? Did something happen to Joey?"

He hadn't been prepared for her to already comprehend so much, but that, of course, would've been the first thing to cross her mind when she heard their name announced in the restaurant.

"They say he's going to be okay," Sam said.

"They?"

"The doctors." He could've kicked himself for not

leading up to it more gently, but he'd already screwed that up. There was nothing left except to tell her. "Rose, we're at Grady with the baby. He fell down the stairs and hit his head pretty hard."

There was a pause.

"Rose?"

"But he is alive? You wouldn't keep that from me, would you, Sam?"

"Oh, yes, God, he's alive. He's very alive." Why hadn't he made that plainer? "His breathing is steady, and his pulse is real strong." He paused. "He has a concussion."

"We'll be there in five minutes."

"Rose?"

"Yes?"

"I don't know how it happened." His voice cracked. "I just don't."

There was a long pause, and he could hear the noise of the restaurant in the background.

"We'll be there in five minutes." She hung up.

He stood in the phone booth a minute more, his head slumped against the glass.

Sam carried a cup of coffee up the hall where Kate and the doctor talked in low voices outside Joey's room. He thought Kate stiffened when she saw him. She slid her hands down into the pockets of her white coat. She hadn't looked him in the eye all night.

"How's Joey?" he whispered.

Behind them, through the cracked door, Rose stood over the crib, still wearing that black dress, except now it covered her shoulders.

"Still not responding." Dr. Franklin put his hand on Sam's shoulder. The doctor had been friendly to Sam but hadn't given any sign that he remembered him. But then doctors were professionals at not giving signs. "It's too soon to expect anything." The doctor squeezed Sam's shoulder.

"I brought her some coffee. Can I take it in to her?"

Kate scratched her forehead. "Maybe it'd be better if I took it in."

"I don't mind doing it," Sam said.

"That's okay." Kate took the coffee and went quietly into the room.

Sam felt awful. Rose hadn't spoken to him since she'd arrived at the hospital. She hadn't really had time. Why should he think about that now? The baby was all that mattered right now. Why should Rose pay him any attention when her son's life was in the balance? Still, he couldn't stand the thought that Rose resented him, maybe even hated him.

He saw Kate set the coffee on the night table and then stand next to Rose, hugging her and looking down at Joey. When she came back out, the three of them moved away from Joey's door.

"How's she holding up?" Sam asked.

Kate had dark circles under her eyes. "Pretty well, but I wish she'd get some sleep."

"What about you?" Dr. Franklin said to her. "You've been here since eight this morning. Why don't you go home? Sam will call you if anything happens."

Sam nodded to the doctor, appreciative to be assigned a way to help. He put his arm around Kate. "Why don't you? You look wiped out. I'll call if something happens." *When* something happens, he told himself.

"I wouldn't be able to sleep, anyway." She walked off in the direction of the waiting room, leaving Sam alone with the doctor. She sat down next to Lamar and massaged his shoulders. Something she said to Lamar made him smile.

"Don't take this too hard." The doctor patted his back. "These things happen." The doctor squeezed Sam's shoulder, then walked up toward the nurses' station. He walked on his toes, a slight bounce to his step.

Left alone outside Joey's room, Sam moved toward

the door, glanced up and down the hall, then slipped inside. Rose didn't hear him. He stood inside the door; his pulse raced. The room was still except for the blinking heart monitor over the crib. The room was very warm, almost hot. Pictures of clowns stared down from the walls.

Rose leaned on her elbows over the crib, her dress clinging tightly to her back. Her whole body arched toward the still baby, and she talked to Joey in a hushed tone she might use if he'd just drifted off to sleep.

Sam heard nurses' voices in the hall. He shouldn't be in here. He felt he was watching something he shouldn't, intruding, spying even. He started to slip out.

"Stay, Sam." Rose didn't turn around but held out her hand for him.

He stepped up and took her hand.

Joey lay on his back, a wire taped to his chest. The color had come back into his cheeks since the first moments on Virginia's kitchen table.

Joey's hair curled down the back of his neck, several long strands Rose hadn't cut since he'd been born.

"I am so sorry," he whispered.

"How's Lamar?" she asked in a tired voice. She stroked the baby's head. A wisp of her hair had come unpinned, falling across her eyes.

"Kate's with him."

"If anything happens to Joey, Lamar will never get over it." With a stab of grief, Sam remembered his conversation with Lamar out by the grill.

Sam put his arm around her shoulder.

She leaned against him.

They stayed that way a long time. Out in the hall the intercom echoed a doctor's name. They stayed that way until Joey—his eyes still shut—began to whimper, then cry and thrash his arms in the air, elbowing his way back.

Chapter Five

When Sam glanced up from the special orders Jessie had asked him to go over, a giant bouquet in slacks walked into the store. It was Carl, hidden behind two immense floral arrangements. He set the flowers on the counter and stepped back to admire them. "What do you think?"

"They're big." They swallowed the counter.

"I get a professional discount." He put one arrangement in the window and the other in front of a card table set up in the middle of the store, which was stacked with neat pyramids of Bill Gullard's latest book. Carl had ordered a hundred extra copies for the signing. Jessie had asked him if he thought they needed that many. Carl told her he was worried that there wouldn't be enough, that the signing would put Brilliant's on the map.

Carl had also printed and mailed out several thousand announcements to regular customers. To Jessie's irritation, he'd tied up the whole staff for a week, addressing, folding, and stamping. (Sam could still taste the stamp glue.) This past week he'd gone around town taping up announcements in bars, grocery-store windows, and Laundromats. Sam had even noticed one in Mr. Berkowitz's window. In the meantime, he'd been on the phone to Bill Gullard at least once a day, asking him crucial questions: What kind of pen did he use? What color ink?

At the weekly staff meeting yesterday, Jessie had

asked Carl if he didn't think that he'd spent too much of the store's time and money on the signing in proportion to anticipated sales. Carl assured her they'd make it all back and more.

"We'll be mobbed," Carl had said.

Paula leaned over to Sam and whispered, "Remind me to wear my riot gear."

Carl had Sam turn the floral arrangement in the window as he stood outside the store, yelling through the window. "A little to the left . . . No, that's too far. . . . Back a little to the right. . . . Turn it all the way around. . . ." Finally, he gave Sam the thumbs up. He stuck his head back through the door. "I'm going back out for wine."

"Wine? I didn't know we had wine at signings."

"Sam, this is a literary event. This signing will put Brilliant's on the map." He turned to leave. "If Bill calls, tell him I'll pick him up at eleven-thirty." Then he hurried off, his shoulders thrust forward with a sense of mission. Sam admired Carl's ability to lose himself in these projects, knowing full well that in the end Jessie would kill him.

For the next hour, Sam dusted, shelved, and realphabetized sections, work that he usually found relaxing, almost hypnotic—a repetitive act that freed his mind. But over the past couple of weeks he'd become suspicious of anything that encouraged his mind to wander. Since Joey's fall he'd begun to believe that life wasn't so much a grind as a lulling. Routine was a rug that sooner or later would be jerked out. The trick was to remain vigilant in the present. But he wasn't so sure anticipation helped. What good did it do to expect the worst when it happened anyway?

In the two weeks since Joey's accident, he hadn't been able to muster the nerve to ask Kate to marry him. When she asked him later why he'd straightened the house, dimmed the lights, and gotten out the good china and the tablecloth (which had been ruined with candle wax), he told her he'd planned a romantic evening. From the moment Joey's hand had slipped from the stair rail, Sam had lost his grip, too.

He'd thought Kate would be angry about the messy way he'd handled the emergency, but she was the one who kept reminding him what the doctor had said—that by carrying Joey down to Virginia's rather than waiting around for an ambulance, he probably saved Joey's life. In other words, if he hadn't panicked, Joey might've died. Sam had a hard time believing that there was anything admirable or consoling about stumbling upon the right thing to do, but he had a harder time accepting the fact that Kate did. Her understanding unsettled him. It seemed forced. He almost wished she'd blow up at him, call him every name in the book, say the very worst things.

He'd begun to suspect that beneath her sympathy she cultivated bad feelings toward him, shaping them into a bitter and permanent disappointment. When they went to the Pub or worked in the garden or curled up on the couch to watch TV—doing things they'd always done together— Sam felt left out. When she kept saying over and over, "Things go wrong without our permission," he didn't take it as forgiveness but as a warning.

"Who died?" Paula had come out from the receiving room and was standing in front of the floral arrangement next to the card table. She wore a black leather jacket, and she had a new bright pink streak in her hair.

"Carl got them for the signing." He pointed to the other arrangement in the window.

"Did he ask Jessie?"

"He said he gets a discount at the florist."

"Probably hot off some poor stiff's coffin." She picked up a copy of Bill Gullard's book, thumbed through it, then dropped it on the table. "Carl's finally gone off the deep end. We won't sell a quarter of these."

She plucked a pink rose from the arrangement, came

up to the counter, and cut the rose stem with a pair of scissors. She had Sam pin it to the lapel of her jacket with a paper clip.

"Where is Carl, anyway?"

"He went back out for wine." He had to bend the paper clip to make the rose stay.

"Wine!" She threw her head back and hooted. "When Jessie finds out how much he's spent . . ." She drew her finger across her neck.

Sam patted the rose. "It matches your hair."

"Macon got a job as a clerk at a record store. Let's hope he holds this one down at least until we pay off the MasterCard." She headed out the front door. "Can I get you anything next door?"

"No, thanks." Sam went back to straightening sections. He'd finished the nonfiction hardbacks and started on self-help. He thumbed through a copy of *The Joy of Sex*, looking at the sketches of a man and a woman making love in various positions. The book depressed him. He felt intimidated, not by the lovers' dexterity but by the way they gazed into each other's eyes—an all-consuming passion that reduced the rest of the world to backdrop. He and Kate hadn't made love since Joey's accident. They had even stopped touching. Passion felt out of place; even affection seemed to be stretching it. Although they hugged each other good night, they drifted to the far edges of the bed in their sleep, leaving enough room for another person between them.

Jessie burst out of the office, rattling an invoice in her hand. "Twenty percent!" She shook her fist at the ceiling. "Who the hell do they think they are?"

Sam paused in his shelving, knowing she was talking about publishers. She went through this almost every month when the bills came in.

"I've paid on time for ten years." She smacked the invoice with the back of her hand. "Never missed a payment, never even been late. Suddenly, they cut my discount." Her face turned a deep shade of red. "I can't run a bookstore on twenty percent. I can't run a lemonade stand on twenty percent." She walked up to Sam. "They don't cut Walden's or B. Dalton's. They don't cut the chains because they order in volume. The small, independent bookstore is a nuisance, a thorn in their side. Publishers resent independence, anyway, since they've all been bought out by Gulf and Shell." She walked right past the card table and the floral arrangement and opened the register, fingering the bills. "Hell, there isn't even lunch money in here." She slammed the drawer shut. "If they have their way, one day there will be just one huge chain selling one big fat Stephen King novel."

She slumped down onto the stool behind the register, stared at the floor a moment, then looked up at him. "Your hair's getting shaggy."

"Kate hasn't had time to cut it." She'd been the only one to cut his hair since they lived together. They'd wait for a night when a good movie was on TV, because it took her a couple of hours. They'd spread out a sheet in the middle of the living-room floor. He'd sit in a chair, a towel wrapped around his shoulders, while she parted his hair with a wet comb, then pinned up sections. She was methodical. Even after she'd finished, she'd trail him around the house with scissors, snipping places she'd missed.

"You've been quiet lately," Jessie said. "Are you thinking about giving notice?"

"Is that a hint?"

"Hell, no," she said. "Why do you take everything as if somebody is telling you what to do?" She picked up the clipboard with the special-order list. "I just thought you might be tired of not making money."

"There are more important things than money," he said.

"Yeah, but who can afford them?" She tossed the

clipboard on the counter. "You've been sulking ever since that accident with the kid. I thought you said he's going to be okay."

"That's what the doctors say." Sam blew dust off a book.

"You think they're keeping something back?"

Sam shelved a handful of *Women Who Love Too Much*.

Jessie hopped down off the stool, came over to him, and put her hand on his shoulder. "You think those doctors got together, saying, 'Hey, listen, Sam's not feeling too good. Let's cook up a little lie to make him feel better'?" She rolled her eyes at him. "Nowadays doctors don't practice false hope. They're afraid they'll get sued."

"Kate says the same thing."

"See? The two smartest people you know agree." Jessie glanced out the window at a tall black man who loped past. He wore a red kerchief tied over his head and carried a knapsack. "Oh, shit, he's back. I'd heard he was up for parole." She waited until he walked past, then stepped up to the window, having to look around Carl's floral arrangement. "I don't know his real name. Everybody called him the Bandanna Man. He used to hang around here four or five years ago but was arrested and put away. I'm not even sure for what—drugs or burglary, maybe even assault." She went back and stood by the register protectively. "It wasn't jaywalking."

The door opened, and they both turned around. It was Paula, carrying a bag from Gorin's.

"Why are y'all so jumpy?" she asked.

"We thought you were the Bandanna Man," Sam said.

"That tall dude I just passed?"

"I don't want to be an alarmist," Jessie said, "but I hope you both know that if you're ever held up, give them whatever they want. I'm not into unnecessary heroics."

"Don't worry," he said. "I have enough trouble with the necessary stuff."

Paula waited until Jessie had gone back to her office before asking Sam what she thought of Carl's flowers.

"I don't think she noticed them."

"You're kidding." She unwrapped a ham sandwich. "How could she not notice those monstrosities?"

"I noticed." Jessie's voice echoed from her open office door. "Where is Carl, anyway?" she yelled.

"Out buying *wine* for the signing!" Paula yelled back.

There was a pause.

"Wine?" Jessie roared.

Paula grinned at Sam, drawing her finger across her neck.

In the booth behind Sam's, four carpenters built a house between bites of beef tips and gravy. They roofed, insulated, and Sheetrocked, discussing rooms that didn't even exist yet, speaking in the exclusive language of square feet.

Leila wiped his table, put the salt and pepper shakers back in their wire rack, set out his silverware, and poured him a glass of ice water. "You're early today." She took out her pad.

"We're having a book signing," Sam said. "I have to get back to help."

"BLT on whole wheat and a sweetened tea." She headed back to the kitchen with his order.

Sam thought about last week, when he and Kate went by Rose and Lamar's. The four of them sat in the living room, trying to hold a conversation, but talk trickled off. Everyone's gaze wandered to Joey, who stacked the Styrofoam bricks they'd brought as a get-well present. The only sign of injury was a bandage over the crown of his head, which didn't slow down Joey at all. He'd stack the bricks, then punch them with his fist, squealing as they bounced around him.

"They hate me," Sam had said to Kate when they left Rose and Lamar's.

"No, they don't." Kate traced designs in the dashboard dust of the Tempest.

"They were so quiet."

"They're still recovering. It's traumatic."

"You hate me."

"I do not." She reached across the seat and covered his hand with hers. "It was an accident. It could've happened to anybody."

"Somebody must hate me." They drove home in silence.

When Leila brought his sandwich, Sam asked how school was. She had started back at Georgia State to finish her college degree.

"Compared to life, school is a breeze." She wiped her forehead with the back of her wrist. "If you ask me, they've got it backwards. You should work the first half of your life and go to school the last half. Nobody would drop out then." She refilled his iced-tea glass. "My kids think it's a scream that Mom has homework."

"Leila?" A sunburned man wearing a Black Cat hat held up his empty coffee cup. "I'm running on empty."

"Coming, Martin."

Sam watched her pour the man's coffee. She moved on to fill other customers' cups. His problems seemed paltry next to hers—raising two children by herself on a waitress's salary. He thought of Virginia's raising three children alone. Fathers were a rare commodity, and it didn't look like he'd join their ranks anytime soon.

On his way back to the store, to avoid traffic, Sam cut across Ponce de Leon Avenue and drove through Druid Hills, a quiet neighborhood of large houses set back on golf-course lawns. Sometimes he jogged along these streets because they were so shaded and there were few cars. As the Tempest glided down Lullwater, a tree-lined street that curved along a small, overgrown park, a squirrel ran out in front of his car. Sam swerved, sure he'd hit it, relieved to see it dart up a tree on the other side. He stopped the car, watching the squirrel cling to the tree, petrified and panting, its eyes wide with terror. Sam's heart pounded, too. Lately, everything he felt was framed by the ragged edge of despair. The possibility of Joey's death consumed him. He couldn't help going over the ways Joey might've died. He dug a mental pit that his thoughts kept slipping into. That Joey was alive didn't detract from the possibility of his death. The distinction between life and death seemed too capricious.

Sam drove down Lullwater, sailed under the new green canopy of leaves, and breathed in the gaudy smells of pollen and fresh-cut grass. Overnight, azaleas and dogwood had reached a crescendo of pink and white. He thought of Kate, the dark, sweaty scent of her hair. He thought of her cool breath. He felt a tingle that started at the top of his head, then traveled down the back of his skull and along his spine. Why couldn't he ask her to marry him? He hit the steering wheel with the palm of his hand. He drove on down the street, colors blazing all around him—frozen fires.

Dwarfed by the floral arrangement, Bill Gullard, a small, baggy-eyed man who looked thirty years older than the photo they floated over his column every day, sat alone at the card table, played with his pen, sipped Chablis from a plastic wineglass, and wasn't fazed that in the past two hours only three people had asked him to sign a book and one of them had been Carl. He strolled around the store, browsing.

About an hour into the signing, Jessie had crooked her finger at Carl, led him back to her office, and shut the door behind them. They'd been in there ever since.

"What do you think she's doing to him?" Paula asked.

"Taking the wind out of his sails, I imagine," Sam said.

"They've been back there a long time."

"He has a lot of wind."

Paula and Sam had manned the register all afternoon because Carl didn't think one person would be able to handle the rush.

Finally, Gullard came up to the register with a couple of glasses and the rest of his bottle of wine. "I hate to drink alone." He filled glasses for Sam and Paula. The three of them sat around the register, talking and finishing off the bottle.

"I wonder why the turnout was so poor," Sam said, then realized that wasn't such a thoughtful thing to say in front of Gullard.

"The turnout is always poor," Gullard said. "Nobody buys my books. I can't say I blame them." He'd started to light a cigarette, then remembered he was in a bookstore and put the cigarette away. "My books stink."

At least he finishes them, Sam thought, recalling his own halfhearted efforts.

Paula and Gullard particularly hit it off. At one point, Paula said, "To read your columns you'd think you're a jerk, but in person you're decent."

Gullard laughed. "That's not what my son says."

Paula waved her hand, dismissing his comment. "Every kid thinks of his parents as jerks. All it means is that you're doing a good job."

About an hour later, Carl emerged from the office, looking paler than usual. "Mr. Gullard, I'll take you back to the newspaper now."

"Just a second." He went back to the card table,

autographed a couple of copies of his book, then handed them to Paula and Sam. "Makes a great doorstop."

That night, after work, when Sam pulled into his driveway, Willy's VW was parked in Kate's spot, which wasn't unusual, since Willy often dropped by in the late afternoon to sit around and watch the news and get invited for supper. Sam squeezed his car close to the bus, leaving room for Kate.

He reached into the backseat, getting out Gullard's book and a bouquet of flowers. They'd split up the immense arrangements so that everyone could take flowers home.

He faced his house. Sometimes the shingles seemed to rot before his eyes, the gutters rust, the paint curl away from the house flake by flake. Inside, the ceilings sagged, and walls quietly crumbled. Termites nibbled at the foundation, feasting on the mortgage. He walked out into the middle of his mangy yard; tufts of uncut grass sprouted between vast expanses of brown dirt. A dead limb clawed his pant leg. He dragged it out to the curb. The house wasn't falling apart; it was disintegrating, molecule by molecule, atom by atom, until one morning he'd wake to a pile of fine dust.

The front steps trembled with the Talking Heads: " 'Is this my beautiful house?' " He crossed the porch, hesitating in the doorway, the door wide open. He leaned into the living room; the music was a stiff wind.

The coffee table was littered with an empty Miller bottle, an opened bag of Fritos, and sections of the afternoon paper. Sam turned off the stereo. He grabbed a handful of Fritos and continued on through the dining room, out to the kitchen, where the back door stood open. Through the screen he saw Willy out back walk up and down the dark neat rows, the hose trailing him as he watered the garden. He kept his thumb pressed over the end, spraying a mist. A rainbow hung in the air. The screen door diffused the whole scene into a pointillist painting, and for a moment Willy seemed in danger of evaporating into dots of pure color.

Sam got a couple of beers out of the refrigerator and went out to the backyard, the screen door slamming behind him. Willy had just turned off the water and coiled the hose up against the house.

"I didn't realize you were into irrigation." He handed Willy a beer.

"Kate called and said the garden needed watering." He sipped the beer. "She said she's going to be late again tonight. She wanted me to remind you to go to the Farmers' Market."

They stood on the edge of the dark patch of wet earth. Just the other morning Sam had been fixing breakfast when Kate had called him outside to show him the rows of pale seedlings that pushed up from the ground, hooded by their seed cases.

"Has Kate seemed moody to you lately?" Sam asked.

"Try the past thirty years."

There was a rustle in the high grass at the far end of the yard. The Siamese crept through the hedge.

"If it hadn't been for that damned cat, Joey wouldn't have fallen, and I would've asked Kate by now."

Willy took a swallow of his beer. "That is one influential cat."

DeKalb Avenue was thick with commuters filtering back into the suburbs as Sam weaved the Tempest in and out of the reversible lane, his eye on the green arrows and red X's.

Willy hunched over the dashboard, trying to find music on the radio. He'd leave it on a song for a couple of notes, then cut the singer off in mid-phrase, switch to another station long enough to recognize the song, then switch it again. He settled on the Braves game and sat back and drank his beer. There was deafening applause. Someone for the Braves had just hit a grand slam.

"They're great this year," Sam said. "People say they might even win the pennant."

"I liked them better when they were pathetic."

On their way to the Farmers' Market, they passed Agnes Scott, Kate's old college—several blocks of graceful nineteenth-century brick buildings set back under the shade of large oaks—where young women walked alone or in couples, carrying books, their heads bent in conversation.

"Did you ever go there?" Sam asked.

"It's for women." Willy sounded offended.

"I mean, did you ever visit Kate there?"

"A few times." Willy sipped his beer. "Women everywhere you turned."

"Is that bad?"

"Too much of a good thing." Willy turned up the game. The Braves had just gotten another run. "Suddenly everybody's a fan."

They drove underneath a crosswalk crowded with commuters filing out of the MARTA station to the parking lot across the street. Some had an hour's drive still ahead. The hardest part of their job was to get there.

"Did you know you had a street named after you?" Willy pointed to a sign that read Sam's Crossing.

He'd driven this overpass for years and never noticed that sign. But that's the way his life had gone lately. Ever since Joey's fall, Sam had begun to emerge from his oblivious cloud. The little boy's accident had given painful shape to an inner absence.

The traffic was backed up; they stopped in the middle of the overpass. The MARTA tracks ran underneath, curving into the distance.

"First we had Jimmy Carter Boulevard," Willy said. "Then Martin Luther King Memorial Drive. Now Sam's Crossing."

"I wonder who Sam was."

"Probably some guy who did something." Willy looked out the window. On the radio there was loud applause. Somebody had gotten a hit.

They walked across the parking lot, pausing in front of long, bright red rows of potted geraniums that looked surreal in the waning light. Inside, they were met by a blast of cold air, a gang of evocative smells, and a loud, steady roar—the collective voices of thousands of shoppers. The Farmers' Market was a cavernous air-conditioned warehouse of food; its aisles extending to the horizon.

Dark-skinned men and women worked the stalls— bagged, sorted, and talked to each other in languages so foreign they sounded improvised. The market hired immigrants—Indians, Africans, Koreans, Vietnamese, Chinese, Mexicans, and Iranians. Immigrants shopped there, too, because the prices were low and it was the only place in Atlanta that sold so many kinds of food. In fact, it was the only place in the South where you could see so many nationalities together, side by side, as they sniffed, squeezed, and felt over the food.

In the baked-goods section, Sam and Willy bought small coffees and cookies from an Indian woman with dark, delicate features who presided over a large pastry case. She stood above the crowd, looking regal as she repeated orders in clipped English and reached into the case with wax paper. Shoppers stopped here first, bracing themselves against the arctic air with a cup of coffee.

Sam leaned over the case, looking at the pastries.

"Nice, eh?" Willy asked.

"Everything looks good."

Willy elbowed him in the ribs. "I was talking about her." He gestured toward the Indian woman.

Sam and Willy started in the vegetable section, with Willy still pushing the cart.

"Shit!" Sam searched his pants pockets. "The grocery list. I left it on the kitchen table."

Willy reached into his shirt pocket and pulled out a piece of yellow paper. He pushed the cart and read the list out loud as Sam went along ahead of the cart, picking out vegetables and bagging them. Sam dropped three bell peppers into a plastic bag, tied the end, and tossed it into the cart.

"Cauliflower." Willy read from the list, crossing items out with a pencil.

Sam picked a cauliflower from a huge mound and tossed it into the cart. "What am I going to do? Every time I think I'm about to do something, I don't."

They had to stand aside for a small lift truck honking its way through the crowd, carrying unpacked crates that dripped with water and ice.

"You'll think of something," Willy said.

"Like what?"

Willy put his hand on Sam's shoulder. "You want me to tell you what you'll think of?"

"Could you give me a hint?"

Sam left Willy in the coffee section, where he'd struck up a conversation with a black woman waiting to have her coffee ground. Taking the list from Willy, Sam saw that a pound of turbot was all that was left. He wandered off to the fish section, where customers tapped on the glass cases, indicating which fillet. Behind the cases, an assembly line of Oriental men and women in rubber aprons cleaned fish on a long, wet counter, slitting, beheading, and gutting in one swift motion.

He had always liked to come shopping here with Kate. To be here with her, in this immense place, among all these different kinds of people, made them feel intimate somehow.

Sam squeezed his way toward the front, trying to get the clerk's attention. Then he heard a familiar voice: "Two pounds of red snapper, please." Grace Smith stood at the counter down from his, ordering fish. His first impulse was to sneak away and lose her in the crowd, but he was pinned against the counter. She waved. "I loved the books," she yelled to him across several heads.

"Good." He waved back.

"Can I help you, sir?" one of the Oriental clerks asked.

Sam turned to the clerk. He held up one finger. "One pound of turbot." When he looked back, she was gone. He came away from the counter, holding his bag of fish. Her phone number was still in his wallet.

The next afternoon, Kate called Sam at the bookstore, saying that Rose had called the hospital to see if they'd meet them at José's for supper.

Since it was only a few blocks away and the weather was good, Kate wanted to walk. They strolled along Moreland Avenue, past two immense concrete bridge supports on either side of the road that were overgrown with vines and kudzu, monuments to the aborted Presidential Parkway, a commuter's shortcut that would've led past the Jimmy Carter Library, cleaving Little Five Points in two. The community had organized and held marches; some protesters had even lain down in front of bulldozers or chained themselves to trees. Kate had been very involved and had even gotten carted off to jail when she chained herself to an oak tree that was about to be cut down. Sam marched once for about half an hour but went home when it started to drizzle, his Save Our Neighborhood sign having gone limp.

Sam and Kate walked down Euclid Avenue and passed

by the Pub; the smell of dried beer and stale cigarettes wafted through the open doors. The pawnshop was dark and locked up tight; its barred windows and chained doors harbored a junta's worth of weaponry. One sad light burned in Roger's Cafe, where the little man sat alone in his closed diner, hunched over rows of baseball cards—his hoard of obscure, even forgotten faces.

"Joey isn't even going to be there," Kate said. "Rose's mother is watching him." Kate had changed out of her work clothes into a pair of old jeans and a long-sleeved T-shirt of his.

"They're afraid to have him near me."

Kate didn't seem to hear him. "Rose did sound a little odd on the phone."

They paused by the boarded-up movie theater, reading the yellowed posters of what would've been upcoming attractions if the theater hadn't gone out of business. They'd seen *Never Cry Wolf* here, which was their favorite movie. They'd gone out to a restaurant to celebrate their one-year anniversary, but the waiter was rude, they'd bickered over which was the salad fork, and then Kate nearly choked to death on one of those miniature corncobs. By the time they'd gotten to the movie, they weren't speaking. But there was something about the movie's sweeping landscape that calmed them. The sad plight of the wolves also seemed to diminish their own troubles. In the middle of the movie, Kate leaned over and whispered, "At least we aren't an endangered species."

José's was tucked into the bottom of Euclid Avenue, next to the post office. It was a low brick building, like the Rainbow, except smaller, and José had made some effort, painting it white with green trim. Menus were taped to the window, the printed prices scratched out and new prices written in.

"I don't see them." Kate shaded her eyes and peered in.

"Maybe we missed them," he said hopefully.

"There they are." She rapped on the window, waving at Lamar and Rose, who sat at a corner table, wineglasses lifted as if toasting something.

I was playing with him on the bed," Lamar said, "and he starts to kiss my face all over." He touched his face with his fingers. "These light little kisses all over my face." Lamar ate a forkful of black beans. "It was better than sex."

Sam had never seen Lamar quite so animated, and Rose was almost radiant, a drastic change from their sullenness the other night. Rose kept her hand on Sam's, saying how good it was to see him.

"Could we get some more coffee?" Lamar asked María, the waitress, a fifteen-year-old who sat across the room at an empty table, thumbing through *US* magazine and eating a piece of pie. She rolled her eyes. María rolled her eyes often and in such a way that you could never be sure if she rolled them at herself for forgetting or at the customers for asking. She got up and poured their coffee.

José's was a small Cuban restaurant run by one family. José, the father, cooked, the mother ran the register, and María, their daughter, waited tables. She was a bad waitress. She was insolent, sloppy, and absentminded, but because she was the only one of the three who spoke English very well, she was indispensable. If you wanted to eat at José's, there was no getting around María.

Finishing his chicken and rice, Sam thought what a good time he'd had. Even Kate, who seemed to be trying to catch Rose's eye about something, had allowed herself to lean back and relax.

As María cleared the dishes, she asked if anyone wanted dessert.

"What do you have?" Lamar asked.

"I'm not sure."

"Could you ask somebody?"

María rolled her eyes. She sauntered back toward the kitchen, and they heard her talk to her father in Spanish.

"What is she saying to him back there?" Lamar asked Rose.

"If they have any dessert," Rose said.

"You sure she's not saying something insulting about me?" Lamar asked.

"I thought you were on a diet." Rose patted his stomach.

Lamar lifted his shirt, pushing out his stomach. "I eat for two now."

"Put that away." Rose pulled his shirt back down.

"Maybe *you* ought to get a dessert," Lamar said to her.

"Because you're eating for two?" Kate leapt at this.

Lamar reached across the table for Rose's hand.

Kate smacked the heel of her hand on the table. "I knew it. I knew it." She hugged Rose. "But I thought the doctor said that after you had Joey you wouldn't be able to have any more."

"The doc underestimated my virility," Lamar said.

María trudged back out to the table. "We don't have dessert."

"What about that piece of pie you were eating?" Lamar asked.

"The last piece." María finished clearing their table.

"My wife's pregnant," Lamar said to María. "It's going to be a girl."

María turned to Rose, said something to her in Spanish, looked at Lamar, and said something else in Spanish that made Rose laugh.

María smiled a genuine smile, then sauntered back to her empty table to finish her pie and resume her magazine reading.

"What did she say?" Lamar asked.

"She said, 'Let's pray she looks like the mother.' "

Kate was very quiet when they walked back home.

They went to bed early that night, stayed awake and read. This was one of their favorite pastimes, to lie facing each other, their books open on the bed. Kate was reading a new biography of Martin Luther King. Sam was reading the letters of Flannery O'Connor. He liked to read the letters of writers, hoping to find some clue to the mystery of his own inabilities.

After about a half hour, Kate put her book down and cut off her lamp. She turned over on her side, facing away from him. "I can't get that baby off my mind."

"Rose's?" Caught up in his book, he turned the page.

"A new baby at work was born without vocal cords."

Still reading, Sam patted her back. "It'll be okay."

Kate got up out of bed and yanked her robe off the closet hook.

"What'd I say?" He put down his book.

"You don't know that baby will be okay. Nobody knows that." She slipped into Sam's sandals. "You just want it to be okay so I can be okay so you can be okay." She knotted the tie on her robe and marched out of the room and down the stairs.

He got out of bed, still wearing the same shirt he'd had on all day, his briefs and socks. He found her sitting at the kitchen table in the dark. Sometimes he'd wake in the middle of the night, find the bed empty, and come down here and find her sitting in the dark.

"What can I do?" He pulled a chair up next to hers.

"I don't want you to do anything. A baby born without

vocal cords is sad. There's nothing anybody can do. All I want is for you and me to sit here and know how sad it is." She sighed. "Avoiding sadness has become a national pastime. Don't want to be sad? Turn on the TV, turn up the radio." She nodded at the book still in his hand. "Read a book."

They sat in the kitchen, listening to the old electric clock over the stove scrape away the minutes. Finally, Kate looked up at him. "I wonder if there's a late movie on TV."

"But you just said—"

"You think I'm above a happy ending?" She led him out to the living room, where they curled up on the sofa and watched *True Grit* until two in the morning.

It was just light when Sam heard the radio–alarm clock click on, followed by strains of familiar classical music. He turned over to Kate, whose eyes were wide open. "Who wrote this?" she asked.

"McCartney?"

"I think it's Handel."

Sam yawned. "You're asking me?" Her eyes were slightly red. She'd been crying. "Are you okay?"

She went into the bathroom and turned on the shower. He got up and washed his face, noticing the time on the clock. "Why are we getting up so early?"

"It's Friday." She talked over the shower.

"Oh, right, your staff meeting." On Friday mornings the entire neonatal staff met—doctors, physician assistants, respiratory therapists, physical therapists, nurses, and social workers.

"You want breakfast?" he asked over the sound of the water.

"I can get something at work."

"Not that hospital slop." He pulled on his pants. "I'll go down and whip up something."

He made a big breakfast, but she ate very little. "Grits cold?"

"Everything's fine." She folded her napkin and smoothed it beside her plate. She glanced up at the kitchen clock, said something about being late, and hurried off to the bedroom to get dressed.

The phone rang. "I'll get it." Sam picked up the phone in the kitchen.

"Sam, this is Jessie." She yawned. "I'm sorry to bother you, but Carl just called and said he had to drive to Valdosta this morning to pickle some distant cousin who kicked the bucket yesterday. . . ."

"Sure, I'll open this morning."

"I'd ask Paula, but she probably just got to bed. I'd do it myself"—she yawned—"but Sylvia and I stayed up half the night patching the living-room ceiling where the guy stuck the pitchfork through at the last party."

"I'll open. Go back to sleep. Catch a few more z's."

"My z's thank you." She hung up.

Sam finished clearing the breakfast dishes, then hurried upstairs to get ready for work. "Jessie wants me to open," he said as he came into the bedroom.

"Shit!" Kate whispered to herself. "Shit! Shit! Shit!" She stood in front of her dresser mirror, tears streaming down her face.

"Kate?"

She turned to him, shaking her head. "It's all wrong."

"You and me?"

"I've got it buttoned all wrong." She pulled on her blouse.

Sam started rebuttoning it for her, but she pushed him away.

"There's nothing you can do." She wiped her tears away and rebuttoned her blouse.

"Maybe this is something we ought to talk about?"

"I'm late." She jerked a brush through her hair. She

grabbed her purse and ran down the stairs and out the front door.

"Kate?" Sam followed her.

She'd stopped halfway across the yard and stared down at something.

Sam came up behind her. At her feet lay a small dead robin.

"I need a vacation." She stared down at the bird.

"That's an idea," he said eagerly. "Jessie'd be willing to give me a couple of weeks off—"

"From us."

He nodded slowly. "For how long?"

She shook her head. "I don't know."

"Maybe it's Atlanta." He heard the panic in his voice. "Maybe we should move someplace new."

"We'll have to talk about it tonight." She got in her car but had trouble strapping on her seat belt. She threw the seat belt back. "I give up." She started the car and, as she pulled out of the driveway, rolled down her window. "We have to remember that this is nobody's fault." She drove away.

His head swimming, he watched her car disappear up the street. On his way back to the house, he picked up the dead bird. There was no blood, no wound, no visible sign of anything wrong.

For a split second Sam wasn't sure whether the furious ringing wasn't his subconscious, an inner alarm: Poe's bells gone berserk. The flashing strobe lights in the window cued him that he'd forgotten to disarm the store alarm. In four years he'd never set off the alarm. But driving to work this morning, he'd accidentally run a red light and wouldn't have noticed then if he hadn't found himself in the middle of an intersection, cars honking and screeching all around him.

Someone rapped on the window. Ronnie pressed his face against the glass, and behind him, several street people peered in, no doubt thinking it was a robbery. The street people never missed a car wreck or a fire or a robbery.

He punched in the code on the alarm panel, and the ringing stopped. There was a stunned silence, followed by another ringing. The phone. That would be Kate saying she didn't know what came over her, that she was sorry, that she hadn't meant what she said. He let it ring a few times to gather himself. When he finally answered, he tried to sound casual. "Hey."

"This is Grace," a voice said. "Do you have a message?"

Grace Smith? Why would she be calling him. "Grace from Stone Mountain?"

"Do you have a message?"

It didn't really sound like the woman who'd come into the bookstore. Maybe she had a cold. What kind of message would he have for her?

"Sir, if you don't have a message, I'll to have to notify the police."

"The police? Who is this?"

"Gray's Security." The woman sounded impatient.

"Oh, Gray's." It was the alarm company calling for the false-alarm code. They never came right out and asked for the code. They always asked for a message because they didn't want the thief to know there was a code. Jessie kept the code on the bottom of the phone. He read the numbers to the woman. "Sorry about the mix-up."

"We get all kinds." The woman hung up.

That night, when Sam got home from work, Kate's car was in the driveway, and a row of suitcases was on the front porch, lined up like orphaned children. Smoke poured out the front door. He found a pot of charred pork and beans smoldering on the stove. He grabbed the pot, but the handle was too hot. Wrapping the handle in a dish towel, he threw open the back door and slung the pan into the yard.

"Kate?" He heard something upstairs. He found her in the bedroom, arranging some photographs in a box. "Trying to burn the house down?"

She whirled around, her eyes wide. "You scared me."

"Are you trying to collect the fire insurance?"

"What?" Her eyes were red and puffy. "Why are you holding your hand?"

He cradled it against his chest. "I guess I sort of burned it . . . getting rid of your beans. . . ."

"The beans!" She started to get up.

"Hope you like 'em charbroiled." He noticed the suitcase on the bed. "What gives? What're all those suitcases on the porch?"

"Let me see your hand." She took it gently in hers.

"Where are you going?"

"We have to get this under cold water, now." She guided him to the bathroom.

He tried to pull away. "You're leaving tonight?"

"It might even be a second-degree burn." She held his hand under the water. "Feel better?"

"I thought you said we'd talk." Panic squeezed his chest.

"It's not swelling, but we better wrap it, anyway."

"Where are you going?"

"To Maggie's." She got the gauze out of the medicine cabinet.

"She's in the Everglades."

"Willy's there."

"How long will you be gone, Kate?"

"I don't know if it'll help." She led him back to the bedroom, where she sat him down on the bed, wrapping his hand. "At least it'll remind you it's hurt."

"Who needs reminding?" He looked at how neatly she'd packed her suitcase. "I can't believe this is happening."

"We need to explore other opportunities." She closed her suitcase.

"Is this a career change?"

She sat down beside him, gently holding his bandaged hand. "It's starting to hurt?"

"A little."

"That pork and beans was supposed to be our supper."

"The Last Supper?" His voice cracked. "Kate, give me another chance." He tried to hug her, but she stood up.

"It might get better for a little while, and then it'll get worse again, and I won't have the energy to do anything about it." She picked up her suitcase and carried it downstairs.

Sam helped her load her car. She'd mostly packed clothes. "I'll leave the furniture for now."

"This is crazy. We've been together for such a long time." He hugged her, but she stiffened.

She pulled away. "If you need me . . ."

"But I do," he pleaded. "I need you more than anything."

"I'll be at Maggie's." She took his hurt hand and held it gently. "Be careful with this, and if it gets infected, go to the doctor." She got in the car and started to back out of the driveway. "I'll call in a couple of days to see how you are."

"Don't leave me like this." He trotted along beside her.

She started to cry. "I'm sorry. I don't know how else to do it." Then she was gone.

He went inside, turned on the TV, turned it off, and walked back outside, thinking he'd heard her pull in again. The driveway was empty. He went inside, put a record on, turned it up loud, and then just wandered through the house, which reeked of burned beans.

He sipped from his beer as he sat in the broken La-Z-Boy, staring at the TV while Dylan blasted from the stereo. Four empty beer cans were lined up on the coffee table. Someone tapped his shoulder. It was Willy.

"She sent you," Sam said.

Willy went out to the kitchen and came back with a beer. He turned down the stereo. "She didn't send me."

"I don't need anybody to check up on me." He got up and turned off the TV. "I'm not going to do anything to myself. Is that what she thinks?"

"You already have." Willy pointed his beer at Sam's bandaged hand.

"Shit." He felt very drunk. He'd never been able to hold his alcohol.

"She's really upset, if that's any consolation." They stared at the darkened TV screen. Willy sat up. "Do you hear something?"

Sam went to the front door, thinking maybe it was Kate pulling into the driveway.

"It's coming from the backyard."

They both went out to the kitchen and stood at the screen door. "Sounds like a dog in the garbage can."

"Sounds like a pot being banged around," Willy said.

Sam remembered the pot of beans he'd slung into the backyard. The racket kept up, so he got a flashlight. They stepped out into the backyard. It was pitch-black except for the flashlight, which he waved back and forth across the yard.

"Shine it over there," Willy whispered.

Sam moved it across the yard, stopping it on a gray hump with a long skinny tail. Whatever it was had its head down in the pot, scraping it against the ground. "A possum." Sam handed Willy the flashlight.

"What're you doing?"

Sam came back with a garbage can. "Is he still there?"

The possum seemed oblivious. Maybe it didn't hear them with its head down in the pot. Sam walked off into the dark, carrying the garbage can.

"What're you doing?" Willy whispered.

"We're going to catch it." Sam didn't know exactly what had come over him—probably four and a half beers. Still, it felt good to do something, to take matters into his own hands, even if he didn't have much experience in catching possums.

They must've spoken too loudly. The possum lifted his head, staring into the flashlight beam. It didn't move, entranced by the light.

"Sam?" Willy called, but Sam had disappeared in the dark behind the possum. The possum bared his teeth and hissed. "Sam? I think he's about to charge."

"Possums don't charge." Sam's voice came out of the darkness. "Just keep the light on him." He appeared right behind the possum, holding the garbage can in front of him. He was about to bring it down when the possum bolted. Sam lunged but missed.

"Shit," Willy said as it ran in his direction.

"Keep the light on it." Sam got back to his feet. His bandage had come undone, and his hand throbbed.

Willy followed the possum across the yard with the flashlight as it ran, its fat sides shaking. It ran through the garden and back toward the toolshed, where it squeezed through the cracked door.

Sam ran up and pulled the door shut. "Got him!"

Coming up behind him, Willy gave him back the flashlight. "Now what?" They listened for any sound from within, but the toolshed was silent.

"Playing possum. We have to go in and get him."

"What'll we do with him once we have him?"

"Eat him."

"I hear possum is high in cholesterol." Willy backed away from the door.

They heard a scratch at the door, then a hiss.

Sam handed the flashlight back to Willy. "When I open this door, shine it right in his eyes. Blind the son of a bitch."

"What if it charges?"

"It's not a damned rhino." He turned back to Willy. "Kate left me. I can't believe it."

"I'm real sorry." He noticed Sam's bandage. "It's come undone." He started to tie it back for him.

The scratching behind the door was louder. The possum hissed again.

"Ready?" Sam gripped the door handle.

Willy shined the flashlight right at the door as Sam shoved it open. There was nothing there. "Maybe it crawled out a back way," Willy said hopefully.

"There isn't a back way." Sam stepped inside the toolshed. His heart pounded. He could smell the possum's dankness.

"Be careful," Willy said. "They carry rabies."

"Now you tell me. . . ." The possum, which had hidden behind a sack of flour, bolted to the right, then to the left, then straight at Sam, scraping his pant leg as he passed between his legs. Sam dropped the garbage can and ran, knocking over Willy, and the possum scrambled between them and disappeared into Mrs. Smeak's hedge.

Willy and Sam lay there on the ground, looking up at the stars.

"It got away," Sam said.

"Thank God. I thought we were going to have to roast it."

A silence fell between them as they lay catching their breath. In the distance, sirens started at the fire station.

"How's your hand?" Willy asked.

"It hurts." Sam sighed. "She really left me."

"Maybe only for a while."

"Do you think so?" Sam sat up. "Do you think she'll be back soon?" A nauseous feeling crept up the back of his throat. "She's got to come back."

"I wouldn't wait around for water to turn to wine," Willy said.

Sam quickly got to his feet, stumbled off behind the toolshed, and threw up. He kept throwing up, his stomach retching. He deserved it, he told himself. Everything that goes around comes around.

He felt a cool hand on the back of his neck. "You okay, man?" Not having the energy to speak, he leaned on Willy's shoulder and let him lead him back to the empty house.

Chapter Six

Sam walked past the parked train, with its empty cars, that in a few hours would be filled with tourists and families circling the foot of Stone Mountain. He crossed the tracks and started up the trail in the soft predawn light, thinking, This is the hour for bird-watchers and suicides.

At the front gate, an old man in a Parks Service uniform had asked him if he was with the Audubon group. "Maybe I'm shallow, but I've never understood why anybody would leave a warm bed at such an ungodly hour to count birds."

The man drank from a cup of coffee and eyed Sam in a way that made him a little nervous. "To each his own." Sam worried that the man was about to ask, if he wasn't here for the birds, what was he here for? He glanced at his watch. "If you hurry, you'll catch the sunrise." So Sam drove on around to the immense parking lot, which was completely empty.

As he walked up the side of the mountain, he felt light-headed. He hadn't gotten much rest the past two nights. He'd resisted sleep, because he dreaded waking or that moment right before waking when he'd reach across the bed and gather air in his arms.

This morning his eyes had popped open at five o'clock, and he hadn't been able to go back to sleep. He couldn't stand the thought of a Sunday morning alone in the house. Without Kate, breakfast felt pointless, Sunday morning evangelists weren't funny, and Charles Kuralt was pedantic. In just two days without Kate he'd lost whatever perspective he'd had. He woke to a half-empty closet. Barely giving him time to pull on some pants and tie up his shoes, the sadness drove him out of the house and onto a dark, empty eight-lane expressway. He glimpsed his face in the rearview mirror. He hadn't shaved since she left. It hadn't seemed worth the effort. He had the scruffy, unwashed look of Charles Manson.

He'd had enough of the city and was about to drive the 140 miles back to Greenville, look up his old girlfriend, and find an apartment with enough light to sustain a rubber tree. He took the Stone Mountain exit, surprising himself. The Tempest veered onto the ramp.

Halfway up the mountain, there was a break in the trees, and Sam could see the sun edge over the top of the mountain, lighting Robert E. Lee's forehead. He remembered one morning when he and Kate had first started seeing each other, before she'd moved in; she'd arrived at his door at six one Sunday morning. "Get dressed. You're coming with me." As they moved along the expressway, he sipped from a thermos of coffee she'd made. She drove to Stone Mountain, and they'd climbed to the top to watch the sun rise. Afterward, they'd gone to the Rainbow and had breakfast. She raised her coffee cup to him. "To our first sunrise together." That was the first time she'd implied that they might have a future.

When he reached the ledge, the sun had fanned out over the immense field below—the same field where people spread their quilts at night to watch the laser show. He leaned against the rock wall and watched a lone hawk float across the sky. A new stab of loneliness made him catch his breath. He didn't know if he'd ever felt this bad. How had he screwed it up? He felt awful. This sadness wasn't something he could drive away from.

He leaned out over the wall where Kate had danced

that night when the three of them had come up here. He looked down at the field far below and remembered how he'd felt when Kate slipped and he grabbed her and felt himself being pulled over with her. In that split second when he was sure they would both fall, he'd felt closer to her than ever. And in a way now, he wished they had fallen; at least they would've been together. He also thought of Grace.

He stepped up onto the wall and felt dizzy when he looked down. He closed his eyes. So that was why he'd come up here. He nodded to himself. Ever since he'd awakened this morning this had been his intention, and he hadn't even realized it.

A breeze lifted his hair, and the sunlight glowed red through his closed eyelids. Just one step, one simple step, and he wouldn't have to feel anything anymore. Surely he could manage that. He lifted his arms straight out. Maybe he'd glide across the field like that hawk. Even if he sank like a stone, there would be a symmetry to it that Kate would understand. He wouldn't need to leave a note.

He imagined his funeral. Kate and Willy would be there. Maggie and her friend Claire, Paula and Jessie. Carl would take care of the arrangements. He opened his eyes. It was a little sobering to think of Carl injecting preservative into his veins. But what would it matter? He'd be dead. He wouldn't feel a thing. He closed his eyes, inching forward on the wall. He opened his eyes again. He couldn't stand the thought of Carl's gaudy flowers tackying up his coffin.

On his way back down Sam sat on a rock to gather himself. He knew he wouldn't have jumped. He'd been grandstanding, trying to demonstrate to himself how awful he felt. When he was a child and found himself alone in the house, he'd sometimes get out his mother's carving knife and hold it to his chest, the point pricking his ribs, about to plunge it in, knowing the whole time that he wouldn't, couldn't. For as long as he could remember, he'd been given to these private demonstrations of despair.

A covey of bird-watchers passed him on their way up the trail. With binoculars slung around their necks, they were quiet and kept their eyes to the sky. If he had jumped, these guys would've had the sighting of their lives.

He pulled out of the parking lot and waved to the old man in the guard house. "Great sunset!" he called out. "I mean sunrise!"

As he got back on the expressway, he glanced at his watch. It was only eight o'clock, and already he'd had a long day. Still, he couldn't bring himself to go right back home to that empty house. That was the depressing thing about not committing suicide. He'd continue to feel this way for some time. Having given up that drastic option, there was nothing he could do about these waves of desperation except ride them out.

He drove aimlessly for a while, got off the expressway, and followed roads out into the countryside just to see where they led, as he and Kate did. He caught himself: as he and Kate *used* to do. Overnight they had become past tense.

Some Sundays they left the house with the intention of getting lost. They drove until they didn't know where they were. They never asked directions, the idea being that they would find their way back without anyone's help. Sam enjoyed these afternoons of getting lost together. Besides, Kate was never really lost. Without even looking at a map, she'd just say, "Turn here. . . . Turn left there. . . . Take that second right. . . . Go left at the fork. . . ." Within a few minutes they would be back on a familiar road. She said she imagined herself hovering over the countryside and was able to see in all directions.

Obsessed with Kate's leaving him, Sam had driven for more than an hour, oblivious to the plush golf courses, the upscale shopping centers, and the elaborate entrances of new subdivisions with Open House banners flapping in the wind.

Why was he so stunned by Kate's departure? How had she come to mean so much? Their four years together couldn't be characterized as rosy. They fought a lot and bickered even more. They were about as different as two people could be. But he'd been attracted to her in the first place because she shook him up, because she asked hard questions and expected a lot. He loved her because she included him in her expectations, because she believed in him. But now that she'd left, it was as if most of him had packed up, too. He was a shell of himself driving through the Georgia countryside.

When he finally did look around, he'd driven beyond the wide belt of Atlanta's suburbia and entered farm country at the edge of the mountains. He passed acres of hilly, plowed fields and small farmhouses—a country of kudzu, satellite dishes, and cars on cinder blocks.

He stopped to ask directions at a little grocery store-gas station. Inside, there was no one around except an old woman in a Braves cap who sat behind the counter smoking a cigarette and watching Oral Roberts on a tiny black-and-white TV on the counter.

Exhausted and very sleepy, he poured himself a cup of coffee from the self-service coffee machine, then went up front to pay.

"Excuse me, ma'am. Could you tell me where I am?" He noticed that his own accent thickened whenever he went into a place like this.

"Tate, Georgia." The old woman didn't look away from the TV.

"Yes, ma'am, and where is that?"

"Here," the old woman said.

"I mean, where is it in relation to anywhere else?"

She stubbed out her cigarette in an ashtray. "Well, we're north of Ball Ground and south of Jasper."

"Let me put it this way. I need to get back to the highway."

"You can't get there from here." She looked up at him and winked.

If Sam had been in a better mood, he would've used this comment as the old woman intended, to start up a conversation. She was lonely, and being evasive with out-of-towners was probably one of her few joys in life. He knew that if Kate had been there, she would've joked with the old woman, talking about the weather and anything else, until finally their conversation wound back around to directions to the highway, which Kate wouldn't have needed in the first place. Already Sam missed her sense of direction.

The old woman pulled out a map from underneath the counter, which from its yellowed condition made Sam wonder if it showed anything but wagon trails. Thirty minutes and half a dozen wrong turns later, he found himself on an expressway, headed into Atlanta. It occurred to him that the reason he hadn't heard from Kate might be that she was waiting to hear from him. As he closed in on the city, he felt something like hope rise in his chest.

Sam turned down the alleyway that divided Maggie's block. He cut off the engine so that the Tempest glided quietly into the back driveway and stopped next to Willy's VW, where Maggie's Land Rover was usually parked.

Sam liked the startled expressions of other drivers when they looked up and saw Maggie's small gray head barely clearing the massive steering wheel. Sometimes she would take Kate and Willy and him up into the mountains, pull onto some logging road, put the Land Rover into four-wheel drive, and drive deep into the woods. She'd mow down saplings, grind through rocky creek beds, and accelerate around hairpin turns. She'd find a pretty meadow. They'd put down a quilt and set out sandwiches and beer. After a couple of beers, Maggie would tell stories about Kate and Willy when they were kids.

"Don't torture the poor boy," Kate would groan.

"Home-movie time." Willy would yawn and pretend to be bored.

But they loved it, and Maggie loved it. She'd go on with whatever story, talking to Sam, who didn't mind being a convenient excuse. But it was understood that the stories were for Willy and Kate. It was Maggie's way of reminding her children that no matter how old or how smart they thought they'd become, they were still her children.

When he didn't see her Land Rover in the driveway, Sam remembered that Maggie was spending two weeks in the Everglades. He guessed Kate's car must be parked around front.

Maggie's house was a modest single-story, a lot like Rose and Lamar's, except that instead of brick, the house was wooden. Maggie and her husband had designed it together thirty-five years ago. Shaded by several oaks, it was a low, airy house with an Oriental feel that made Sam want to take his shoes off at the door. He'd never understood how Kate's father could've left Maggie or this house; both had a comfortableness about them. Sam felt more at home here than in his own house.

He shut the car door quietly. How strange it felt to not know if he was welcome. He walked up the steps to the side door, hesitated, then turned the doorknob. Kate gave Maggie hell that she didn't lock the side door, but Maggie maintained that a burglar would never think about walking right in.

Sam walked inside, careful not to let the screen door

slam, and stood in the kitchen, listening to his heart race. It was almost noon, and no one seemed to be up yet. The house always had a gritty, slightly burned toast smell. Wind chimes hung in front of an open window, tinkling with the breeze. He crossed through the breakfast nook to the bedrooms; both Kate's and Willy's doors were closed. He put his ear to Kate's door. There was a drone. She liked to sleep with the fan on.

He knocked lightly on her bedroom door, but she didn't answer. He pressed his ear against the door, and all he heard was the fan. He slowly opened the door. Her room was a wreck, at least for Kate. Her suitcase was open on the floor, with underwear, blouses, and socks scattered in various directions. Her shoes were piled in one corner. A couple of dresses were draped over a chair. The throw rug beside her bed was balled up. A brown half-eaten apple lay on its side on the dresser, and a couple of plates with crumbs on them were stacked on her night table. Also on the night table was her beeper. She'd probably gotten called to the hospital last night.

He opened the door wider and saw Kate, asleep, the sheet pulled up over her head. He studied the white curve of her ankle that poked from beneath the bottom of the sheet. He noticed that her toenails were painted. She must've done that in the past couple of days—a statement to herself. He ached to touch her, to lie down beside her. A wave of immense exhaustion came over him. He tiptoed over and, careful not to awaken her, slipped down beside her, put his arm over her, and fell asleep. He must've been asleep only a couple of minutes, because he was awakened by Kate's voice.

"They've taken him off the ventilator," she said. She was talking in her sleep. "He might not live."

Sam got up gently, careful not to jostle the bed, pulling the sheet back over her. He should leave. He couldn't just sneak into her room and lie down beside her.

He was violating her privacy. Wasn't it really a subtle form of rape? She'd kill him if she knew he was here. Wouldn't she?

He couldn't tear himself away, and he stood in the middle of her room, watching her sleep. Her jaw flexed slightly, making a low, grinding noise. She'd had to wear a mouth guard ever since she was a child. The dentist had said that eventually she might need corrective surgery. But when she moved in with Sam, she'd stopped grinding her teeth and didn't need the mouth guard. Sam had taken this as a sign that he was good for her and was more than a little proud that, inadvertent as it was, he'd saved her molars.

She started to mumble in her sleep again, and he decided to leave before she woke up. Looking at her one more time, he tiptoed out of the room and quietly closed the door behind him. He hurried through the house, jumped in his car, and sped away, wondering if he would ever be trusted with her sleep again.

When Sam got home, he collapsed onto the living-room couch and slept until the phone rang at seven o'clock that night. He ran to the phone, his heart hammering. He thought it was Kate. Instead, it was a nasal-sounding woman calling on behalf of disabled veterans. Out of desperation, he bought fifty dollars' worth of light bulbs.

Groggy and hungry, he shuffled into the kitchen, made himself some eggs and toast, turned on the TV for the sake of voices, and then sat out on the front steps eating. No one walked past. Everyone was inside having supper. He sopped the eggs up with the toast. He smelled the onset of spring, a combination of dank ground and new-cut grass. Inside, Harry Reasoner interviewed some woman who was having her hundredth birthday.

Everything he did reminded him of her. He'd made four eggs, two for him and two for her. He put out two mugs for coffee. He'd even poured her coffee, putting in cream and sugar—the way she liked it. He felt her presence in the house and had to keep reminding himself that she wasn't off in the other room, reading a book.

When he finished eating, he wandered through the house, which overnight had become a museum of their relationship. In the kitchen, he remembered a breakfast when the tie to her robe caught on fire over the stove and the look of astonishment on her face when he'd drenched her with the pot of cold water he'd just drawn for the grits. In the dining room, he remembered an elaborate Indian meal he'd spent all day cooking, but he'd gone overboard on the hot peppers, and beads of sweat collected on Kate's forehead as she'd valiantly tried to eat it. In the living room, there was the time they'd been watching TV when a screech owl came flapping down the chimney and perched, its wings soot-covered, on an andiron.

He walked through the unfinished rooms where Kate, wearing a dust mask, had helped him rip out old plaster. He'd planned to replace it with new Sheetrock, but right now the walls were nothing but ancient two-by-fours and dusty wiring—the innards of an old house.

Sam was tempted to rope off all the rooms so that everything would remain just as Kate left it—a paperback open on the night table by the bed, washed stockings hanging over the bathroom radiator, a used tea bag wound around a spoon on the kitchen counter, a Reese's cup wrapper balled up in the ashtray on the coffee table, and next to it a *People* magazine open to a black-and-white picture of Cary Grant.

Tired of the plaintive voice of Mike Wallace, Sam turned off the TV and sat down on the couch to try to read, but he'd only managed a few sentences when one of those waves of depression caught him off guard. The house's resounding emptiness drove him outside, where, not knowing where else to go or what else to do, he went for a long walk. He hurried through the dark, narrow streets of Little Five Points, past people talking on their porches, past stereos pounding across yards, past windows bathed in the blue light of TVs.

When he came back, he couldn't bring himself to go inside the house. He got into the Tempest and drove downtown, along Peachtree Street, where gleaming sky-scrapers edged up to the sidewalk. He pulled into the small brick Amtrak depot. Kate always said she thought it was ironic that a city that was once the railroad capital of the South had such a dinky depot. He went inside. There was no one there except a bag lady who huddled in one corner, rummaging through a shabby Rich's shopping bag.

He sat down on one of the benches. He and Kate had taken the train on their trip to Boston, leaving from this station in the middle of the night with a quiet crowd of yawning travelers.

It had been a long trip, dark through Georgia and the Carolinas and dawn somewhere in Virginia. Kate slept well into the morning. He woke her somewhere around Richmond with a cardboard tray of coffee and powdered-sugar doughnuts from the snack bar. They dunked their doughnuts in their coffee as they whispered Boston plans, crumbs falling onto the unfolded map draped over their laps.

He remembered how good he'd felt that morning, with the landscape in motion out the window, and their heads almost touched, touring Boston by finger. Kate seemed happy, too, the way she smiled whenever the conductor strode down the aisle to announce another city: "Wash—ing—tonnn!" "Bal—teee—mooore!" "Phil—a—del—phiaaa!!"

Kate had said that the way the conductors pronounced the cities made her want to visit each one.

"Hey, buddy?" The bag lady had come over to him,

holding a cigarette to her lips. "Got a light?" She was younger than he had first thought. She had a slightly sour smell.

"Sorry." He patted his pockets to show her.

"Can you spare a dollar?" She wore layers of clothes, like the woman who'd come into Brilliant's asking for a book about training cats.

He opened his wallet, took out a dollar, and handed it to her.

"The train won't be for a while." She stuffed the bill in an inner pocket. She started to go back to her bags, but his presence seemed to trouble her. "Waiting on somebody?" She dug a pack of matches out of another pocket and lit her cigarette. "It'd be better for you to go away and come back. The train ain't for hours." She pointed at the big yellow clock in the center of the station. She inhaled her cigarette, and he felt her keep glancing in his direction. "Ain't exactly Grand Central, is it? Of course, I done seen Grand Central."

He nodded, then got up and walked outside to the empty platform. It had gotten chilly. The tracks were illuminated by bright anticrime sulphur lights. Detached train cars stood on side tracks, dark, hulking forms. The train tracks cut a trough through this side of the city. He faced the direction he and Kate had ridden away in and wished they had stayed in Boston or some other distant city where the unfamiliar might've kept them together.

"Hey, buddy." The bag lady had come out after him. "If you're waiting on somebody, you got a mighty long wait."

Chapter Seven

Out on the sidewalk, Carl balanced on the top rung of a stepladder, hanging a sale banner in the front window, as Paula planted her foot on the bottom rung to steady it. If it had been a month ago, Sam would've worried that she'd kick the ladder out from under him, and at that time Carl would never have put himself in such a vulnerable position. Ever since Jessie had dressed Carl down about the Gullard signing, he'd been much more tolerable. Paula, too, had become more malleable, partly because of Carl's turnaround and partly because Macon had hung on to his job at the record store and they'd made a two-hundred-dollar payment on their MasterCard bill.

As he arranged a sale table of new remainders, Sam kept an eye on Carl and Paula through the window and thought, If anyone has been hard to get along with the past few weeks, it's been me. Kate's leaving had driven him into a deep funk, and the more he tried to extricate himself, the deeper he sank.

Jessie came out of the back, showing Sam a catalog. She'd been in her office all morning with a sales rep. "How many copies of le Carré will we sell?"

"At least fifty."

"What about the Baldwin essays?"

"Twenty-five." Sam liked the fact that Jessie consulted her employees. While she made most of the final decisions, she included staff members in meetings with sales reps. It was Jessie's philosophy to familiarize anyone who

122

worked at Brilliant's with all aspects of the book trade. At staff meetings she always said, "I want everyone who works here to know this business so that when you think about having a bookstore of your own, you won't make the mistake I made and go through with it."

Paula and Carl came inside from hanging the banner.

"It must be in the mid-nineties out there." Carl set the stepladder by a bookshelf, mopping his forehead with a handkerchief. "And it's only May."

"At least the store is air-conditioned," Jessie said.

Paula wiped her forehead with the back of her hand. "I told Macon he'd better stick with this job so we can buy an air conditioner for the bedroom."

"You don't have air conditioning?" Carl was horrified.

"Neither do we," Jessie said. "It gives Sylvia a headache."

"Gerald's from Minnesota, and he'd melt if we didn't have central air," Carl said.

"We don't have it either," Sam said. "*I* don't have it." She'd been gone for weeks, and he still lapsed into the plural.

"Well . . ." Jessie clapped her hands together. "These books won't sell themselves." She turned to Paula. "There are a couple of boxes of Viking in the receiving room."

Paula nodded and headed back to the receiving room.

"Carl, I'd like you to help me finish the Random House order," Jessie said. "The rep is in my office. I'll meet you back there."

Jessie and Sam were the only ones left in the front of the store. He felt her look at him, but he kept on arranging and rearranging sale books.

"Have you heard from her?"

"No."

"How long has it been?"

"Three weeks."

She came over and put her arm around his shoulder. "If you need somebody to talk to about it . . ."

He nodded.

She patted his back, then walked to her office. Only after he heard the office door close did he shove the stacked books onto the floor.

Half an hour later, Jessie, Carl, and the sales rep went to lunch. Paula received in the back, and Sam restacked Updike's *Witches of Eastwick*. He heard the door open and without looking up asked, "Can I help you?"

There was no reply. He turned around and saw the doorway darkened by the tall figure of the Bandanna Man. He wore the red bandanna around his head; sweat glistened on his forehead. He had a knapsack slung over his shoulder. He stood there, making his mind up about something.

"Can I help you?" Trying to appear casual, Sam made his way over behind the register. With Carl and Jessie at lunch and Paula in the receiving room, he was alone in the store.

"History," the Bandanna Man said.

"If there's a specific book you're looking for, maybe I could help you find it."

"Just show me where history is." He took a step inside the store. "U.S. history."

Sam fingered the hidden alarm button under the register, then decided he was being ridiculous. What would he tell the police if they showed up? He didn't like the guy's tone of voice? As he started to lead him back to the history section, he decided he shouldn't leave the register unguarded, so he pointed. "To your right . . . Back a little to your left . . . Okay now. There, in front of you."

The Bandanna Man pulled a book off the shelf, settled back against one of the sale tables, and began to read.

A flurry of customers kept Sam busy for the next half hour, checking titles and ringing up sales. When he looked back toward the history section, the Bandanna Man was gone. He'd left without Sam's even noticing and had probably taken half the history section with him. Sam hurried back to check the shelves. Nothing seemed to be missing, although a few books were scattered around the floor, all of them about Vietnam.

When he got into the car, the steering wheel was so hot he could hardly keep his hands on it. The car had baked in the parking lot all morning with the windows rolled up. Luckily, the lunch-hour traffic was over; otherwise, the Tempest would've overheated. He passed the flower man, whose shirt was darkened with circles of sweat under his arms; his buckets of flowers looked tired in the heat. Sam bought a bouquet, anyway. As the old man counted back his change, he wondered what he was doing meeting Maggie behind Kate's back.

He circled the Rainbow's jammed parking lot a couple of times before a pickup backed out. He pulled in next to her Land Rover, a canoe strapped to the top and the bumper covered with stickers from Yellowstone, Mount McKinley, the Okefenokee, and a new one—the Everglades.

Maggie sat in a booth, sipping iced tea, reading over a menu. "Sam." She stood up and hugged him. In her khaki shorts, knee socks, and hiking shoes, she must've just come in off the trail. She smelled of campfire smoke. She guided him over to the booth, the way she did at her house when about to serve him a big bowl of her lentil soup. A serious-looking couple, who must've been in their mid-forties, held hands in the booth across from theirs. They hadn't touched their food.

"You just got in?" When Sam called her at the beginning of the week, she was going on a two-day camping trip in the Cohutta Wilderness.

"Pretty rank, aren't I?" She picked at her shirt and sniffed.

"How was the weather?"

"It was cool up there." She cast a disparaging glance toward the window. "Nothing like this." She smiled to herself. "Claire brought mushrooms." Claire was Maggie's best friend. They'd met hiking the Appalachian Trail. Both divorced and both campers, they found they had a lot in common and spent most of their time together, on camping trips or in Maggie's kitchen, drinking coffee and pouring over topo maps. Sam had liked sitting in on these sessions. They'd even taught him how to read a topo map—the closer the lines, the steeper the trail.

"Have you ever done mushrooms?" Maggie asked. "We spent two whole days just sitting in a clearing, being." Her eyes widened. Whatever misgivings Sam had about seeing Maggie again vanished with her enthusiasm. She was a hardy woman. She was a shorter, sturdier version of Kate. And Maggie's mother, who at the age of ninety still lived alone in a farmhouse in the mountains of North Carolina, was even huskier. The women in that family never died, but thickened like trees.

"The first day, a copperhead crawled under my knee, lay right in front of me, sunbathed on a rock for a couple of hours, and then slithered away into the grass. What an impressive snake. Claire got a picture."

Another thing Sam missed was Maggie and Claire's slide shows. When they took a picture of a tree, nobody was leaning against it. When they took a picture of a rock, nobody sat on it. When they took a picture of a sunset, no one was in the foreground, trying to look moved.

"I was bitten by a copperhead when I was a kid," he said. This is the way it was with Maggie. He hadn't seen her in a month, since Kate left. Some big changes had taken place, and yet here he was telling her a story about his childhood.

"I never knew that," she said.

"I was five years old. I was playing with a pipe in

my great-aunt's backyard. A baby copperhead fell out and bit my ankle."

"What'd your aunt do?" Stories were never wasted on Maggie.

"Stomped the snake's head with her shoe, whisked me up, carried me inside, cut my leg open with a paring knife, and sucked the poison out."

"So you're probably immune to copperhead poison."

"I haven't tested it." He told everyone that story. It was one of the few things about his life that seemed the least bit exceptional, and even then, he couldn't take credit for it. The snake had inflicted Sam with some small sense of identity.

Maggie reached across the table and covered his hand with hers. "I'm really sorry."

"It was twenty-five years ago. I'm pretty much over it."

She smiled sadly.

"Oh, that." He crossed his arms, remembered he'd read somewhere that standing with crossed arms was a defensive posture, and uncrossed them. He caught himself starting to cross his legs. Not knowing what to do with his hands, he tucked them under his thighs. He spent most of his waking hours arranging himself.

"When Henry left me," she said, "I thought I'd never get over it."

Surely she wasn't comparing Kate's leaving with her divorce? The breakup of a twenty-five-year marriage to a temporary rift between him and Kate? Did she know something he didn't? Or was she just being melodramatic? Maggie assumed that people felt things as intensely as she did. She never belittled others' pain. Sometimes she over-empathized, making him feel that he didn't feel enough.

"And while I hate people who say, 'You'll get over it,'" she said, "the thing is, you do."

When Maggie went to the rest room, Sam noticed the couple in the booth across from them. He slowly cut his eyes to the couple. Kate used to say it was impossible to carry on a conversation with him in a restaurant, he was so busy listening to everybody else. He wondered if things might have been different if he'd paid more attention to Kate and less to everyone around them.

Maggie hadn't come back from the rest room when Leila brought Sam's iced tea. "I guessed you wouldn't want coffee on a day like today." She refilled Maggie's glass. "Her mother?" She nodded at the empty place. Over the past few weeks, he'd confided a few things to Leila. There was an easiness about her that made it almost impossible not to talk to her—the way she'd pause in front of his table, her tray tucked under her arm, her head cocked slightly, her eyes not quite meeting his. She listened. She even knew when he didn't want to talk about it and would talk about her children or school.

"She doesn't look like a retired anything." He'd told her she was a retired schoolteacher. Leila set out the silverware.

When Maggie came back, Sam introduced her to Leila. "Leila's in school at Georgia State. She's finishing her degree."

"So I won't lose my tenure at the Rainbow." She slid her pad out of her pocket. "The way things are going, pretty soon you'll have to have a Ph.D. to bus tables. You were a teacher?" Leila asked Maggie.

"Leila wants to teach high-school English," Sam explained. "I've told her a little bit about you."

"What grade did you teach?" Leila asked.

"Tenth," Maggie said. "It's a good age. They're not totally jaded. Teaching isn't a bad job, although sometimes you're more of a zookeeper."

Leila looked around the crowded diner as waitresses dashed from one table to the next, serving food, pouring coffee, clearing dishes. "What is a job if not the zoo of our choice?"

Maggie laughed. "What drove me crazy were all those education courses."

"If you ask me, education has given school a bad name." Leila clicked her pen with her thumb. "What can I get y'all?"

After they'd ordered and Leila had hurried off to wait on someone else, Sam felt an awkwardness come over him. He picked up the salt shaker.

"What is it?" Maggie sipped her iced tea.

"I didn't ask you here just to visit." He smoothed his napkin.

"You want me to talk to her."

"Am I that transparent?" He threw up his hands. "I know it's underhanded to talk to you behind her back. I feel like a real sneak. I've felt crummy ever since I called you, skulking around with this ulterior motive."

She set her glass down. "There's nothing ulterior about love."

There was a loud crash on the other side of the diner. A red-faced waitress crouched on the floor, picking up a tray filled with dirty dishes she'd dropped. The busboy came out of the kitchen, lugging a mop.

"I shouldn't have asked you to meet me," he said.

"I'd be disappointed if you hadn't."

"I can't ask you to talk to her."

"I already have."

His heart leapt. He was surprised to find Maggie in his corner. "What'd she say?" He held up his hands. "Maybe I don't want to know."

She pushed her gray hair away from her eyes. "She thinks the world of you."

"Come on."

"She didn't leave you because she was mad at you. Y'all want different things."

He sighed. "I don't know what I want."

"She does." She shrugged. "She doesn't want to

make you want what she wants. She respects you. In a way, her leaving was for your benefit."

"Benefited isn't exactly how I feel."

"I'm not saying what she did was altruistic. She did it for herself." She twirled the band on her ring finger.

"If I learned anything from my husband's leaving, it's that self-sacrifice can be an insidious form of selfishness." She stared out the window at the heat wriggling up from the parking lot. "We spend our lives waiting for people to think about us and hate them when they don't."

It dawned on Sam that if Kate wasn't angry with him, then what was there for her to get over? If she hadn't left him because of something she felt, it must've been for what she didn't feel.

"What can I do, Maggie?"

She blinked and looked back at him. "Have faith, but don't count on anything."

"Who had the meat loaf?" Leila had come up to their table, plates balanced on her arms.

Two days after his talk with Maggie, Kate appeared at his doorstep one night with her suitcase. He was upstairs taking a shower, having just come back from his jog. Since he didn't have anything else to do with his evenings, he went for a run and then came back and sat in his study and read until he got sleepy. He didn't like reading in bed alone.

His usual jogging route was down McClendon Avenue and through Candler Park, where couples pushed strollers along the edge of the public golf course, teenagers huddled around cars in the parking lot or sailed Frisbees back and forth in the waning light, old men walked their dogs, and children hung upside down by the crook of their knees on the jungle gym.

Tonight he'd noticed fewer people out. Storm clouds had been building since he'd gotten home from work. On the news, they'd said a cold front that swept through Alabama had spawned a series of tornadoes and was expected to pass through Georgia later that night. He'd felt strange because the park had been empty. When he'd jogged up the long hill, he saw that the usually crowded tennis courts were abandoned. As he looped around, along a wooded path, he felt singled out, exposed. The air had gotten heavy. The whole park was bathed in an eerie yellowish tinge. He had the distinct impression that something sinister lurked nearby. He decided to cut his jog short, especially since the distant rumble of thunder was not so distant anymore.

As his foot hit the porch steps, a crackle of lightning split the air. More people were struck by lightning in Georgia than any other state—one of Willy's statistics. Sam paused on the porch to slip off his running shoes and watch the lightning flash across the neighborhood. It began to rain.

He listened to the radio as he showered. There was a tornado watch but no sightings. Strong thunderstorms were moving through Atlanta and could spawn a tornado. If you heard a loud locomotive sound approaching, you were to take shelter in the basement or in the center of your home, or if outside, throw yourself in a ditch. He'd just stepped out of the shower when he heard a pounding downstairs. At first, he thought it was the storm. He turned the radio off. Someone knocked at the front door.

He ran down the staircase, a towel wrapped around his waist, his wet feet slapping the floor. "Coming." He stood on his tiptoes to see out the top window of the door. He fumbled with the dead bolt, finally opened the door, and found Kate standing there, an apparition in her white lab coat. She'd come from work.

"You're leaking." She pointed to the puddle at his feet.

He gawked at her a minute, amazed that she still existed. It had been only three weeks (twenty-two X's darkened his calendar), and while he had talked to her a couple of times on the phone, the suddenness of her absence had the shape and completeness of a death. To see her on his porch, resurrected, shook him up. Her suitcase sat beside her.

"You didn't get caught in the storm?" Her hair wasn't even damp. He looked behind her and saw that not only had the storm passed, but the sky had cleared, and there was a faint twilight glimmer left in the neighborhood.

"What storm?" That was the thing about Atlanta. It could pour in one part of the city and fifteen minutes away might not rain a drop.

"Why'd you knock? Why didn't you just come in?"

"I want to respect your privacy," she said in a determined voice.

"I wish you'd respect it a little less." His heart pounded. She'd come back. What else would she be doing with her suitcase? She'd left unannounced; that's how she'd return. He'd tried not to bother her since that morning he'd crept into her bedroom. He'd refrained from calling her when he thought he couldn't stand it anymore. He believed that the more pressure he put on her, the less likely she'd want to come back.

"Come on in." He tried to control his excitement. He lifted her suitcase, surprised how light it was.

She glanced around the living room, which, in her absence, had dissolved into a wreck: Half-read newspapers were strewn all over the sofa, dirty socks marked the spot where he'd taken off his shoes, clothes were draped over chairs, and crumpled potato-chip bags and half-empty diet Pepsi cans littered the coffee table.

"I'm a little behind in my housecleaning." He wished he'd kept things neater, anticipating her return. He shivered.

"You must be freezing," she said.

"Go fix us some coffee while I run upstairs and put on some clothes." He'd started up the stairs.

"Sam."

"Yeah?" He whirled around.

"I can't stay." She followed his gaze to her suitcase. Her eyes widened. "You thought—" She picked up the suitcase. "Oh, Lord, no." She realized what he thought. "I'm sorry. It's empty."

"You've always traveled light." He shivered again.

"I've come for the clothes I left in the dresser."

"Clothes?" He sank down on the steps. She'd left some clothes in the dresser, but he'd thought of that as a hopeful sign that she planned to return. Half-empty drawers he'd thought of as half full.

"You thought . . . ?" She picked a couple of dirty socks off the floor and folded them into a neat ball.

He sighed. "That's what I get for thinking." He carried her suitcase upstairs for her, feeling just how empty it really was.

He dried off and put on some pants while she packed her suitcase, which she'd opened onto his unmade bed. He dressed in the bathroom, feeling a weird modesty around her. He tried to think of what he should say. Something told him he'd lost his chance. She was leaving all over again. Her first leaving had been too quick, too precipitous to be felt. It took seeing her again to know she'd really gone.

He came out of the bathroom tucking in his shirttail.

She lifted a neatly folded stack of different-colored panties out of a drawer. He'd once asked her why she folded her underwear. "Because it's there."

"Your hair is different." It was a little shorter and wavier.

She touched her hair. "You think it does anything for me?" Kate talked about permanents the way some people talked about religion.

"How's your writing going?" she asked.

"How has it ever gone?"

"I just thought with more time on your hands . . ." She wedged a stack of blouses in her suitcase. "I have to level with you. I didn't come here just to get my clothes."

A faint hope stirred in him. "You didn't?"

"There's something I needed to say in person." She glanced at herself in the mirror. "I've started seeing people."

"People?"

"Men." She pushed the blouses down in the suitcase. "Nothing really serious."

He walked to the window, put his palms on the sill, and leaned out. Rain dripped from the maple next to the house. The streetlights had come on, shining on the wet pavement.

"Sam?"

He'd been so busy missing her that, in a way, he hadn't given her much thought. What had she been doing since she left? A dozen painful possibilities opened up. "Did you leave me for someone?"

"I left you for me." She lifted a knot of colorful belts from a drawer, started to untangle them, but then just dropped the whole knot into her suitcase. "There was no one else."

"Was?" He turned back around.

"Was no one else. *Is* no one else."

"What about the future tense?"

She refolded a green sweater that used to be his, but he'd accidentally put it in the dryer, and it had shrunk to her size. "I want you to start going out, too."

"The three of us?"

She rolled her eyes. "I mean, with other women."

"I don't know any other women." He knew how childish he sounded.

"Come off it, all kinds of women come in the book-store. That's where we met, remember?"

"Among the remainders." He sighed. "That should've been an omen." He sat down on the bed, beside the suitcase. It was an old brown suitcase that Maggie's father had bought her to take to college. He fingered the broken handle he'd wired back together on their Boston trip. They'd been crossing the Common, and the handle snapped. The suitcase fell open, and the wind scattered her clothes across the sidewalk. It was one of his fondest memories—the two of them chasing Kate's electric-colored underwear on the Boston Common.

"It makes me tired to think of going through all that again—the rigmarole of asking somebody out," he said. "It's not easy being a man, always expected to make the first move, to take the initiative."

"*I* asked *you* out." She closed the suitcase. She snapped one side, and he snapped the other.

"It's the principle of the thing." He pulled Kate down in his lap, holding her. He patted the suitcase. "Remember our Boston trip?"

She sighed. "Don't do this."

"That night we strolled around Harvard Square, listening to street musicians and drinking coffee at that Cafe Algiers?" He touched her hair, coarsened by the permanent. "That early-morning walk along the Charles . . . those guys sculling up the river in the mist?"

"We've had good times." Her voice had softened. "But . . ."

"I was afraid that word was coming."

"You can't build a relationship just on good times."

"We've had plenty of bad times."

"You know what I mean."

"I know I've missed you." He hugged her as a month's worth of misery spilled out of him. "I didn't know I could feel so lousy."

She walked over to the window, looking out.

"Stay," he said.

Her eyes gleamed with a skim of tears. "You think this has been easy for me? You think I haven't been miserable, too?" Her voice cracked. "You think I haven't wanted to call you? That I haven't wanted to see you?" She stared at him. "You think I haven't missed you? Good God, Sam!" She stomped the floor. "I've missed you from the moment we met!"

The rain dripped on the maple leaves just outside his window, making a sad tapping sound.

She went into the bathroom and came out with a wad of toilet paper, dabbing her eyes. She set the suitcase on the floor. "I shouldn't have come. It's too soon. I should've sent Willy or Maggie or waited till you weren't here."

He held her hand. "I know I've fucked up royally."

"I fucked up, too."

He stroked her cheek with the back of his hand. "Why can't we go on fucking up together?"

She smiled sadly, stooping to pick up her suitcase. "I don't like leaving you."

"Then stay, if not for me, for your conscience's sake." His voice cracked. "Relieve some of that guilt."

"I have to go." She glanced at her watch.

"Is it because I'm terminally wrinkled?" He tugged at his shirt. "What if I promise to press my clothes every morning for the rest of our lives?"

"I don't think you're ready for that kind of commitment." She kissed his cheek, then backed out the door, knocking her suitcase against the night table. "You don't have to see me out." She paused in the doorway. "Take care of yourself."

"I don't have much choice." He sank down on his bed, listening to her footsteps descend the stairs. He heard the front screen door slam and her car pull out of the driveway. He smelled her permanent on his fingers.

Chapter Eight

Sam salvaged a few peas and diced carrots, picking through the charred remnants of a Stouffer's pot pie, as he ate by the flickering light of the evening news. The burned smell lingered, even with the kitchen fan sucking out the smoke—an acrid replay of that night two months ago when he came home and found beans smoldering on the stove and Kate upstairs, nearly packed.

He set down his fork and felt the small, smooth scar on his hand where the pot handle branded Kate's departure into his palm.

Staring down at the greenish yellow pile of exhumed vegetables, his appetite faded. He got up from the couch and cut off the TV, interrupting Dan Rather in mid-international crisis. In the kitchen, he scraped the plate in the sink, which overflowed with crusted dishes submerged in murky water. A sinkful of "barnacles," he thought, remembering Kate's word.

He glanced at the kitchen clock. He was going to see *The Mission* tonight, one of those movies he'd heard a lot about but somehow missed. He'd seen more movies in these two months than in the past two years. Since he spent days at the bookstore, evenings were the hardest time for him. If he wasn't out jogging or in his study, he was at a movie theater. In the beginning, he and Willy had gone out drinking a few times. Actually, Sam drank, and Willy waited to drive him home and put him to bed. One morning, he awoke to an elephantine hangover and the sobering conclu-

137

sion that having no one else to live with, he'd have to live with himself.

He hurried upstairs to change into more comfortable clothes, tossed his dirty clothes into a pile in the corner, and plucked a ragged pair of shorts from the clean pile. Over the past two months his wardrobe had sorted itself into three piles—dirty, washed, and no-man's pile, where he tossed clothes whose status was uncertain. He dug a short-sleeve, button-down shirt out of this last pile, sniffed the armpits, and put it on.

Halfway out the front door, he remembered to go back and turn on his answering machine, which he'd bought a month ago when he realized he was hanging around the house waiting for calls, a specific call. Kate and he had talked on the phone a few times since she'd come over that night to get the rest of her things. They had halting conversations, spending half the time asking each other, "Are you still there?" As torturous as these calls were, he couldn't abide the thought of missing one.

He cut the porch light on, locked the front door, and was walking out to the car when he noticed Raymond and two other boys playing marbles on the sidewalk. He recognized Bobby, a boy about Raymond's age who lived down the street, and Chris, Bobby's little brother.

Intent on the game, they didn't even glance up when Sam walked over.

Raymond cradled his marble in his finger, squatted down, checked the lay of the sidewalk, curled his tongue against his lip, and with a flick of his thumb, sent his marble across the circle, where it popped against a big blue cat's-eye.

"Nice," Sam said.

"Not if you're on the receiving end," Bobby grunted.

Sam knelt down beside them. "Can I have a shot?" The sidewalk was still warm with the day's heat.

Raymond loaned him a couple of marbles.

"I didn't see your mother today," Sam said.

"She took the day off."

"Is she sick?"

Raymond shook his head. "She called it a mental-health day."

"Are you going to shoot or what?" Bobby asked Sam.

He took aim at the chalk circle of marbles. He'd seen more of Virginia since Kate left. She'd stopped and talked to him a few times in the evenings on her way back from the MARTA station. Last week she'd even come up on the porch and drank iced tea with him. He suspected that since Kate worked with her, she'd asked her to check on him, which was the same feeling he got with Willy and Rose and Lamar, that through them Kate orchestrated his life from afar.

His shot bounced over the whole circle and would've rolled into the street drain if Chris hadn't caught it.

Bobby laughed at Sam's shot.

"He's just a little rusty." Chris handed the marble back to Sam.

Bobby took aim at one of Raymond's green pureys. He glanced up at Sam. "What happened to that nice lady who used to stay with you?"

Raymond jabbed Bobby with his elbow.

Bobby scowled at Raymond. "I just asked the man a question. You made me miss my shot."

"She moved out," Sam said.

"Where'd she go?" Chris lay on his stomach to take aim at a cat's-eye.

"To live with her mother," Sam said.

The boys frowned at this.

"Who'd want to live with their mother if they didn't have to?" Bobby asked.

"I don't plan on eating meat loaf the rest of my life." Chris still took aim.

That part of it had been awkward. Sam hadn't been over to Maggie's since that morning months ago. It felt strange to be cut off from a place he'd grown accustomed to.

"You're better off without her." Bobby aimed at a rainbow on the opposite end of the circle. "Women tie you down."

"And do what to you?" Chris asked.

Raymond and Bobby shook their heads.

"I have a couple of girlfriends." Bobby's marble rattled through the circle, missing all the marbles.

"*They* have *you*," Raymond said.

Bobby leaned over to Sam. His breath reeked of bubble gum. "Just remember to wear a rubber."

Raymond put his head in his hands.

"Yeah," Chris said, down on his stomach, taking aim at a marble. "Everybody needs a rubber."

The boys turned to Chris. "You don't even know what a rubber is," Bobby said.

Chris closed one eye to take better aim. "Do too."

"What's it for?" Bobby asked.

The little boy didn't say anything, didn't move, but just lay there, squinting at the circle of marbles and breathing deeply. This was the Zen of marble shooting.

"I told you he didn't know," Bobby said.

"Leave him alone," Raymond said. "He's just a little kid."

"That's what he gets for talking big."

"And he's the only one around here who does that." Raymond jabbed Bobby in the chest.

"I know what it's for." Chris calmly took aim.

"What, big man? What's it for?"

"Protection." Chris's shot glided to the far side of the circle and clicked against his brother's last cat's-eye.

Down the street a mother called her children inside, her voice cutting through all the other noises. The boys paused in their game—as children paused in their play all through the neighborhood—then realized it wasn't their mother and bent back to the marbles.

Streetlights bleached Elmira Street in a yellow light. A breeze rattled the leaves overhead, a cool reminder that although it was the middle of summer, autumn wasn't that far off. Sam usually looked forward to the fall, but now seasons stretched out ahead of him. He didn't miss Kate with the same urgency he'd missed her the first few weeks, when he'd wake in the middle of the night, clutching sheets. He slept now. Maybe even a little better, since he had the whole bed to spread out on. He missed her in quieter ways. If he was having a slow day at the bookstore and would console himself with the thought that at least he had the evening to look forward to, then he'd remember that when he got home his house would be empty, emptier than the bookstore. He was amazed how many times during the day he had to correct the course of his thinking and remind himself that as tedious as it sometimes was to shelve a shipment of cookbooks or rearrange the religion section, doing so was the high point of his day. Without Kate, time lacked emphasis. Breaking up was painfully monotonous.

Sam stood in the long ticket line for twenty minutes. He'd glimpsed a woman who looked a lot like Kate standing far back in the line, but he often thought he saw her. He had seen her a couple of times, and neither time had been exactly coincidence, since he never went anywhere if he didn't think there was a chance she might show up. He made a point of shopping at the same grocery store he knew she'd shop at, driving the same route home she'd take, going to the same drugstore, the same mall, the same bank, the same post office, the same library branch. He didn't seek her out as much as position himself so that their paths might intersect. He'd seen her in the frozen-food section of the Winn Dixie and followed her around the grocery store for twenty minutes. Another time he'd found himself driving right behind her on his way home from work. He'd followed her a couple of blocks toward Maggie's, decided he was being too conspicuous, and turned toward home.

In fact, that was why he was standing in this long ticket line. He hadn't really wanted to see this movie, especially right now. He wasn't in the mood for a movie about martyr-priests. But he'd remembered that Kate had said several times that she wanted to see it because Jeremy Irons was one of her favorite actors. For some reason, they'd never gotten around to it. The last of the old big-screen theaters in Atlanta, the Columbia, had been one of their favorite theaters.

"How many, please?" asked the gum-chewing high-school girl in the ticket booth.

"Two, please." He corrected himself. "I mean, one." He hadn't made that mistake in a while.

He stopped at the concession stand in the lobby to get a Coke and a box of popcorn, which he almost dropped when Kate walked in. He whirled around so that the man behind the counter asked him, "Did you need something else?"

"Milk Duds." He pointed to the glass case. He watched Kate cross the lobby. She was with a tall blond man who looked vaguely familiar. At first, he was sure Kate had seen him, but she was so busy talking that she hadn't noticed him.

He paid for the Milk Duds, ducked around a couple of posts, and since the lobby was crowded, was able to loop around behind Kate without her noticing. He ended up right behind them. With his heart in his throat, he followed them. The man had a beeper clipped to his belt. A doctor, Sam told himself. He remembered now. He'd met him at the neonatal Christmas party. In fact, the doctor had had the party at his house, a swanky three-story deal on West Paces Ferry with tennis courts and an indoor pool. The whole time Sam had felt like he was walking around inside a *New Yorker* ad.

He followed them into the theater and nearly bumped into them as they stopped to decide where to sit. The Columbia always felt cavernous, especially after those ten theaters in one, what Kate called "sub-theaters." The screen seemed the size of a football field.

He waited till they'd sat, started to cross to the other side of the theater, and then, not knowing quite why, slid along the row immediately behind theirs and sat down behind them.

Kate and the doctor talked in low voices, laughing now and then. Sam noticed she wore a pair of silver earrings he'd given her for Christmas. Through the space in the seat he could see she had on a bracelet he'd given her for their second anniversary. He was sure that at any moment Kate would turn around and see him; the doctor did glance back but didn't seem to recognize him. The lights dimmed.

When the previews started, Kate and the doctor slid down in their seats. The doctor put his hand over Kate's on the armrest.

She left it there for a moment, then pulled her hand out from underneath his.

Sam ate his popcorn. He thought his heart would beat out of his chest.

Fifteen minutes into the movie, which Sam hadn't noticed except for the sound of an immense waterfall, the doctor slipped his hand onto Kate's knee. Again she waited a few minutes, then picked up his hand and put it back on his knee.

Five minutes later, he put his hand on her knee again.

Sam waited for Kate to put it back. He waited through several dramatic scenes, none of which really registered with him, although whenever he thought back to this moment in the theater, he would always picture Jeremy Irons trying to put the move on Kate in a lush Brazilian jungle.

Kate didn't remove the doctor's hand. About halfway through the movie she covered it with hers. At this point, as Sam was about to get up and leave, the doctor turned to look at Kate, but she kept watching the movie. He touched her chin and turned her face toward his. He was about to kiss her.

Sam jiggled the doctor's seat with his foot.

The doctor turned around and frowned.

"Sorry," Sam said in a muffled voice.

Fifteen minutes later, he tried to kiss her again. Sam nudged his chair. The doctor turned around.

The third time, Sam kicked the seat a little too hard.

The doctor leaned over to him. "Would you please . . . ?"

"Keep your hands off her." The words were out of Sam's mouth before he even knew it.

"Pardon me?" The doctor turned around.

"I said, keep your hands off her," Sam said louder.

Kate turned around. "Sam! What're you doing here?"

"Shh!" hissed several people in the audience.

"I came to see the movie."

"That's funny, so did I," said a middle-aged woman sitting next to them who'd been among the hissers.

"I don't need a chaperone," Kate said without rancor.

"Who is this guy?" the doctor asked.

"The man I used to live with. Richard Scales, this is Sam Marshbanks."

"I remember you from the Christmas party," the doctor said. "You alphabetized my bookshelves."

"Even if y'all aren't going to watch the movie," said the woman next to them, "would you mind if the rest of us did?"

"Yeah," said several people around them.

"I've heard a lot about you," the doctor said to Sam, and turned back around.

Kate reached over the seat and squeezed his knee, then turned back around to watch the movie.

Sam was mortified. He'd followed them into the theater and spied on them. Kate knew it, the doctor knew it, the whole theater knew it. He was an idiot, an immature idiot. Even worse, he'd revealed his desperation to her.

Kate and the doctor sat stiff in their seats, staring self-consciously at the screen. They stopped holding hands. The doctor didn't try anything else for the rest of the movie. Sam hated the fact that he'd spoiled their date instead of allowing it to ruin itself.

He slipped out of the theater as up on the screen the Spanish savagely annihilated the defenseless Indians. He couldn't stand to watch any more. As he passed through the abandoned lobby, he decided that instead of rating movies PG or R, they should be rated Hopeful or Hopeless.

It drizzled on his way home. He had to reach around the outside of the windshield and flick the wipers to keep them going. He'd meant to fix that. He passed by the Rainbow; its big windows of yellow light cut through the drizzle, inviting him in for a cup of coffee. He wasn't eager to get home—not with the answering machine waiting for him: If there wasn't a message, he'd be depressed, and if there was, what would the message be? Did they make a machine that answered your answering machine?

He picked up his slightly burned grilled cheese, then put it down. He didn't have an appetite. He sipped coffee, looked out at the steady drizzle, and listened to this young punk couple who sat in the booth catty-corner from his.

The couple might've been some of Paula and Macon's friends. They were in their late teens or early twenties, Georgia State students probably, like a lot of the late-night customers, a real contrast to the early-morning crowd, workmen in their forties and fifties who would be amused or appalled if someone roused them and dragged them over to the Rainbow in the middle of the night to show them the generation they'd fathered.

The girl's skeleton earrings danced a morbid little shuffle as she turned her head to blow cigarette smoke away from her boyfriend, who wolfed down scrambled eggs—a dead smiley-face frowned on his T-shirt, a bullet hole in its yellow forehead.

"Who said anything about marriage?" the boy asked between bites.

"Do you have any better ideas?"

"I gave you my suggestion."

"That's not an option." The woman crushed her cigarette in the ashtray with quick little jabs. She glanced at Sam.

"Since when did you turn into a right-to-lifer?" The boy with the dead smiley raised his voice to his girlfriend. His face was red.

"I'm not saying what anybody else should do. I'm not even saying what you should do." She took another cigarette out of the pack of Camels on the table, tapped the end of it on the table, and put it in her mouth. "But I know what I can't do." She lit the cigarette.

"Hell, you've probably already stunted its growth."

She held the cigarette in front of her, stared at it, then ground it slowly in the ashtray.

Willy sauntered into the diner and eased down into the booth. "You called?"

Sam slid his plate with the untouched grilled cheese over to Willy.

"You called for me to come eat your cold grilled-cheese sandwich?" Willy took a bite of sandwich as the waitress came over and filled Willy's coffee cup.

"What can I do for you?" Willy sipped his coffee.

"I think I'm losing it." Sam leaned across the table.

"How so?"

Sam waited until the waitress was out of earshot.

"Tonight I went to the movies. I saw Kate there with this doctor-guy, and I followed them into the theater and sat down right behind them. This guy kept trying to put the move on her, and finally I told him to keep his hands off her."

"So?"

"I made a fool of myself. The weird thing is it isn't bothering me as much as I think it should."

"Come again?" Willy poured sugar into his coffee.

"I saw Kate with this guy. It isn't tearing me up as much as I thought it would. Willy, I've been thinking about this ever since she left—that sooner or later I would see her with some other guy and that I would fall to pieces."

"You look okay to me." Willy took another bite of sandwich.

"That's what's so strange. I feel sort of relieved."

Willy sipped his coffee and poured more sugar into it. "That's a problem?"

The punk couple smiled at each other about something. A group of high-school girls in short skirts huddled around the jukebox, dropped quarters in, and punched songs.

"I don't know what's going on with me." Sam had to talk louder over the music.

Willy rubbed his bleary eyes. They had been bloodshot a lot lately, and the dark circles had become more defined. Sam worried about him. Willy couldn't enter a room anymore without bringing the crisp, smoldering scent of marijuana.

"I miss Kate," Sam said. "I really do, but lately I haven't missed her quite as much." He sighed. "There are even moments in the day when I catch myself not thinking about her."

"Maybe you're getting over her."

"I don't want to get over her," he said a little too loudly. The punk couple glanced in his direction. He lowered his voice. "It's only been a couple of months. I couldn't have gotten over her that fast. Or if I have, I must be pretty damned shallow."

"One can feel lousy for only so long."

"You think it's okay that I feel better?"

"You have my permission."

The punk couple walked out of the restaurant arm in arm. Sam wondered what he'd missed. What had they agreed upon? How could something so momentous be settled over a late-night breakfast in the Rainbow Cafe?

Chapter Nine

Lamar lifted Joey onto the fence so he could stand eye level with the flamingos wading on the other side of the lagoon like a flock of pink-plastic yard ornaments.

"See the pretty birds?" Lamar said.

"Birds!" Joey explained to Sam. "Birds!" he announced to the birds.

Rose had gone to the gift shop to find a hat to protect Joey's head from the sun. It was a hot, still Sunday afternoon when most of the animals napped in the shade of a tree or a rock, and the only sound, besides the people, was the murderous cry of the peacock that echoed across the zoo.

Sam mopped his brow with his handkerchief. In Atlanta, summer waxed redundant in September, and fall seemed as unlikely as in July.

"You've done a hell of a lot of work on your house." Lamar lifted Joey down.

"I haven't had much else to do," Sam said. In the past couple of months, he'd finished all the downstairs rooms. Every evening, after getting home from the bookstore, he'd fix a quick supper, go for a jog, and then start back in the room where he'd left off the night before. He put up new Sheetrock, painted the walls and the ceilings, sanded and polyurethaned the floors, replaced the molding, and installed new light fixtures. On the weekends, he threw himself totally into work on the house, so that he lost track

149

of time. He'd start early in the morning, sometimes not even break for lunch, and the next thing he knew, it was dark outside.

This afternoon, he was working on the stairway, tearing out the old plaster, when he thought he heard the front screen slam, then light, quick footsteps running around downstairs.

"Who's there?"

There was a silence.

"Who's there?"

"Up," said a familiar voice. Sam had a nightmarish sense of déjà vu. There was a pause. He heard someone breathe. The door opened, and there was Joey at the bottom of the stairs. "Sam."

Rose and Lamar had come by to see if he wanted to go to the zoo. He showed them the rooms he'd finished. The only room he didn't show them, the only one he hadn't worked on, was his study. He didn't know what to do with it—books all over the floor, magazines open to articles he meant to read, and stacks of unfinished stories spilling off his desk and onto the floor.

For a while after Kate left him, he had gone in, sat at the desk, rolled in a new sheet of paper in the typewriter, and actually typed a few sentences. But they were such terrible, hopeless sentences. They were sentences without a future. The writers on the wall frowned at him in disappointment. After a while, he stopped going in there altogether.

Rose returned from the zoo's gift shop with a tiny pith helmet, which she strapped onto Joey's head. Across the front of the helmet was printed: Safari in the City—Zoo Atlanta. "That's all they had," she said. She wore a backless sundress that fit her tightly enough to see that she'd hardly begun to show. The only real differences Sam could detect were her fuller face and an assurance in her step. She walked for two.

Joey ran ahead to the orangutan exhibit, with Lamar

trotting behind him. Lamar caught him and swung him up on his shoulders so he could see over the crowd at the exhibit, which was a grassy playground. At one end of the yard a young orangutan flipped on a wooden jungle gym; at the other end, a shaggy adult climbed slowly up a rope into the top of a tree, where a couple of other orangutans huddled in the shade. As in most of the exhibits, a deep ditch separated the animals from the people, or the people from the animals.

"Lamar and I feel bad that we haven't had you over." Rose sat on a bench, and Sam sat beside her.

"Why should you feel bad?" Sam said. "I could've had y'all over."

"Anyway, I'm glad you decided to come with us." She took Sam's hand.

When Kate first left, they'd asked him over to supper at least once a week, but it felt so awkward without her. They were almost as stunned as he by the breakup, and their get-togethers had the sad reverence of a memorial service. As time went on, they saw each other less, which was okay with Sam, who preferred loneliness to weirdness.

A crowd had gathered to watch the young orangutan swing from the platform. On Lamar's shoulders, Joey sat above the crowd in his pith helmet.

"Have you seen her?" Sam asked Rose.

"She came by last weekend."

The crowd laughed as the orangutan flipped over the bar three times, hamming it up.

"Is she seeing someone?" He'd tried not to ask Willy about Kate so much anymore. He didn't want Willy to feel used.

"A doctor from the hospital," Rose said.

"She's still seeing him?"

"We haven't met him." Rose picked up on his disparaging tone.

"The guy's okay." He rubbed his forehead with his

hand. "But he's not her type." He looked at Rose. "He has a car phone."

She laughed. "He's a doctor. Maybe he needs it."

"I'm telling you, I've been around this guy," Sam said, "and even if he weren't a doctor, he'd have a car phone." He put his head in his hands and groaned. "You're smiling at me."

"I'm sorry, but I can't believe you don't see it."

"See what?"

The peacock's cry echoed across the zoo.

"She picked somebody she can't get serious about," she said.

He wrinkled his nose. "Why would she do that?"

She put her finger on his chest. "*You* connect the dots."

The young orangutan had decided it was time for a nap, climbed on top of the platform, and disappeared. The other adult apes still sat in the tree, not moving. With nothing left to look at, the crowd dispersed.

Lamar put Joey down to let him walk.

"Come on, Sam." Joey took Sam's hand and pulled him off the bench.

"I can't believe he remembers my name."

"We still say good night to your picture," Lamar said. Every night before they put Joey to bed, Lamar or Rose lifted Joey up to the mantel, where he said good night to a crowd of relatives and close friends.

"Joey, don't we say, 'Night-night,' to Sam?"

"Night-night, Sam and Kate." Joey tugged him toward the elephant exhibit.

Lamar's face reddened. "I guess I need to take another picture."

They spent a couple of hours wandering past the outdoor landscaped exhibits, with grass and man-made concrete boulders and trees. No cages, no bars, just deep ditches divided animals and people. The animals were out in the open, free to run around, climb trees, and lie in the sunshine. The Atlanta Zoo was in the middle of remodeling, so a lot of exhibits weren't completed yet. Still, Sam was impressed by the improvements. The last time he'd come here was with Kate on one of their first dates. Back then, most of the animals, including the big cats and the apes, were caged in grim cinder-block buildings. Even Willy B., the zoo's pride and joy at that time and its only gorilla, was locked away in a dreary cell, where he lounged on the floor, ate peanuts, and stared at the TV that flickered at one end of his cage. It had been a seedy motel for wild animals.

After taking Joey through the petting zoo, where he petted a donkey, a llama, and a couple of rabbits, they found an umbrellaed table outside the Okefenokee Cafe. Lamar went in to get them all drinks.

Joey investigated a little black girl about his age sitting with her mother and father at the table next to theirs.

"Joey doesn't seem to hate me," Sam said.

"Why should he hate you?" Rose asked.

"I nearly killed him."

"Sam." Rose reached over and took his hand. "You're going to have to get over this."

"You and Lamar don't hate me?"

"We make a point of spending our Sunday afternoons with people we hate."

"Maybe you asked me to come along because you feel guilty about hating me."

Joey and the little girl chased each other between the tables. The parents of the little girl watched.

"I think they're in love," the woman said.

"She's beautiful," Rose said.

There was an odd moment when the black couple and Sam and Rose watched the children chase each other; then the black couple smiled at Rose and Sam and turned back to their own conversation. Sam realized they thought he was Joey's father.

Lamar came back from the cafe, carrying a trayful of drinks.

"Tell Sam we don't hate him," Rose said.

"We don't hate you." Lamar handed Sam his glass. "Didn't you want a root beer?"

"Thanks."

"And here's your Sprite." He gave Rose her drink. "Hey, Joey, here's your Coke."

Joey and the little girl crawled underneath the table.

"The kid isn't even two and he's already chasing women." Lamar leaned over to Sam. "Is there some reason we should hate you?"

"He thinks we're still mad about Joey's accident," Rose said.

"Are you kidding?" Lamar waved his hand, dismissing any such idea.

"He thinks we're just being nice or something," Rose said.

"Nice?" Lamar asked, incredulous. "Nice? You think Rose and I don't have better things to do with our time than to be *nice*?" He wiped his forehead with the back of his hand.

Joey climbed up into Sam's lap to drink his Coke.

"I suppose you think the kid's in on it, too?" Lamar asked.

When they reached the gorilla exhibit, a large crowd had already gathered along the wooden fence. This exhibit had gotten a lot of coverage in the newspaper, first as Willie B.'s new home and then, more recently, when two of the new female gorillas gave birth. The exhibit was the largest, shaded with trees and extended so far back over a rocky hill that it afforded the gorillas their privacy. You could only be sure to see them at feeding time.

With Joey on his shoulders, Lamar squeezed into the crowd to get close enough so Joey could see. Rose followed after them. Sam became separated from them in the crowd.

He wriggled his way toward the fence. The only gorilla in sight was Willy B., who lay on his back in the grass, playing with a stick. The only thing between him and the crowd was the fence and a very deep ditch.

"He can jump that," a middle-aged woman with a beehive hairdo said to a younger couple.

"Mama, there's no way Willy B. could clear that," the man said.

"Don't worry, Mrs. Neal," the younger woman said. "If he could get out, he would've gotten out a long time ago."

"I know gorillas," the middle-aged woman said. "They can jump." In a huff, she forced her way back through the crowd.

There was a general "Awww . . ." from the crowd. Sam looked up to see the two mother gorillas making their way down the hill, each cradling a baby.

A zoo assistant climbed onto a platform to throw down pieces of cut-up oranges. Willy B. walked over and picked up a handful of the oranges, then sat back on his haunches to eat. He had a bored expression. The mothers waited until he'd finished and had wandered over to lie in the grass before they came closer to pick up the food.

Half-hidden by their mothers' furry arms, both babies suckled. Now and then a foot or a hand would dangle that resembled a human baby's so much that one woman said, "It looks like they just stole somebody's baby."

The zoo assistant said that the mothers never set their babies down for the first six months. The mothers didn't seem encumbered by the babies, but moved easily, scooping up pieces of orange with their free hand.

He wished Kate were here to see Willy B. outside, with these other gorilla families to keep him company. He still had this interior dialogue with Kate, measuring everything by what she would've said, what she would've thought. She was part of him in a way that had nothing to do with her absence or presence.

Willy B. lay with his back to the crowd. People called to him and whistled, but he didn't turn around. Sam imagined what it must've been like when they took him out of his cinder-block cell where he'd been cooped up for twenty years and set him loose here, out in the open. For a minute, he must've just sat there and sniffed the air, turned his face to the sunshine, and stared up at the sky, sure he'd wake up soon, that this was just another dream of being back home in Africa.

A couple of weeks later, Sam came home one night from the bookstore and found a note wedged in his front door from Virginia, inviting him to supper. Like Rose and Lamar, she'd asked him over several times when Kate first left, but he'd always made up excuses, and she'd stopped calling. It had been months since she'd invited him, and he wondered why she did so now. What had changed? Did she have something to tell him? Or did she think enough time had passed that he might accept her invitation? He hadn't set foot in that house since the night of Joey's fall, a night that accumulated significance in his mind the further it receded. He was sure that was the night he'd lost Kate, not the night a month later when she tossed her bags into her car and drove to Maggie's.

He went inside and started to call Virginia to tell her that he had to finish Sheetrocking the upstairs bathroom, that he appreciated the invitation. He'd dialed her number but then hung up. If he turned her down now, she'd know it was more than just getting over Kate that kept him away. He opened his freezer. Did he really want to face another chicken pot pie tonight?

He stepped onto the Brennans' porch, started to knock, then paused to listen through the screen door to Deborah practicing her cello; the dark notes traveled down the hallway, riding a steamy waft of cooked vegetables. The den was dark, too. Light came from the kitchen. He saw the gleaming white table where Virginia had breathed life back into Joey that night. She was out of his view, but he heard her lift pot lids and replace them, open the oven door and close it. She called to Raymond to set the table.

"I'm in the middle of a problem," he yelled to her from the dining room.

"That'll be the least of your problems if you don't get in here and set the table this minute, young man!"

Charles yelled from his room that there weren't any clean towels. Virginia yelled back that there would be if he'd done the laundry. She said to check the hamper.

"Raymond!"

A chair scraped the floor in the living room. Raymond ran right past the front door, where Sam stood, and out to the kitchen. He heard the rattle of silverware. Deborah's cello played on.

He didn't knock. He turned around, walked to the edge of the porch, and stood there as the streetlights flickered on along Elmira. It was dark earlier, and the evenings had a new chill. Autumn, while not quite here, closed in on the city, tinged the dogwood leaves, and restored hazy skies to their original blue. Fall was such a crucial season. He hadn't seen Kate in some time now, and while he didn't feel as bad, he didn't feel as much, either.

Raymond must've seen him at the screen door. He ran up, unlatched the door, and pushed it open. "Supper's almost ready." He sat back down at the dining-room table, where he had his schoolbooks spread out before him.

Virginia came out to meet Sam, wiping her hands on her apron. She'd done the same thing when she came out on the porch that night he ran up the steps with Joey in his arms.

"It's almost ready." She touched Raymond's shoulder. "Go tell your sister it's time for supper."

"Deborah!" Raymond shouted. "It's time for supper!"
The cello played on.

"I said *go* tell her."

Raymond got up and walked down the hallway.

Virginia showed Sam into the kitchen and pulled out a chair. It was a little eerie being back in this kitchen— pots boiling on the stove, iced-tea glasses lined up on the counter, the table set, the same bowl of plastic fruit.

"I hope you like ham. A friend of mine at work gave us a ham."

"I love ham."

"How about some iced tea?" Virginia took a glass pitcher out of the refrigerator, filled one of the glasses, and handed it to him. Then she filled the rest of the glasses.

As he sipped his tea, he counted six places set at the table. He only counted five people—four Brennans and him. From where he sat, he saw through the kitchen door, through the hallway and the screen door to the street. Headlights swept past.

"I appreciate the attention you give Raymond," she said. "He comes home almost every day excited about a new book you've shown him." Raymond still came into the bookstore after school. Sam let him borrow books. Jessie didn't mind.

"All my children read," Virginia said, "but Raymond's like his father. Gene devoured books. He read at breakfast, lunch, and supper. On his lunch break, he'd be perched way up in the crook of some tree, a sandwich in one hand and a paperback in the other."

She lifted the lid on a pot; a puff of steam veiled her face. A silence descended on the kitchen. He counted the places set at the table again. Who was the sixth place for?

"How was the hospital today?" He used to ask Kate the same question.

She lifted another pot lid and shook pepper into the

pot. "Pretty quiet. We had one little girl admitted who'd shot herself in the foot with her father's pistol."

"Good grief."

"Poor thing was more scared than anything." She took a stack of plates from the cabinet. "Her father is the one who ought to be shot." She slapped the cabinet shut. "Leaving a gun around within a child's reach." She tore a paper towel off a roll over the sink and dabbed the beads of perspiration on her forehead. "If I think about it too much, I can't sleep, and if I can't sleep, I can't do my job, and then what good am I to anybody? It's not responsible to worry too much."

"I've never thought about it that way," he said. "But then the biggest worry at the bookstore is whether a book is out of stock."

She turned off the flames under the pots on the stove. "In my line of work, the people who learn to leave it at work don't burn out." She set the plates around the table. She took the butter out of the refrigerator door. She glanced through the kitchen door, looking out through the screen to the porch. "But then you know all about that."

"I always like to hear about what happens at the hospital." When Kate left, she took all those stories with her. "It made me feel not so out of touch."

"Kate said you were good to come home to." Virginia poured the beans in a white bowl and set them on the table. "She said you listened well." She glanced through the kitchen door every time a car passed. "She used to brag how you fixed her breakfast every morning." She opened the oven and slid out the pan with the ham. "Of course, it's only right," she said, a hint of irritation in her voice. "If women help bring home the bacon, men better help fry it." She stabbed the ham with a fork and set it on a platter. "Gene was a pretty mean cook himself." She wiped her hands on her skirt. "Kate thought a lot of you. Still does." She glanced out to the street again.

"Is Mama grossing you out with another hospital horror story?" Deborah came into the kitchen, helping put the food on the table.

"I was not." Virginia turned to Sam. "Tell her."

"Mama's seen it all." Deborah patted her mother's back. "And she's not going to let anybody forget it."

Virginia grunted.

"Your playing sounded wonderful," he said.

"Oh, Lord, don't feed her ego." Virginia put a steaming bowl of creamed corn on the table. "How did I wind up with such big-headed children?"

"We inherited it." Deborah set a basket of hot rolls on the table.

"They blame everything on blood," Virginia said. "Culpability went out with the discovery of genetics."

The two women set the food out on the table. The easy way they moved, the way they knew what went where, and the way they included him in their gentle kidding warmed the kitchen with a kind of good-humored generosity that made Sam feel, if not at home exactly, at least welcome.

"Where are those boys?" Virginia asked.

"Raymond can't tear himself away from his homework," Deborah said. "And Charles can't tear himself away from the bathroom mirror."

"Supper's getting cold," Virginia bellowed. The dishes in the sideboard rattled.

Raymond was in the kitchen in his seat at the table before she finished yelling, and Charles was two steps behind him, drying his hair with a towel.

"Put that towel down so we can say the blessing, Charles," Virginia said.

Charles hung the towel over the back of his chair. They held hands around the table.

"Would you say the blessing, Sam?" Virginia asked.

Everyone bowed their heads.

"You go ahead," Sam said to Virginia.

"The guest is supposed to say the blessing," Deborah said.

"In that case." Sam cleared his throat. He racked his brain, trying to remember a blessing. His family had never been very religious. "God is great," he began, "God is good . . ."

The children burst out laughing.

"That's a kindergarten blessing," Raymond said.

Sam shrugged at Virginia. "It's the only one I could remember."

Virginia bowed her head, and the children quickly quieted. "Lord, we thank you for seeing us through another day." Her voice rose. "We thank you for giving us a roof over our heads and food for our stomachs. We thank you for bringing Sam to our table tonight so that he might share our bounty." Then her voice softened. "We thank you for looking after Gene till we can be reunited in our final resting place." She opened her eyes and looked at the empty place set at the end of the table.

Raymond leaned over to Sam. "Now that's a blessing."

Virginia carved up the ham, serving everyone's plates as they passed around the bowls of food.

"How's your baby?" Charles passed Sam the bowl of creamed corn.

"It wasn't his baby." Raymond spooned beans onto his plate.

"It wasn't?" Charles grabbed the basket of rolls just as Deborah reached for them. "He knows who I mean."

"He's fine," Sam said.

"I'll never get over it." Charles passed Sam the rolls. "The way Mama knew exactly what to do, the way she breathed the life back into that baby."

"That's enough about that, Charles." Virginia passed Raymond his plate with ham on it.

"I was just trying to make conversation." Charles cut into his ham.

"Mama, tell me I'm not related to him." Deborah had covered her eyes with her hands. "You found him in a Dumpster, right?"

"She didn't have any trouble owning up to me when I won senior class president," Charles said to Sam. "She introduced all her little sophomore friends to me."

Deborah passed Sam a bowl of applesauce. "He ran a smear campaign."

"I smeared that guy, too."

"Raymond, are you trying to drown it?" Virginia cried.

Raymond was emptying a bottle of catsup on his ham.

"Y'all straighten up and eat," Virginia snapped.

The children sat up in their chairs and ate.

Virginia leaned over to Sam. "See what you have to look forward to."

As everyone settled into the meal, he felt less conspicuous. The food itself made him feel at home. He liked the way the food looked—a golden puddle of applesauce, which ran into the green beans, which seeped into the creamed corn, which cushioned the ham.

Charles and Deborah were in a heated discussion about who was more famous—Prince or Mozart. Everyone passed the bowls around for seconds and thirds until they were empty. The oven ticked with heat, filling the house with the sweet smell of what Raymond told him was peach cobbler. Sam remembered that night when he'd stood by feeling so inadequate as Virginia breathed into Joey's mouth, his chest rising and falling.

Virginia opened the back door to allow a breeze in. It had gotten dark outside, but inside, the kitchen radiated light. Sitting at this table of family, he felt at the center of the world, even if it was someone else's.

He excused himself to go to the bathroom down the

hall. On his way back, he passed Virginia's bedroom. Her door was open, and the light was on. He paused in the doorway, listening to the conversation in the kitchen. He stepped into the bedroom, which smelled of peppermint and mothballs and some other darker smell. The lamp from the night table cast the room in a soft yellow light, making the rose-colored wallpaper look rusty. The furniture—a dresser with a mirror, a chest of drawers, and a four-poster bed—seemed like appendages of the room, grown out of the floor. The floor was bare except for a small throw rug beside her bed.

He paused at her closet and ran his hands over her crisp uniforms, her soft dresses and softer robes. Pairs of nurses' shoes were lined up at the bottom, invisible nurses standing at attention.

He heard Charles say something in the kitchen in a low voice, then Deborah; then all of them laughed.

Virginia's dresser wasn't crowded so much with hairbrushes, lipstick, and makeup as with things the children had made for her over the years: a bouquet of faded construction-paper flowers, a small, crookedly woven basket, a miniature Christmas tree made of a large pinecone painted green, a lopsided clay ashtray. When Sam picked it up and turned it over, it read, "To Mama on Mother's Day, From Charles, Miss Freeman's Fifth Grade."

She used the mirror as a bulletin board, sliding in Raymond's drawings, programs from Deborah's concerts, a small poster that read: Don't Be a Loser! Vote for Charles Brennan, Class President. The rest of the space was filled with photographs: school pictures of the children, a picture of the Brennans in front of the house—Gene patted Virginia's pregnant stomach, while Charles and Deborah knelt in front of them, sticking their tongues out at the camera. It was the same picture Raymond had drawn that had been taped to the refrigerator, except Raymond wasn't in the photograph, or he was inside Virginia. She'd been pregnant with Raymond when Gene died. There were several older black-and-white photographs—one that Sam first thought was Deborah and her date at her junior-senior but then realized it was Virginia and Gene. Another of Virginia and Gene on the beach in their bathing suits and one of Virginia on a beach blanket, making eyes at the camera.

In the corner of the mirror were a few smaller, very yellowed photographs: one of a little boy sitting on the porch of a shack alone. Sam guessed it was Gene as a child. Another of a man pushing a woman in a tire swing—the man resembled Charles—Virginia's parents, he guessed. Then there was one other faded picture of a family standing in what looked like a cotton field. A little girl with plaited hair stood in front of a man who had his hand on her shoulder. The little girl held a handful of cotton out toward the camera. Sam was sure this was Virginia and her father.

Sam sat on the four-poster bed and ran his hands along the quilt. It was covered with houses, the same pattern over and over but in different colors, and different women had signed each square. So this was the room where Virginia would retreat with Gene when the children became too much. He laid back and stared up at the dimly lit ceiling. He heard Gene's deep, soothing voice talk about places he wanted to see, places he'd read about and knew better than the people who'd been there.

"Sam?" Virginia stood in the doorway of her bedroom. "Do you feel okay?"

He sat up so fast his head swam.

"Are you all right?" She came into the room.

His face burned red.

She walked over to the dresser, leaned on her fists, and looked at the photographs he'd just been looking at. How long had she been standing there? She pointed to a picture of Gene cutting limbs high up in a tree. "At Christmas, he didn't shoot down mistletoe; he just shimmied up the tree." She nodded. "There's something to be said for a man who goes after his own mistletoe."

In the kitchen, the children stood at the sink in assembly-line fashion, washing and drying the dishes, while Sam and Virginia lingered over their coffee at the table. Sam scraped up the last of his cobbler from the bowl. A quiet had settled on the house. He couldn't tell if the children were thinking about other things or if his presence made them feel awkward. He told himself he shouldn't have come. On the other hand, if he didn't do everything that made him feel awkward, he wouldn't get out of bed in the morning.

The children finished the dishes, said good night, and filed back to their rooms to do their homework. Sam and Virginia carried their coffee cups out to the porch. Moths flitted against the yellow porch light as the two rocked on the porch, sipping their coffee. An old steam engine echoed in the distance. The night was crisp, and a breeze shook the hedge. Deborah's cello started up; the music curled around the house.

"Kate still talks about you," Virginia said.

"I bet." Sam laughed.

"Fondly."

One lone white boy rode his skateboard down the middle of the deserted street. The wheels rattled on the pavement. He leaned almost imperceptibly, steering himself on down the street, his arms flat against his sides, his hands empty.

She stopped rocking in her chair. "Y'all's problem was that you lived in sin." She sipped her coffee. "Young people nowadays, they want all the easy and none of the hard." She leaned over to him. "Well, I hate to break it to you, Sam, but there's no way around the hard, and the longer you put it off, the harder it gets."

The screen door opened, and Raymond came out on

the porch to his mother. "I need help with a math problem."

She pulled him into her arms, holding him against her. She stroked his head. "Did you ask your brother or your sister?"

"Deborah's practicing, and Charles is studying for a test."

"This is when I miss Gene most. He was a whiz at math."

Sam shrugged. "I'm no whiz, but I used to be pretty good."

"Don't you need to get home?" she asked.

"The Sheetrock will keep," he said.

"Come on back in," she said. "I'll put on some more coffee."

Sam followed Raymond into the dining room, where he had his books spread out on the table. Virginia went back into the kitchen to put the coffee on.

He pulled a chair up next to Raymond's, rested his hand on the boy's back, and for half an hour lost himself in the intricacies of the problem in front of them.

Chapter Ten

Sam dimmed the store lights, as he did every night at five minutes before seven o'clock, and announced to the few remaining customers that it was time to close.

Ronnie wandered in at the last minute, asking Sam to change a dollar bill.

"I used to have a radio." He stared at the radio behind the counter as Sam opened the register and pushed four quarters across the counter. Ronnie dropped the quarters into his pocket but kept his eyes on the radio. "I played those call-in games. The ones if you're the nineteenth caller you win a hundred dollars?" He looked rougher than usual. His hair was matted, his clothes were soiled and torn, and his skin had a sallow pallor that made Sam wonder if he was sick. When he walked out of the store, he left behind a stifling, too sweet smell.

Sam rang up the last couple of sales, straightened the remainders, shelved a stack of books that had accumulated by the register, and held the front door for the customers, watching them disappear down the darkening street, past the lighted windows of closed shops. He walked through the store and checked behind both the bookshelves and the register, making sure everyone was out. When he was sure the store was empty, he lingered in the doorway a minute more, thinking that over the past six months he'd become used to himself. He'd grown into his loneliness. He wasn't being self-congratulatory. He knew that whatever

167

had changed in him was not the result of anything he'd done.

In the distance, sirens howled, and Halloween firecrackers popped, sounding like skirmishes across the city. Fallen leaves tapped along the sidewalk in front of the store, scattered by a warm breeze. It had been a balmy fall. Of course, Willy said it was the greenhouse effect. He said the polar ice caps were melting, the oceans rising, and that in a couple of thousand years the Atlantic would lap the foot of Stone Mountain. Sam couldn't worry globally. He knew it was myopic, but he wasn't nearly as concerned about the ozone layer and whether it would exist in two millennia as he was about Jessie's party tonight and whether Kate would be there.

As he locked the front door behind the last customer, Sam was startled to see the Bandanna Man walk past the store. He hadn't been around for some time. For a while he had come into the store almost every day. He'd saunter past the register, drop his knapsack beside the counter, then head for the history section and disappear behind a shelf, where he'd squat Indian style, his head bent over a book about Vietnam. Then, one day, he just stopped coming, disappearing from the streets altogether. Someone said he'd shot somebody. Someone else said he'd stolen a car. The last story Sam had heard and the one he gave the most credence to was that he'd been caught smuggling a package of barbecued chicken out of the Big Star.

He probably wouldn't have felt as uneasy about the Bandanna Man if he hadn't been closing alone tonight. He had volunteered, since Jessie had stayed at home today, preparing for the Halloween party, and Paula and Carl had left early to change into their costumes. He hadn't given a costume much thought these past weeks. He'd been too busy deciding whether to go at all. At first, he wasn't going because Kate might show up. Then he was, to prove to himself he was over her. Then he wasn't, for if he was really over her, he didn't need to prove anything. Then he was, to prove to himself that he had nothing to prove.

"I'll understand completely if you don't come," Jessie had said to him yesterday. "I should never have invited Kate. You know why I originally invited her?"

"Because you're fair."

"Because I'm meddlesome. I wanted to get y'all back together. I thought if I could just get y'all in the same room, the rest would take care of itself." She pushed her glasses back up with her thumb. "It was none of my business."

Although he was irritated that she'd tried to manipulate him, he was touched that she'd cared enough to interfere. "I'll come," he said.

As he locked the day's receipts in the safe and cut off the store lights, he wondered if, by confessing her plan, Jessie hadn't hoodwinked him into going. What was trickier than the truth?

Coming from the office to the front of the store, Sam saw the Bandanna Man's face pressed against the store window, shading his eyes from the streetlight as he scowled into the darkened store. He pointed his finger at Sam as if it were a gun. He banged on the window and shouted something through the glass. Then he hitched up his knapsack and walked on down the street.

Sam almost called the police, but when he waited a moment and the Bandanna Man didn't reappear, he decided against it. He'd seemed drunk or maybe high on something.

He stepped out onto the sidewalk to make sure the Bandanna Man was gone; then he armed the store alarm and hurried out. Jessie said the alarm didn't activate for two minutes. It was triggered by movement; even the ceiling fans had to be absolutely still. In spite of Jessie's reassurances, Sam's heart raced during the moment between setting the alarm and getting outside. Whenever he pressed in the code that changed the steady green light to a blinking red, he remembered the furious ringing of the morning months ago when he'd set it off. That had been the day Kate moved out. This electronic gadget had been more sensitive to the subtle motions of their relationship than he.

He tugged on the door to double-check that it was locked, then headed down the street, walking home, glancing over his shoulder. Last week he'd watched, with a real sense of mourning, as a tow truck hauled the Tempest out of the Rainbow's parking lot. He'd put off calling the shop, afraid his old car had expired under the wrench, but when he mustered enough courage to call, they said all it needed was a new clutch. He could pick it up next week. He'd be out $300 but he'd spent nearly that much on Onion, his ungrateful cat. He realized that his emotional attachment to this erratic machine was greater than the sum of its rusted parts. But on the other hand, the Tempest had never left him, which was more than he could say for women or cats.

He stopped at the Treasury Drug to buy a bag of miniature Snickers bars. Most parents wouldn't let their kids trick or treat in his neighborhood. In fact, trick or treating in general seemed on the decline. When he was a kid, Halloween had been a night of roaming free through the neighborhood, and the only thing to fear were the ghosts and goblins of his imagination. Now the monsters were on the inside, waiting to answer the doorbell.

In the drugstore, the radio played over the PA system, and Sam heard a news bulletin that a line of intense thunderstorms had swept across Alabama this afternoon, spawned several tornadoes, and injured thirty people and killed two. The news announcer said that the same line of storms would pass through the Atlanta area at about ten o'clock tonight.

Sam stopped in at Berkowitz's liquor store, thinking that it wouldn't hurt to fortify himself for the party tonight.

Scribbling furiously on a yellow legal notepad, Mr. Berkowitz didn't look up until Sam had actually gotten the bottle of Jack Daniel's off the shelf and set it on the counter. Sam guessed he was in the middle of another letter to the editor and wanted to finish his thought.

When the old man finally did look up, there was fire in his eyes. "Who are we to tell women what to do with their bodies?"

Sam was caught off guard by the old man's vehemence.

"The administration tells the Supreme Court that now is a good time to overturn *Roe v. Wade*. Who are we to tell women whether they can have an abortion? Who are we to control women's bodies?" The old man's face reddened, and the cigar butt worked up and down in the corner of his mouth. "Who is this joker in the White House? This kinder, gentler schmuck?"

Mr. Berkowitz rang up the bottle of Jack Daniel's. "How's your wife?"

"Fine." He bent to tie his shoelaces. Not only hadn't Sam told him they weren't married, but he couldn't bring himself to tell him she'd left. He'd considered killing her off, but he couldn't decide on the method. A brain tumor would be too drawn out, a car accident too violent, suicide too sad. He couldn't bring harm to Kate, even if imaginary.

"How's her condition?" the old man asked.

"Her condition?" Sam rubbed his forehead.

The old man held his hands out in front of his stomach.

"Oh, that condition."

The old man gave him a quizzical look. "Is it so easy to forget?"

"She went to the doctor last week, and everything looks good." He felt his face redden. Last month sometime, during his conversation with Mr. Berkowitz, he'd inexplicably concocted Kate's pregnancy. He never would've believed he was capable of such a story. Mr. Berkowitz had come from behind the counter, clapped him on the back, shook his hand, and sent him home with a bottle of champagne, warning him that Kate should only have a sip of it because of her condition. He'd never seen the old man so excited. Ever since, when Sam stopped in, the old man asked after the baby. He wondered how to extricate himself from this new lie. Easy enough, he could tell him Kate had a miscarriage. But Mr. Berkowitz would be crushed. No, he was stuck with this baby, and if he wasn't careful, he might have to concoct an entire family.

"When's the baby due?" Mr. Berkowitz bagged the Jack Daniel's.

Sam hesitated. "July."

Mr. Berkowitz whistled. "Eleven months? That must be some baby."

"May." Sam counted backward from July. "She's due in May."

"She? They know it's a girl already?" Mr. Berkowitz frowned at him over his glasses.

Sam nodded. Ever since he'd invented this baby, he'd pictured a girl.

"The miracles of modern science." The old man sat in his chair. "Pretty soon they'll be able to tell which college they'll attend."

Sam said good night to Mr. Berkowitz and was on his way out the door when the old man called out. "Sam." He crooked his finger for Sam to come back. Mr. Berkowitz smiled a sly smile that made Sam sure that the old man knew he'd lied. He put his arm over Sam's shoulder. He took the wedge of unlit cigar out of the corner of his mouth and pointed it at Sam. "I consider myself a pretty good judge of character." His breath smelled of garlic. "You think you have everybody fooled." The old man's eyes hardened. "But son, I know about you."

"You do?" Somehow he'd found out, or maybe he'd known all along.

"You forget when the baby's due. You forget

whether it's a boy or a girl. You even forget your wife is pregnant." He thrust his cigar butt at Sam. "You act so nonchalant about the whole thing. You don't fool me, son, not for one minute." He hugged Sam harder. "You're going to make a good father in spite of yourself."

A brown bag cradled in each arm (Snickers in one, Jack Daniel's in the other), Sam hurried along the sidewalk of Ponce de Leon Avenue, a main escape route from downtown that in the evening pumped commuters back out into the northern suburbs. He cut across a small park, where a swing set and sandbox stood empty. He zigzagged his way home along quiet back streets. The air was thick and sticky. All day the sky had had a sickly yellowish pallor, a muggy afterthought of summer.

He didn't like deceiving Mr. Berkowitz. He'd just wanted to save the old man's feelings, which was getting more difficult. This single untruth had reproduced exponentially. It had all started years ago when he allowed Mr. Berkowitz to assume that Kate and he were married. He hadn't wanted to offend the old man's sense of propriety, and he didn't see the harm in letting him think what he wanted. In fact, for the longest time Sam told himself he hadn't lied because he never actually said he and Kate were married. It was an assumption on the old man's part. Only recently had he realized that reticence didn't free him from liability. What one said and what one didn't say were not two different things.

When he turned down Elmira, he was startled by three small ghosts drifting across a yard, coming toward him and moaning his name.

"Sammm! Oooo, Sammm!" They flailed their arms and circled him. They held out their plastic Kroger bags, sagging with loot. "Trick or treeeattt! Trick or treeattt!" It was Raymond, Bobby, and Chris with old bed sheets pulled over them.

Sam tore open his bag of candy and dropped a handful of Snickers in each bag. "Y'all are pretty spooky looking."

"Treat or trick." Chris readjusted his sheet so he could see through the eyeholes.

"Don't you have that backwards?" Sam asked.

"That's what we keep telling him," Bobby said from under his sheet.

"He's been saying it at every house," Raymond said.

Chris ran off toward the next house, screaming, "Treat or trick! Treat or trick!"

Their heads bowed in resignation, Raymond and Bobby slowly followed. "It's embarrassing," Bobby said.

"I'll never show my face in this neighborhood again," Raymond said.

As Sam watched the three small ghosts float across lawns in the gathering dark, he remembered reading about a man who was a ghost therapist, a professor at some big university who traveled the world counseling ghosts. He said ghosts were really souls who'd lost their way, and what he did was reassure them that they had an emotional existence in the hereafter. He said ghosts experienced a lot of self-doubt because no one believed in them.

As he headed down the sidewalk toward home, squashing acorns under his feet, he thought how lately he'd been impatient to get home to work on the house or go for a jog or just sit in the kitchen and read. Kate had lived with him for four years, and when she left, she'd left him alone with a vaguely familiar stranger—himself. Over the past six months he'd gotten reacquainted with himself. Almost without his knowledge, his life acquired a certain evenness. He discerned a melancholy pleasure around the edges of his loneliness.

He walked up the driveway, pausing in front of his house. He'd had the outside painted and the gutters replaced, making the house look new and silver-edged in the twilight. Inside, he'd about finished all the rooms. Almost everything was done, but with each improvement the house had felt less lived in, less his.

Inside, Willy lounged on the sofa—a beer in one hand, a slice of pizza in the other. He gestured toward the TV with his beer. "A sixty-year-old woman jumped off Stone Mountain."

"You're kidding." On the TV, they showed Stone Mountain, then men dragging a body bag through the woods at the foot of the mountain.

"She owned some real estate company," Willy said.

Sam remembered the morning he'd gone up there to throw himself off. As he saw this grim procession of rescue workers struggle with the sagging load of the woman's body, he was embarrassed by his histrionics on the mountainside.

"That could've been you," Willy said as the men loaded the body into an ambulance.

Sam looked at Willy. "How did you find out?"

"Who the hell do you think had hold of your belt?" Willy stared at the TV. "I wonder if they make queen-sized body bags."

Willy referred to the night at the laser show when Kate had slipped and he with her. The three of them had dangled from the ledge. That was why Sam had never really been able to believe how close they had really come to falling. It would've been such a slapstick death.

He went out to the kitchen to get a dish for the Halloween candy. He poured himself a Jack Daniel's and Coke. He set the candy dish with the miniature Snickers on the little table in the foyer, then sat on the couch next to Willy.

"How about some pizza?" Willy picked up another piece out of the greasy box on the coffee table.

"Not hungry." Sam sipped his drink.

"What's in the glass?"

"Bourbon and Coke."

On the TV the weatherman prodded a swirling map, pointing to the cold front and the system of storms ahead of it that had spawned tornadoes in Alabama. He said the system should reach the Atlanta area within the next couple of hours and that the National Weather Service had already issued a tornado watch until midnight. He warned that if you heard a loud, roaring noise to go to the basement or the lowest floor of your building. He said, if you're in a car, not to try to outrun the tornado but throw yourself into a ditch or lie on the northeast side of a hill.

"I'll check my compass." Willy walked out onto the porch. He seemed restless.

Sam followed him outside. They sat on the porch steps, observing the sky. The air was thick, almost steamy. A ceiling of low clouds moved over the city, reflecting downtown's dingy glow.

"Storms never happen when they predict them." Willy waved his hand dismissively at the sky.

Sam stirred his drink with his finger.

They listened to the firecrackers and sirens in the distance. There was an uneasy stillness in the air, or perhaps the uneasiness was his, about the party tonight. He felt a little of this all the time, a subtle dread that lurked beneath everything. A dread not so much of what people might think of him as that they wouldn't think of him at all, that whatever he did or said would not register with the rest of the world. A dread not of the worst but of a redundant and featureless indifference.

Mrs. Smeak's Siamese crossed the yard cautiously, then picked its way up the porch steps, carefully avoiding Sam's legs and rubbing Willy's.

"I get the message," Sam said to the cat.

Willy stroked its back. Willy'd hung around a lot lately. Not that Sam objected. He was good company. Most of the time he entertained himself, but he was around if

Sam wanted to do anything. For instance, the other night Sam had gotten it in his head that he wanted to play Putt-Putt, so they played Putt-Putt, no questions asked.

"Are you coming to the party?" Sam asked.

"Nothing better to do." Willy leaned against the banister and sipped his beer.

"Jessie says Kate might show up."

Willy nodded, looking down at his beer can. "There's something you ought to know." He cleared his throat. "She might marry that doctor guy."

Sam's drink slipped out of his hand; ice and glass shattered on the porch steps. "She what!" He walked out into the middle of the yard and just stood there, feeling stunned. "She's going to marry that heel?"

Willy shrugged.

"Why him of all people? This guy lives in a mansion on West Paces Ferry and buys a new Mercedes every other week. Why would she want to marry someone like that?" He scratched his head and took a couple of steps back toward the porch. "Willy, this guy is Gatsby without the shirts!"

"I'm not sure we're talking the same doctor here." Willy leaned back against the steps. "He's short, about five-eight, I guess . . ."

"I don't think it is the same guy," Sam said. "So you've met him. What's he like?"

"He's a pretty good guy."

"Definitely not the same guy." Sam sighed and looked up at the swirling clouds overhead. She'd gone on to someone else, someone he didn't even know. Rose's theory about Kate's seeing someone she couldn't love no longer held water. Whatever faint hopes he'd had about Kate were extinguished by this news. He was hurt, not so much because she didn't come back to him—he'd all but given up on that long ago—but because she'd decided on someone without consulting him.

Sam went inside, got a broom and a dustpan, and swept up the glass on the steps. He made himself another drink and came back out to sit with Willy.

"So you say this guy is nice?"

"He's okay." Willy rubbed his eyes with the heels of his hands. He leaned back on his elbows against the porch steps. The clouds had thickened over the city. Firecrackers popped in the distance. A slight breeze stirred tree limbs overhead, but it was balmy.

"I've been dreading something like this," Sam said, "but you know, I'm not as depressed about it as I thought I'd be. Do you think I might be over her?"

"You sound disappointed," Willy said.

He scratched his head. "Is it possible to be sad about not having anything to be sad about?"

"The human heart is a convoluted organ."

"I'd hate to think I'm one of those people who isn't happy unless he has something to be depressed about."

"The evening news must make you ecstatic," Willy said. The cat butted its head against Willy's hand, wanting to be petted. He stroked its back.

The breeze had picked up, and low clouds looped in and out of each other, threatening to tie the sky in a knot.

Sam jumped up and went back inside.

"What?" Willy followed him.

Sam rummaged through the den closet until he found a big box marked "Goodwill" in Kate's script. (He'd never known anyone who could make Magic Marker look so elegant.) Filled with slightly shabby clothes, the box was the final resting place for many of their yard-sale "finds," which, tried on again in the practical light of their bedroom mirror, lost their bargain luster. Sam pointed out to Kate the futility of buying clothes at yard sales, only to give them away. Whenever he mentioned this—usually when she was in somebody's front yard, winnowing through a rack of twenty-five-cent blouses—she'd shrug. "Think of us as buyers for the Salvation Army."

"Spring cleaning in the fall?" Willy nodded at the pile of old clothes Sam had poured onto the floor. They gave off a musty smell, a mixture of mildew and mothballs.

"We need costumes for tonight." Sam picked through the pile.

"Do we have to have a costume?" Willy changed the channel on the TV, flicked past every station, then turned it off.

Sam held up a cotton print dress with yellow roses on it. "What do you think?"

"Not my colors." Willy dropped down on the sofa. "I'm a summer."

From the street, Jessie's house—with its long, well-lit porch and blazing upstairs windows—was a giant jack-o'-lantern casting its luminous grin across the neighborhood. The party had burst it seams, overflowing onto the porch, down the steps, and onto the lawn, where guests nursed their drinks and carried on animated conversations behind their masks.

Sam and Willy paused on the curb, taking swigs from the Jack Daniel's bottle. Sam had been the one who hesitated. Suddenly, it had hit him that Kate might actually be here, behind any of these masks. She liked parties. She could be in a lousy mood, but if he took her to a party, her eyes brightened and her face shone as she sought out new people to talk to.

He didn't like parties. He could never think of anything to say. When on occasion something occurred to him, it seemed so trivial and unrelated that he couldn't imagine anyone would be interested.

"Quite a crowd." Willy passed the bottle back to Sam.

"We wouldn't be missed." Sam took a swig, replaced the cap, and put it inside his coat.

"That's not what I meant." Willy put his arm around Sam's shoulder and steered him toward the house.

When they first parked the car, Sam couldn't remember which house was Jessie's. He'd noticed an elderly couple walking arm in arm on the other side of the street.

"Excuse me."

They didn't seem to hear him, so he crossed to the other side.

"Pardon me."

The old man whispered something to the woman, and they quickened their pace.

Sam followed after them. "Hey, all I want—"

The old man swung around, roughly grabbed Sam's hand, and slapped a crumpled piece of paper into it. "Will that do?" He put his arm protectively around his wife's shoulders, and they hurried up the sidewalk, glancing back at him.

He held the crumpled piece of paper up to the streetlight. "It's a five-dollar bill," he said, astonished.

"You make a convincing bum," Willy said.

He'd forgotten he had on a baggy, torn old suit coat, pants big enough for two or three of him, and an old aviator's cap with huge earflaps. He also wore an old pair of Kate's gardening boots and, on Willy's suggestion, had smeared his face with chimney soot.

Willy wasn't wearing a costume. "Just call me the control," he said.

As they crossed Jessie's lawn, Sam saw two people dressed in fluorescent skeleton costumes bickering underneath the big oak in the front yard. He guessed they were a married couple. Then he recognized the voices.

"Why don't you ever leave me anything interesting

to receive?" the tall one said. "Even just a box of calendars?"

"I receive what needs to be received," the short one said.

"Man cannot live on Schaum's Outlines alone. And if I receive one more shipment of Cliff Notes, I'm going to turn into a synopsis."

Sam crept up on them. "Y'all are a couple of walking X rays."

Paula and Carl both took a step back, not recognizing him. Carl reached into his pocket. "Listen, buddy, I'm all out of spare change."

"I might have something in my pocketbook inside." Paula started toward the house.

"Hey, guys, it's me," Sam said, incredulous.

"Sam?" Paula turned to Carl. "It's Sam."

"You sure you didn't wander out of some soup kitchen?" Carl said.

"Where'd you get the costumes?" Sam said.

"At a funeral directors' convention at Myrtle Beach a couple of years ago," Carl said. "Gerald never comes to Jessie's party."

"And Macon had to work tonight," Paula said.

"So we decided to come as matching skeletons." Carl draped his arm over Paula's shoulder.

"I would've never recognized you," Paula said to him.

"Hell, I was ready to empty my pockets for you," Carl said.

"Maybe I ought to go into panhandling professionally," Sam said.

"Make more than working at a bookstore," Paula said.

Sam passed around the Jack Daniel's. He was beginning to experience the warm glow he felt whenever he drank anything more potent than a beer or two.

Willy had wandered off to a group standing by the porch. Some guy laughed at the fact that he was the only one who hadn't worn a costume.

"It's the ultimate costume at a costume party," another woman said, defending Willy. "No costume at all."

After taking a swig, Paula passed the bottle back to Sam.

"Any sign of Kate?" he whispered. He slid the bottle inside his coat.

"Not yet," Paula said.

"Of course, she could be behind any of these masks," Carl said.

Sam put his hand on Carl's shoulder. "You do wonders for a body's paranoia. I better say hello to the host so she'll know I put in an appearance."

People backed away from Sam as he walked up the front steps. He overheard one woman in a witch's costume ask another woman dressed as Medusa, with papier-mâché snakes in her hair, "How'd he get in here?"

He made his way through the guests with great care, keeping his gaze on the ground. Carl was right. She could be behind any mask. He felt at a disadvantage.

At the front door, Jessie and Sylvia welcomed guests in matching devil suits, complete with horns, pointed tails, and pitchforks. They'd even drawn mustaches over their lips. They wore these costumes every year, calling themselves the Hosts from Hell. They greeted guests, introduced them around, then pointed them in the direction of the hors d'oeuvres with their pitchforks.

Several guests passed in front of him as he paused in the doorway, thinking maybe he'd just slink away. He'd turned to leave when a svelte woman in a tight black satin dress walked in. Across the front and back of her dress was a spiderweb of string. She wore a black mask over her eyes. She looked familiar, but he'd been to so many of these parties that he'd probably seen her last year or the year before. Jessie hugged and kissed her and told her how good it was to see her again but never said her name. She directed her toward the food. She was with the Ayatollah, in a turban, a fake long gray beard, and immense bushy eyebrows.

"Who's that with her?" Sylvia asked.

Jessie shrugged. "Well, it ain't Salman Rushdie."

Sam had decided to leave when Jessie came toward him, took his arm, and firmly led him out on the porch.

"Now, sir, I don't know how you wandered in, but I would appreciate if you'd wander right back out." She pulled a wad of dollar bills from a pocket in her suit and handed it to him. "That'll buy you supper, and if you need a bed tonight, St. Mary's on Ponce de Leon has a shelter . . ."

"Can I consider this a raise?" He fanned the dollar bills in his hand.

She squinted at him. She wiped her finger on his cheek and looked at the soot, then at the white streak on his face. "Sam?" She snatched the wad of bills out of his hand. "Give me that." She laughed. "People told me a bum had crashed the party, so when I saw you . . ." She took a couple of steps back, looking him up and down. "You and Ronnie could be twins." She fingered the collar of his red plaid coat.

Sam followed Jessie down the porch steps and out to the edge of the yard, where they stood facing the house.

"What is it with these clouds?" Jessie looked up. "Somebody said something about bad storms in Alabama." The clouds had piled up in the sky.

"Who's the woman in the spiderweb dress?" Sam asked.

"I don't know."

"You sure acted like you knew her."

"Sign of a good host." She coiled her devil's tail around her hand.

He reached inside his coat, pulled out the bottle of Jack Daniel's, unscrewed the top, and held it out to her.

"You've got this bum persona down." She sipped from the bottle.

"Comes naturally." He tilted the bottle back, taking a big swig. The more he drank, the smoother it felt.

"Better go easy on that stuff."

"I'm sick of going easy." He took another swig. "I've been going easy all my life." He felt the bourbon burn down his throat and then warm his stomach.

"Then plan to spend the night. We've got a pullout sofa."

The witch and Medusa crossed the lawn over to them.

"What's going on up there, Jess?" Medusa asked, tilting her snake-laden head up to the sky.

Jessie introduced them to Sam, but he forgot their names immediately. He made small talk without much effort, surprising himself. The bourbon had already put a fuzzy distance between what he said and what he thought.

"They're lovers," Jessie whispered to him when the two women had ambled off. "They break up on a regular basis."

Carl and Paula passed by in their skeleton costumes.

"Can you believe those two—one minute they're at each other's throat, the next minute they're a skeletal Mutt and Jeff." She put her hand on Sam's shoulder. "You'll be relieved to know Kate's not coming."

"She's not?"

"She called a little while ago. Her doctor friend got called to the hospital, and she went with him." She put her hand on his back. "Are you okay?"

"I'm disappointed." He shrugged. "I worried about seeing her for so long, I'd like to think my worrying amounts to something."

"Jessie?" Somebody called from the front porch. "Jessie?" They saw Sylvia's silhouette lean over the banister.

"Out here, darling."

"What're y'all talking about?"

"You."

"My horns were burning." Sylvia lingered on the porch a moment more. "I miss you," she said, then turned and went back inside.

"What would I do without her?" Jessie watched her go back in, then turned to Sam. "Forget about Kate." She hit Sam on the back. "Come on in and join the party." She turned to him as they started up the porch steps. "You're the only bum here."

Witches crowded the avocado dip, ghosts hovered over the melon balls, and demons piled their plates high with finger sandwiches. There was something unsettling about a roomful of evil incarnations standing around making small talk. Evil spirits should be about the serious business of haunting, tempting, and casting spells. As he watched the Ayatollah ladle cups of pineapple punch, Sam thought, If you can't count on the bad to be really bad, what can you count on?

Jessie introduced him around, but he could tell by the unenthusiastic way people shook his hand that they weren't certain whether he'd really just come in off the street. Sam enjoyed the uneasy looks people gave him as they tried to skirt him.

The room was so packed that he and Jessie got separated. He didn't see Willy anywhere. He glimpsed the woman in the spiderweb dress, but every time he tried to make his way toward her, she disappeared. He was pretty sure she'd glanced at him, maybe even nodded at him, but in a houseful of people, it was impossible to tell who eyed whom.

"Sam! Sam Marshbanks? This is you?" Mr.

Berkowitz's costume consisted of a party hat angled jauntily on his bald head. He'd confused Halloween and New Year's. The bright pointed hat looked so out of place over his thick-lensed glasses and the cigar wedged in the corner of his mouth. "The book business doesn't do so well?" The old man fingered the frayed lapel of Sam's coat. "Kate is here someplace."

"She is?" He looked around.

"I'm asking you." The old man frowned at him over his glasses. "She embarrassed to be seen with you?"

Sam hoped the conversation might end on Mr. Berkowitz's joke, but Jessie walked up and patted the old man on the back.

"Glad you made it, Mr. Berkowitz."

"Jessie, you should do better by your employees." He put his arm around Sam's shoulder. "Especially for a young family man."

Jessie laughed. "I'll wait till he acquires a family."

"It's only a matter of months," the old man said.

She gave Sam a quizzical look. "Is there something you haven't told me?"

Mr. Berkowitz turned to Sam. "You haven't told her when Kate is due?"

"Kate is due?" she asked.

"I need a drink." Sam slipped into the crowd, occasionally glancing back at Jessie and Mr. Berkowitz. He'd get Jessie alone later and explain everything. He was glad Kate wasn't coming so that Mr. Berkowitz wouldn't inform her she was expecting.

He passed by the den, which was empty except for a baggy-eyed Dracula who sat alone in the corner, watching a football game on television, a cigarette in one hand and an empty glass in the other.

Sam slipped the bottle out of his coat and took a long swig. "Who's winning?"

"The Falcons by a field goal." The plastic fangs in his mouth made him lisp.

Sam recognized the voice as belonging to the columnist whose disastrous signing Carl had arranged. "You're Bill Gullard." He held out his hand. "Sam Marshbanks. I work at Brilliant's."

"Oh, right," the little man said. "I thought maybe you were one of the guys I'd interviewed down by the tracks for that piece on the homeless."

On the TV, the stadium crowd roared as a Falcon tight end ran the ball in for a touchdown, while underneath, a printed message ran along the bottom of the screen—"the National Weather Bureau has issued a tornado watch."

"I don't like football," Gullard said. "But I like parties less."

"*Yo comprendo.*" Sam knew he must be drunk if he was speaking Spanish. He refilled Gullard's glass from the bottle of Jack Daniel's.

"So why am I here?" Gullard said rhetorically. "My wife fished the invitation out of the garbage can. She likes parties. She likes to mingle." He gestured to the crowded living room. "She's out there somewhere. The last time I mingled was before Watergate."

They watched the game for a while. Sam kept Gullard's glass full, taking an occasional swig himself. In the other room, conversations buzzed at an almost delirious pitch.

During a commercial Sam leaned over and put his hand on Gullard's shoulder. "I admire the hell out of you."

"You do?"

"Because you can write books."

Gullard gestured with his cape. "Hell, anybody can write books, especially the kind of books I write."

"I can't." Sam slapped his knee. "I tried, but I can't. I can't sustain anything."

"You have kids?"

Sam shook his head.

"You married?"

"Nope." Sam sipped from the bottle.

"Hell, son, no wonder you can't sustain anything; you don't have anything to sustain." Gullard stood up, throwing his cape over his shoulder. "I better go look for my wife. I've got a column to write in the morning." He shook hands with Sam. "Thanks for the bourbon." He started out the door but then turned around. "Want advice about writing?"

"Sure."

"Never take advice about writing." Gullard disappeared into the crowd.

Sam was about to turn off the TV when the game was interrupted by a weather bulletin. A weatherman appeared and pointed to a radar screen behind him, showing a line of severe thunderstorms sixty miles south of Atlanta. He said the system should reach the city within the next hour to hour and a half. He said that this same system had spawned tornadoes in Alabama and that Atlanta residents should be prepared to take precautions.

Having lived in Atlanta so long, Sam was accustomed to such storm warnings, which were almost a weekly threat in the spring and summer. Still, he should probably tell somebody. When he stood up, he felt dizzy. What did he expect? He'd been drinking on an empty stomach. He'd better eat something. He fought his way to the hors d'oeuvres table, piled melon balls and ham biscuits on a small plate, then retreated to the sill of an open window, where he positioned himself half in and half out of the party. The curtains billowed around him from the breeze.

As he studied people's costumes, he remembered that last year Kate came as a daffodil. For the stem she wore a tight green leotard. She cut petals out of yellow construction paper and taped them to a piece of wire that fit around her face. The petals radiated from her face. She got so drunk at the party that she hung all over him, asked him to kiss her, and cursed him when he wouldn't. Everybody thought it was hilarious—this daffodil telling him he was a "fucking prude." Later, he found her alone in Jessie's bedroom, slumped at the dresser, staring into the mirror. The petals hung limp over her face. "Is this what people see when they look at me?" She pouted in the mirror. "Do you love me?" As she spoke, one petal slowly drooped over her forehead.

He stood over her, massaged her shoulders, and told her in the mirror that everything was all right, that she'd had too much to drink.

"I know I've had too much to drink." She pulled away. "What I don't know is if you really love me."

"Of course."

"When we're in public, why do you roll your eyes at me and act like I'm a pest?"

"I'm not demonstrative."

"I don't expect an emotional exhibition, just a clue now and then." She blew into a Kleenex. "A squeeze of the hand, a nod in my direction—any signal that I'm not in this alone."

He bit into a ham biscuit, thinking it had only been a year since he'd found Kate staring at herself in Jessie's bedroom. He'd been touched to see her so susceptible to him. Still, if he'd been more observant, he would've understood what she'd tried to tell him, that she might be forced to leave him. Ever since that night almost six months ago when he'd come home to her packed bags on the porch, he'd thought of all the ways she'd warned him. In retrospect, their whole relationship became an omen.

Riding a gust of wind, a dead leaf blew through the open window past Sam, lifted slightly, then fluttered down into a woman's hair. Without thinking, he picked the leaf from her hair. She whirled around, touching her head. It was the woman in the spiderweb dress. Her eyes glared at him from behind the black mask.

"This blew into your hair." He held up the leaf. "Through the window." He looked at the leaf, then at the window it came through. "Pretty unlikely, huh? Actually I plant this leaf in a woman's hair if I want to talk to her."

Her eyes softened, and the corners of her mouth turned up in a slight smile. A gust of wind snapped the curtains.

"There's a tornado watch," he said. "Or is it a warning? I can never keep those straight. One means they've seen one, and the other means they're looking for one."

The woman smiled at him.

"I've had too much of this." He slipped the Jack Daniel's from his pocket. "I didn't drink all that by myself. I've had help." He held the bottle out to her.

She drank a couple of swallows. He noticed how red her hair was and how white her throat. His eyes wandered downward to the tight fit of her dress over her hips.

She handed the bottle back to him and with the back of her hand wiped a drop of Jack Daniel's that trickled down her chin.

"Have we met?" he asked.

She didn't say anything, but her eyes shone with amusement.

"I don't usually drink like this."

She didn't say anything.

"I started on this bottle because an old girlfriend of mine was supposed to show up tonight." He caressed the Jack Daniel's. "I finished it because she's not coming." He slumped against the windowsill. "One minute I drink not to feel; the next minute I drink to feel anything at all."

The noise level of the party had risen as more people crowded into Jessie's house, coming in from the porch and the lawn. Someone turned up the music. People danced in the middle of the room.

The woman leaned over, put her hand on his shoulder, and talked into his ear. "Read any good books lately?" She kissed his cheek.

The Ayatollah grabbed her hand. "Let's dance, Grace."

"Grace!" Sam called after her. It was the red-haired woman who used to come by the bookstore. She hadn't come by in a long time.

She squeezed Sam's hand, then let the Ayatollah pull her into the dancing crowd. Blitzed on Jack Daniel's, Sam panhandled party guests. He worked his way through the crowd and held his hand out, shouting, "Spare change? Spare change!" Those who recognized him laughed. Almost everybody gave him a dime or a quarter. His pocket bulged with change. As word got around, people anticipated him and dug into their pockets, and scrounged the bottom of their pocketbooks.

He was in the middle of the crowd when he felt a hand on his shoulder; the touch was light yet familiar.

"Where have you been?" Sam shouted into Willy's ear. "Look at all this loot, man." He patted his pockets. "How many cups of coffee will this buy?"

"She's here, Sam." Willy nodded toward the door.

Sam followed his gaze and saw Kate framed in the doorway. She wasn't in costume but wore his overalls, an old army jacket, and a gray flannel shirt he'd given her. Her eyes swept over him, not seeing him, or maybe she wasn't looking for him? She paused there a moment longer, the night behind her. Thunder crackled, and a hand came from behind and rested on her shoulder. He couldn't make out the doctor's silhouette; all he saw was the hand.

She balanced on her tiptoes, craning around the room. This time her eyes hesitated on Sam, then continued on around the room, unconvinced. The hand tugged her shoulder. She reached up and laid hers over it. She turned away but glanced back over her shoulder right at Sam. For the first time since the moment she walked out of the house, he felt, really felt, that she'd left him. Everything up until now had been a rehearsed pain. The doorway was empty.

"Kate!" he shouted, but the din of the music and conversation drowned out his voice. He pushed toward the doorway, squeezing and shoving, trying to extricate himself from the crowd.

"Let me through, please," he pleaded. "I've got to get through." He was almost to the door when a hand grabbed his coat collar. It was Carl in his skeleton's suit, blocking Sam's way.

"I just saw Kate," Carl said. "She was looking for somebody."

"Let go." Sam snapped.

Carl had to bend over to hear him. "What'd you say?"

"Let go of me!" He screamed in his ear.

Carl stumbled back, his hand over his heart. "Excuse me."

"Kate!" He lunged for the doorway, but just as he did, the Ayatollah passed in front of him, carrying drinks in both hands. Sam accidentally knocked the drinks out of his hands, drenching the Ayatollah in gin.

"What the fuck!" the Ayatollah said as Sam raced past.

The porch was empty. "Kate!" He called across the yard. Lightning flashed, and thunder roared. The trees swayed with a strong breeze. Unsteady on his feet, he lurched down the porch steps and wandered into the yard and around the house to the back, calling her name. The trees sighed from the wind.

A car started out on the street. He ran through the back hedge and around through the front yard, weaving in and out of Jessie's azaleas. He called Kate's name. His foot caught on something stretched out between the bushes. He heard a grunt as he fell onto a soft bed of pine straw. He knew without looking that he'd stumbled over a couple in the middle of making love. He didn't move, couldn't move. All he saw in the dark was one shadow on top of another. He heard a desperate whisper.

"Don't stop," it said.

"But he's right there," whispered another.

"Please . . ."

There was a pause in which the wind seemed to die and the thunder grew silent. Even the steady hum of the party seemed to abate. The world seemed on the edge of something.

"If you stop now . . ."

Her moan was so low that it seemed to come from far off or from down in the earth. A clap of thunder sent him scrambling to his feet. He ran up the walk and out into the middle of the street. The car had already pulled away. He watched the taillights of the doctor's car recede. Overhead the wind tore through the trees. Branches fell. A large limb snapped and shattered on the street. The whole world heaved. Suddenly, the wind stopped, the trees silenced, and an eerie stillness settled over the neighborhood.

He heard a sound that he would never forget—a low, long moan. At first, he thought it was that couple still going at it beneath the azaleas. But it was too loud. There were no trains around here. It grew louder. And then somehow, even though he'd never heard it before, he knew exactly what it was. He sprinted to the house.

"Tornado!" he screamed as his foot hit the porch. "A tornado's coming," he shouted to the few people hanging around on the porch. He shoved his way into the crowded room, shouted that a tornado was coming, but no one heard him over the music. He barged his way to the stereo and ripped the needle off the record. The sudden quiet made everyone stop talking and turn to Sam.

"What in the hell is going on, Sam?" Jessie asked.

"A tornado's coming."

People laughed.

"He's watched *The Wizard of Oz* one too many times," the Ayatollah said.

"No, listen." Jessie held up her hands.

There was the sound he'd heard—approaching.

The curtains snapped in the wind, and the screen opened and slammed. Sam's ears popped.

"Everyone in the basement, now," Jessie said.

As the moan grew to a roar, the party guests filed quickly down the basement steps, not saying a word. Sylvia directed them with her pitchfork.

Willy ran through the house, throwing open all the windows.

"What're you doing?" Sam cried over the roar.

"So the house won't blow up."

The two of them raced through the house, flung open all the windows, then hurried down into the basement to join the others. One bare bulb cast a timid light over the costumed crowd, so that it looked to Sam as though he had descended into somebody's nightmare. Confined by the small dirt basement, everyone pressed in on each other with playful groaning and hushed giggling.

They didn't hear anything. Sam wondered if the storm had passed. Maybe there wasn't a tornado? He thought how foolish he'd feel, scaring everyone down into the basement.

The bulb flickered a couple of times and went out, leaving them in perfect darkness. He pressed against the cold dirt wall. In a way, the musty dankness reassured him. Kate loved that smell. As a child, she licked basement walls. He thought of her, driving around Atlanta in this storm. He shouldn't have allowed the doctor to take her away from the party. He should've insisted she stay. If he had, she'd be safe now.

Outside, the wind howled.

"Hold me," a woman said into his ear.

Unable to see who it was, he put his arms around

her, sensing that all around people hugged or held hands, groping for anybody. It was so dark that even though he felt her breath on his face, he couldn't see her at all.

The house shook and rocked, receiving a glancing blow from the storm. He hugged the woman tighter, ready for the house to cave in on them, prepared to die in a stranger's arms. Overhead it sounded like a barroom brawl as things smashed and shattered.

The woman pulled Sam closer, then pressed her lips against his.

Without even thinking, he kissed her back.

She ran her hand down his back as she opened her mouth, coaxing his tongue inside.

The house shook and rocked.

He kissed her deeper, feeling the edge of her teeth and the soft insides of her mouth. He let his hands slide down to the curve of her waist, thinking, with a certain drunken detachment, This is the last I'll ever feel.

"It's over," someone said.

No one moved right away, not trusting the silence.

When Sam realized the storm had passed, he felt relieved, then tricked. He'd been so sure they were going to die, and he'd seen himself, like in a movie, going out in style. For once in his life he'd risen to the occasion, but the moment had eluded him. Still, out of a drunken persistence, he leaned over and kissed her again.

"Sam," she said.

"Can tornadoes make U-turns?" He tried to kiss her once more, but she put her hand to his face.

"It's me, Grace."

People had begun to feel their way out of the basement back upstairs. Someone found a flashlight and held it at the top of the stairs. Sam tried to hold on to Grace's hand, but as everyone moved toward the stairs, the crowd forced them apart.

Back upstairs, Sam stumbled around in the dark with

everyone else. His feet crunched on broken glass or slid on pieces of food until Jessie and Sylvia set out lighted candles around the house. Aside from overturned chairs and a few crooked paintings, the real mess lay at their feet—broken bottles, shattered glasses, cakes flattened, pieces of broken bowl sticking up in puddles of dip. Chips, cookies, apples, oranges, and several warped cheese balls littered the floor.

Everyone walked around stunned. Sam opened a closet door and looked in.

"Looking for the tornado?" Paula glowed in her fluorescent skeleton's suit.

There was a gasp from the front porch. He and Paula hurried out to join a group that had gathered on the steps. When he first looked out into Jessie's yard, he thought the shrubbery had somehow been rearranged, but then he realized he was looking at tree limbs. They faced the top of an immense oak that had fallen toward the house, missing the porch by a few yards.

He and Paula climbed through the maze of limbs and into the yard to get a better view. The tree, which had shaded the yard for more than half a century, lay the length of the brick walk, torn up by its roots. Standing, the tree had seemed such a natural and hardly noticeable part of Jessie's yard, but sprawled on its side, its trunk nearly as wide as the walk and its limbs spread across half the yard, it seemed gargantuan and graceless.

"Look, Sam." Paula nodded around them. "My God."

Up and down the street, trees, some of them as big as Jessie's, lay across yards, leaned against roofs, covered parked cars, and blocked the street. People had come out of their homes, stepping over the limbs, trying to assess the damage.

"The neighborhood has been clear-cut." Carl joined them on the edge of the yard.

The night air was much cooler now, even crisp. A lid had been lifted on the atmosphere, and fall had rushed in. The sky had cleared, and the moon shone over the neighborhood.

"Lights must be out everywhere," Paula said.

Sam looked up and down the street—no lights anywhere. Even the ever-present glow from downtown was gone. The storm had thrown all of Atlanta into darkness. Kate was in traffic when the tornado hit. He thought of running inside and calling her, but all the lines would be down.

Mr. Berkowitz walked out onto the porch, crawled through the tangle of tree limbs, and shuffled the length of the fallen tree, joining Sam, Paula, and Carl on the curb. The old man's clothes were rumpled, his glasses knocked crooked, but the cigar was still wedged in his mouth. He stroked his bald head as he peered down the street, then up the street, at the fallen trees, the smashed cars, and the scattered garbage cans.

"So." He straightened his glasses. "We had a little wind."

In Dunwoody, the wind had pushed a tree onto a car as a woman pulled into her driveway. She was the only reported fatality, said the tinny voice coming from the transistor propped on the mantel. A fire popped in the fireplace, providing the only light in the house except for the candles and a couple of flashlights.

As Sam picked up the pieces of a shattered glass, Jessie issued rags and brooms. The damage outside was so overwhelming that everyone had retreated indoors, where order was at least within the realm of possibility.

The radio announcer said that trees had fallen all over the city, snapping power lines and blocking streets. The Atlanta Police Department advised citizens not to drive because traffic lights were out.

"I wonder how my house is." Carl swept up a broken plateful of carrot sticks.

Sam wasn't worried about his house. Strangely, he worried about the neonatal unit at the hospital—a roomful of babies plunged into darkness, all the respirators, heart monitors, and other life-sustaining equipment dead. Of course, the hospital had backup generators; still, there would be a lot of scurrying doctors and nurses dashing from baby to baby, checking the equipment.

The whiskey-voiced chief of police came on the radio, warning people to stay off the roads tonight.

Jessie clapped her hands. "We're going to have to make this party an all-nighter. We've got plenty of sleeping bags and blankets."

Willy appeared in the doorway, cradling another load of firewood he'd collected from the front yard. The fire had been his idea. Not only did it provide warmth from the chilly night air, but it created a certain homeyness. As they finished cleaning up the mess, people gathered around the fire to sip bourbon from Styrofoam cups and talk about storms.

Sylvia told of a great-aunt who survived the Galveston hurricane of 1900, when a tidal surge swept some thirty thousand people away. "She was standing out on somebody's balcony when it hit," Sylvia said in a low voice. "She woke on the beach—surrounded by snakes."

Everybody had a storm story, either of a relative or a friend or something they themselves had gone through.

Willy dropped a couple of logs on the fire, which sent sparks up the chimney. Sam felt strange, having passionately kissed a customer.

Grace lay on the opposite side of the fire, her head propped on her hand as she stared into the flame. Willy sat down beside her and struck up a conversation. Sam couldn't really hear what they said, but they moved closer together, talking. The Ayatollah had wandered off to some dark corner with Medusa.

"A match made in hell," Paula had whispered as they watched them slip into the darkness. Paula and Carl sat back to back, holding each other up like skeletal bookends. "I wonder if Macon is okay," she said, yawning.

"I'm not worried about Gerald." Carl stretched his arms and yawned, too. "At the first sign of a storm, he grabs the sherry and heads for the basement."

"I hope the store's okay," Paula said.

Their conversation was accompanied by a soft sawing noise. Mr. Berkowitz's snore. He sat in one of the easy chairs, his head turned to one side, sound asleep.

Alone or in pairs, people began to drift beyond the fire's circle of light. They'd grab a blanket from the pile Jessie had set in front of the fire and wander off in search of a floor to stretch out on. Judging by the rustling, passionate sighs and hushed moans that emanated from the dark, not everyone slept.

After a while, Grace, Willy, and Sam were the only people still awake. Willy and Grace had kept up their conversation with hardly a pause.

Sam decided he was just in the way, so he got up, picked up a blanket and said good night, stepped over sleeping bodies and went into the empty den. It even had a couch. He closed the door so that he wouldn't hear the sounds of lovemaking.

He slid out of his pants, then slipped under the blanket. He lay on the couch, staring out the window at the moon, which illuminated the whole room in a gleaming dustiness. His head swirled from the Jack Daniel's, and he still felt detached. He rubbed the scar on his hand, where he'd burned it on the pot the night she left. He closed his eyes, saw her framed in the doorway, then the doctor's hand pull her away. He sighed. She'd left him again.

He'd just dozed off when he heard the den door open, and for a split second his heart stopped. He thought it was a ghost that appeared in the doorway, for the outline of her body was framed by the moonlight.

Grace shut the door quietly behind her and came over and stood beside the couch.

"Where's Willy?" Sam sat up, yawning.

"Went to bed." Without a word, she unzipped her dress.

"Wait a minute," he said.

She stepped out of her dress.

"We can't do this."

"Everybody else out there is." She nodded to the other room. She unhooked her bra and peeled off her hose, draping them over the TV. She was naked. She stood in the middle of the room; the moonlight filtered over her body, turning it the color of ice. She shivered. "It's cold in here."

He held the blanket up for her as she slipped in next to him on the couch.

"It's warm under here." She moved close to him, then kissed him.

"We hardly know each other."

"We like the same books."

"I'm going to feel bad in the morning," he said.

"You mean a hangover?"

"Guilt," he said.

"Fuck guilt." She kissed him, opening her mouth to his tongue. "On second thought," she whispered, "fuck me."

Sam slipped on top of her, kissed her breasts, and rubbed his hands down her thighs. At first, all he could think was, She isn't quite Kate—she's fuller, more rounded.

A siren sounded in the distance, followed by another, then another. Stunned by the storm, the city reacted now.

Just as Sam thought he couldn't go through with it, she kissed him again, urgently, passionately, and as the blanket slipped off them, he realized he wasn't cold. They'd begun to generate a warmth of their own.

Riding at an angle did not help his dizziness. Streets, yards, and houses leaned inward. The whole world had been blown out of kilter by last night's storm. He knew that the only way Willy could get past trees that blocked the road was to bounce the VW onto the curb and drive with two wheels on the street and two wheels on the sidewalk, but did he have to do it with such maniacal enthusiasm?

Sam stiff-armed the dashboard to keep from falling out of his seat and to hold his head still. It felt as thin shelled as an egg, and when he closed his eyes, he had the sickening sensation of his brain oozing around inside his skull. That sweet, detached drunken feeling had given way to the first waves of a headache that promised to be seismic.

Willy crouched over the steering wheel, swerved right, then left, over curbs, onto the sidewalk, across lawns, handling the bus like a jeep on safari. He drove the same way when delivering papers.

"I appreciate this." He braced for another bump as Willy pulled farther up onto the sidewalk to avoid a huge limb blocking the road.

It hadn't even been half an hour since he awoke to a stinging conscience and the freckled contour of Grace's shoulder blade. They'd slept, curled in on each other, his front pressed to her back, his hands wrapped around her waist. Numb, his right arm tingled as he slid it from underneath her.

He lay awake beside her, his head propped on his elbow as he recalled what had happened, but the whole night was wrapped in such an alcoholic gauze that it seemed a distant memory. He lay his hand on her back and felt her breathe.

As the room took shape under the first hint of dawn, he was gripped by foreboding. His house. Something was wrong with his house. Had it been obliterated by the storm? Of course, the same thought had crossed his mind last night, but with half a bottle of Jack Daniel's coursing through his veins, his perspective had been more cosmic, and his house had seemed irrelevant in the universal scheme of things.

Grace gave a long, heavy sigh in her sleep. He started to wake her, but what would he say? Thanks sounded like a transaction. I enjoyed it, a favor. You were great, a performance.

He eased from underneath the blanket, careful not to step on shards of a shattered potted plant the wind had blown off the sill last night. He put on his coat, its sleeves swallowing his hands, pulled on his pants, and started to tiptoe out of the room, but his feet tangled in Grace's spider-web dress. He draped the dress over the back of the couch. He stood over her. Her red hair swirled over her shoulders and onto the couch cushion.

"Grace." He touched her bare shoulder. "Hey, Grace."

Her eyelids fluttered. "Yeah?"

"I have to see about my house."

She nodded, still half-asleep, and turned over.

He pulled the blanket around her shoulders.

She mumbled something into the cushion but was already asleep.

He closed the den door behind him, zipping up his pants. He caught his breath when he walked into the living room. Wall-to-wall bodies, people layered upon people, sometimes two or three bodies thick. Half in and half out of costume, they were a tangle of naked arms and legs. Masks were strewn everywhere. No one stirred as he picked his way over the still bodies. Carl and Paula, in their fluorescent suits, slept curled up with their backs to each other. Mr. Berkowitz still snored in the easy chair. Sam stopped by the bathroom, then made his way to the porch. He'd walk home. It wasn't that far. He couldn't shake this sense of foreboding. He had to see what was left of his house.

He stepped onto the porch, surprised by the screen of limbs blocking the front steps. Because it had all happened in the dark last night, the storm had the quality of a nightmare. He'd halfway expected that this immense fallen tree and all the fallen trees in the neighborhood would've righted themselves before the light of day. It was cold enough to see his breath.

"Chilly, isn't it?"

Willy rocked in a straight-back chair off to one side of the porch, his feet propped on the banister. He'd wrapped a blanket around his shoulders.

"Have you been out here all night?" Sam leaned against the porch post, waiting for his head to stop spinning.

"Couldn't sleep. These are my work hours." This time of morning Willy was in his VW, flipping rolled newspapers onto dewy lawns. "There won't be a paper this morning. Presses need power." He let his chair fall forward; the legs scraped the porch floor. "What's your excuse?"

"For being up?" Or for sleeping with Grace?

"Some blowout last night, wasn't it?" Willy nodded to the living room. "Hieronymus Bosch's version of the morning after." He pulled the blanket closer around him. "What *are* you doing up so early?"

"I need to see my house."

"Now?"

"I have a feeling something's wrong." He shivered, pulling his coat closer around him. His breath escaped in white puffs. Fall had ridden in on the storm.

"The streets are blocked." Willy gestured out past the tree to the street covered in fallen limbs.

"I'll walk." He started down the steps. He climbed past the tree's limbs out into the yard.

"It's five miles," Willy said from the porch.

"I have to see my house." He didn't understand his own single-mindedness. "I have to see it now." The more he thought about it, the more he was sure it had been damaged, maybe even leveled. Years of restoration demolished in minutes.

"Well, hell." Willy threw off the blanket and jumped the banister, joining him out in the yard. "I'll come, too, but damned if I'm going to walk five miles." He dragged a couple of limbs from in front of the VW.

"You just said all the streets are blocked."

"It'll be a challenge." Willy climbed into the bus and cranked it. Its backfires echoed across the neighborhood; exhaust clouded the air. Even with Willy's deft maneuvers, what was usually a five-mile, ten-minute trip stretched into a forty-minute sojourn. A lot of streets were impassable. Willy'd come to a fallen tree and have to back up and try another street. If that street was blocked, he'd back up again. Their backtracking almost equaled their forward progress. In this way, with a lot of lateral motion, they inched toward Sam's house.

It was eerie to be out. All the traffic lights were dead; not that there was much traffic to stop. The only other vehicles out were a few service trucks—Georgia Power and Southern Bell. Their cherry pickers hoisted men up to the snapped lines. On a couple of streets, city trucks had just pulled up, and orange-vested city workers piled out, armed with chain saws.

From the houses themselves there was little sign of life. No lights. A few people wandered about their yards in their bathrobes, having waited for the first crack of dawn to assess the damage. Most of it seemed confined to the trees and whatever happened to be under them when they fell. A number of crushed cars peeked out from underneath limbs and leaves. Some houses had been damaged—eaves crushed, porches smashed, roofs caved in. A few people had awakened to a skylight where there had been none.

But all in all, at least on this side of Atlanta, the tornado hadn't mowed clean, deadly swaths, as in those "aftermath" TV news pictures, where stunned people sort through the pulverized wreckage. The storm had spared the city, passing over like a buzz saw in the trees.

When Willy finally pulled onto Elmira, which, of all the streets they'd been on, had the least fallen trees, Sam was relieved to find his house still standing. He was surprised to see the Tempest parked in the driveway. The shop must've gotten to it sooner than they expected. They'd even washed it.

Willy started to pull up to the house, then drove past.

"Where are we going?" Sam asked.

"I'm hungry." Willy shifted into third. "Let's see if the Rainbow is open."

"Wait a minute. I want to check my house."

"We just saw it. It's fine. Why don't we go eat breakfast?"

"Just drop me off here."

Willy kept driving.

"Hey, I said stop." Sam pounded the dashboard.

Willy kept driving.

"Stop, damn it!" He grabbed the steering wheel.

The VW veered across to the other side of the street. It bumped against the curb, and the engine cut off.

"Are you trying to kill us!" Willy shouted, his face flushed.

"You wouldn't stop," Sam said, taken aback by Willy's sudden fierceness.

"Now that's worth dying over!" Willy started the VW up again, whipped it around, and pulled in front of Sam's house.

Sam started to apologize, but Willy kept glancing over his shoulder. It wasn't until Sam followed Willy's gaze toward his house that he realized that the Tempest parked in his driveway had whitewalls and a black roof.

"Whose car is that?" He turned to Willy.

Willy ran his fingers along the steering wheel but didn't say anything.

"Come on, Willy." He felt the same dread he'd felt when he'd awakened this morning. Something was wrong at his house.

"Let's go to the Rainbow and grab some breakfast."

"Who's in my house, Willy?" His throat constricted. Sam jumped out of the VW and ran over to the car that was in his driveway. He walked around the car. A Grady Hospital decal was pasted to the front windshield.

He thought he saw a curtain move in one of the upstairs windows. He got the eerie feeling that he stood outside someone else's house when he knew this was his yard, his driveway, his house. Kate and the doctor had moved in while he wasn't looking.

Willy had gotten out of the VW and come up beside him.

"What are they doing here?" Sam asked. "What in the hell is going on?"

"Maybe he brought Kate by to pick up something."

"At six in the morning?"

Willy took his arm. "Let's go grab some breakfast. When we get back, they'll be gone."

Sam pulled his arm away. "This is my house!"

"If you're going to get territorial about it."

Sam marched up the drive.

Willy hesitated, then followed behind him.

"Surely not," Sam whispered. "Surely not," he said, looking up at his bedroom window. "Not in my own house!"

They stepped onto the porch and found the door unlocked.

"We ought to at least knock," Willy said.

"Like hell," Sam whispered.

"You shouldn't sneak up on people. It's not ethical."

"Ethical!"

Willy turned around, walking back down the drive. "I don't like this."

As Willy got into the VW and drove off, Sam quietly pushed open the door. He listened, but there wasn't a sound. The curtains were closed, and the living room was dark. He tried a light switch—nothing. The power was out all over the city.

The living room was empty. There was no sign that anyone had been there. Then he thought he heard a noise upstairs. Voices. He tiptoed up the stairs to his bedroom, having to feel his way in the half-light of dawn. He walked very slowly, avoiding the step that always creaked. What were they doing here? In his house? In his bed? Did she already know about Grace and him? Was this her way of getting back? He stood outside the bedroom door for a very long time, listening. He turned the doorknob until he felt the lock give. He cracked the door and peeked in.

The bed was empty, the sheets and blankets in their usual tangle. Kate and the doctor hadn't been in here, at least. If she'd slept in his bed, it would've been made.

A car cranked outside. He ran to his bedroom window, looking out in time to see the Tempest pull out of the driveway.

"Hey!" he screamed out the window. "Come back here!" He tried to see the doctor and if Kate was with him, but the angle was wrong. All he saw was the roof of the car as it turned out of his driveway. They must've sneaked out the back door as he came in the front. He sat on the edge of his bed. His head throbbed. What was going on around here? Why would they come here in the first place? He walked through the cold house, checking for signs that someone had been here. Everything was exactly as he'd left it, yet somehow nothing appeared the same. The feeling he got as he checked room after room, even opened closets, was that he'd become estranged from his own house.

Too wound up to go back to bed, he decided the only thing left to do was make coffee. No electricity, he reminded himself. But the stove was gas; it would work. A couple of years ago the power had gone out in an ice storm. With the gas stove, he and Kate had been able to make supper, anyway, cooking by candlelight.

He stepped into the dim kitchen, startled to see the coffeepot already on the stove, heated by a bloom of blue flame.

"I'm way ahead of you."

Kate sat at the kitchen table, reading a paperback.

"Shit, woman!" He pressed his hand to his chest.

"Did I scare you?" She sipped from a cup.

"Hell, no," he said. "I'm used to finding strangers in my kitchen."

"Is that what I am now? A stranger?"

A ray of morning sun eased into the kitchen window, pouring light into the room. Kate's hair was uncombed, and she wore the same clothes she'd worn at the party.

"Drop by for a cup of coffee?" He plopped down in the other kitchen chair and faced her across the table.

She warmed her hands on the cup. "Last night he was called to the hospital. We were on our way back when the storm hit. With the wind howling and trees falling all around us, we drove for cover, and since your house was just a block away and I knew you were at the party, I thought we'd wait the storm out here. You'd never even know we'd been here."

"How'd you get in?"

She reached into her trouser pocket and held up a

key. "You never took it back." She poured him a cup of coffee, refilled her own, and set the cups on the table. "When we heard on the car radio that the power was out everywhere and the streets impassable, we decided to wait until daylight. I figured if the streets were blocked, you'd have to spend the night at Jessie's, anyway."

"I saw him pull out a minute ago." He sipped his coffee.

"He had to get to the hospital."

"You're still here." He set the cup down in the saucer.

She looked down into her coffee cup.

"This is a different doctor you're seeing," he said.

"I'm not seeing him anymore."

The flame hissed under the coffeepot on the stove. Chain saws whined in the distance.

"The house is immaculate," she said. "No food cruds in the sink."

"Maid service."

"Right. On a book clerk's salary."

"I guess doctors can afford a pantry full of maids." He folded his arms across his chest.

"That's not what I meant." She swept her hair back out of her eyes. "You're much neater these days."

"Cleanliness is next to loneliness." He spread his hands flat out on the table. "Is that all y'all did here? Wait?" Then he remembered where he'd been last night and what he'd done.

"No, that's not all we did." She opened the back door, standing in the doorway. "We had a fight." A cold breeze chilled the kitchen. "Some limbs fell in the garden."

"Why didn't you leave with him?"

"Is that a question or a suggestion?"

He closed his eyes and massaged his temples. His head felt scraped hollow. "I drank too much last night."

"How was the party?"

"You were there."

"His beeper went off as we walked in the door." She noticed his bum clothes, smiling at the old plaid coat. "I told you those yard-sale bargains would come to some use."

Just the mention of last night made him uncomfortable. Right about now Grace would wake to an empty room. It was bad enough he'd made love to her, but to slip out with hardly a word made what they'd done seem sordid. He should've stayed. She shouldn't have to wake up alone.

Kate leaned against the doorway, staring out at the clear blue sky.

Not knowing what else to do, he made breakfast. He set a big pot of water on the stove, measuring a couple of cups of grits into the boiling water.

"He doesn't want it," she said.

He dug around among the pot lids, trying a couple before he found the one that fit. He took the bacon out of the refrigerator. "Who doesn't want what?"

She sighed impatiently. "He doesn't want—" She kicked the kitchen chair. "God, Sam, sometimes you're so dense!" Her face flushed. He saw how dark the circles were under her eyes.

"What did I do?"

"Nothing." Her tone dripped with sarcasm. "You've never done anything."

"Listen, Kate." He felt his anger rise in him. He took a couple of steps toward her. "I don't know what the hell you're talking about. All I know is that I come home, find a strange car in my driveway and the woman who walked out on me six months ago at my kitchen table drinking coffee and reading Anne Tyler like she never left, telling me she spent the night with some doctor in my house! I don't know what the hell is bothering you, but you have no right to come in my house and have a goddamned baby over it!"

There was a stunned silence as they both stood there,

looking at each other. He hadn't known what he knew until he'd heard himself say it. He crumpled into the kitchen chair.

She sat down across from him, not taking her eyes off him.

He looked up at her, his eyes questioning hers.

She nodded slowly.

"Whoa," he whispered. Amazed, he couldn't think of anything to say for a long time. The grits bubbled on the stove. The chain saw still whined in the distance. His story to Mr. Berkowitz had come back to haunt him. Some part of him had known. "He doesn't want it?"

She shook her head.

"And you?"

"I want it." She sounded determined.

He got up to stir the grits. "Isn't that a lot to take on by yourself?"

"Yes, it is."

"So why do you want this baby?" He slid the bacon out of its package, separated the strips, and crowded them into the frying pan. "If the guy doesn't want it—"

"Because it is this baby, Sam." She pushed her hand against her chest. "I have seen six-month preemies that didn't weigh more than a pound, scrawny little things you could hold in one hand, grow into healthy, beautiful children." She opened a drawer and dug out silverware. "Being pregnant has made me believe in the particularity of life."

Sam cracked a couple of eggs on the edge of the other frying pan and opened them into the sizzling oil. He felt numb. "So what does this doctor have to say about your having it?"

"He said he'd help with the money, but he doesn't want to be the father."

"A little late for that."

Kate set the kitchen table as he finished making breakfast. It was strange to see her back in the kitchen,

familiar with where things were, which drawer held the silverware, which cupboard had the glasses. It was like every
other morning they'd spent together; their six-month separa-
tion had been a bad dream. All along he'd held out what
he now realized had been a childish hope that they'd had
this tacit agreement that even though they were apart, nothing would really change between them. Her news altered
everything. A baby was as irrevocable as you could get.
Someone else's at that.

They ate in silence. He hadn't realized how hungry
he was. She cleaned her plate, too. As he ate, his headache
receded, and the dizziness went away, but her news nagged
him. The more he thought about it, the more upset he got.

"How did it happen?" He blurted out.

"How does it ever happen?"

"You know what I mean." He couldn't control the
irritation in his voice. "What happened?"

She pushed her plate back. "I forgot my diaphragm
one night." She raked a couple of crumbs into her hand,
dropping them on her plate. "I made a mistake."

His hand shot out, grabbed her wrist and held it. He
stared into her eyes.

"I made a mistake." She tried to pull away.

"You never made that mistake with me." He let go.
She looked at him, rubbing her wrist. "You hurt me."

He pushed up from the table and ran outside, slamming the screen door. What in the hell was he doing, grab-
bing her like that? Had he lost his mind? No. He'd lost
her, finally and forever. There was this new permanent
thing between them. There was no going back now. He felt
awful and alone. Until now he'd played at living without her.

He could see his breath. The morning air was cold,
almost frosty. Limbs and branches littered the backyard. He
made his way out to the garden, which was a tangle of
weeds. One of the tangles moved. Out crawled the Siamese.

Its coat was matted, and it lurched unsteadily. He reached down to pet it, but it hissed at him.

"I don't blame you," he said to the cat. "I wouldn't want to be petted by a son of a bitch, either." He went on out to the toolshed. A heavy limb had fallen on it, creasing the roof. As he gripped the limb, trying to pull it off, he heard the screen door slam. Kate walked toward him, carefully stepping over limbs, moving in the deliberate way of pregnant women. She stopped to look over the garden, her hands on her hips.

"What a mess," she said.

"I forgot to weed it."

She bent down to stroke the Siamese, which rubbed her legs. "You're a mess, " she said to the cat.

"I think he was caught out in the storm last night." He tried again to pull the limb off the toolshed, but he couldn't move it.

"Poor kitty." She stroked its back. She walked all the way around the toolshed. "That's a shame."

He turned to her. "How far along are you?"

"Two months." She placed her hand on her stomach.

"I'm sorry I grabbed you." He gripped the limb again.

"You have a right to be upset."

"I don't have a right to be violent."

She laughed. "You're so dramatic." She crossed her arms against the cold. "You're about as violent as Gandhi." She took hold of the limb.

"Not in your condition," he said.

She was already pulling, and together they slid the limb off the shed.

He ran his hand along the dent. It was a big dent, but it hadn't torn a hole.

"What do you think?" She wiped her hands on his old shirt.

"We could hammer it out." He caught himself. "I mean *I* could hammer it out." He opened the door to the toolshed and looked in, wondering what he'd expected to see besides the rototiller, bags of fertilizer, and a wheelbarrow. "The night you left, I got smashed. Willy and I chased a possum into here. We tried to trap it in a trash can."

She looked at him and then, as if she'd caught herself, looked away.

"You still haven't answered my question," he said.

She nudged a tomato stake with her foot. "What question is that?"

"Why are you here?"

She twirled a strand of her hair with her finger. "I wanted to talk to somebody who cares about me." She hugged herself, her mouth set. "I guess that was pretty presumptuous."

There was a chorus of chain saws across the neighborhood.

"Do you want to move back in?" His voice cracked.

"Is that an invitation?"

"Do you want it to be?"

"Do you want me to want it to be?"

They both smiled, but then she got a distracted look on her face. "Shit," she said. "What time is it?"

He held up his watch. "Seven-thirty."

"I don't know what I was thinking. I have to get to work." She started walking back to the house.

"Surely they don't expect you to come in." He followed her.

"I scheduled a meeting with some parents."

"They won't come, not with the power out and trees down."

"They might. Besides, there are a lot of sick babies now." She picked at her flannel shirt. "I can't go like this." She snapped her fingers as they entered the kitchen. "I left a blouse and a skirt upstairs in one of the closets."

He followed her upstairs, where she rifled through his bedroom closet and pulled out some clothes. He sat on the bed and watched her undress. As she stepped out of the overalls and tossed off the flannel shirt, he realized how long it had been since he'd seen her without her clothes. He didn't know whether it was his imagination, but she seemed not really heavier but more substantial.

"How am I going to get there?" She slid into the skirt. "MARTA." She answered herself.

"It's not running."

"It isn't that far to walk."

"Borrow my bike." She'd have to bring it back, guaranteeing he'd see her again.

She pulled on her blouse and had it halfway buttoned when he slipped his arms around her waist and pulled her onto the bed.

She laid her cheek against his shoulder. "Oh, Jesus," she said softly.

He stroked the back of her head, feeling the smoothness of her hair.

They sat on the edge of the bed, holding each other.

He kissed her, then slid his hands under her blouse and touched her breasts, which were fuller than he remembered.

She kissed him, slipping off his old coat and pulling his shirttail out of his pants.

They leaned back on the bed. He opened her blouse and kissed each breast.

She closed her eyes. "You feel good."

He started to slide the skirt off of her, but she pushed him away.

"Cold hands?"

She put her finger to her lips, signaling to be quiet. "Footsteps," she whispered. She pointed in the direction of downstairs.

He listened. At first, there was silence; then he heard

footsteps in the living room and out to the kitchen—slow and deliberate.

She pulled her blouse back over her shoulders. "He's come back," she whispered. "To talk me out of this baby." She stood up, buttoning her blouse in the mirror. "I should go down and face him."

He stood behind her, watching her in the mirror. "You want me to tell him to get the hell out of my house? I mean, who the hell does he think he is, strolling into my house?"

They heard the footsteps cross back and forth downstairs.

"I should talk to him." She straightened her skirt in the mirror. "I owe him that much."

She started to walk out the door, but Sam pulled her back. "Wait. Maybe he'll leave."

They listened for the footsteps. They didn't hear anything. "I think he's gone," he said.

But then they heard footsteps on the stairs.

"I don't believe it. He's coming up here," Sam said.

"I should let him know we're here." She started to call to him, but Sam clapped his hand over her mouth and held her. She didn't struggle.

"Please," he whispered. "Maybe he'll just go away."

It took the guy forever to climb the stairs, gradually getting closer and closer. The footsteps stopped outside the bedroom door. They heard breathing. Sam still had his hand over her mouth. Her eyes were wide. His own heart pounded.

The door creaked open.

Willy's head craned around the door. His face looked horrified, as if he'd expected to see bodies. When he saw Kate and Sam clutching each other, he held up a grease-stained green-and-white bag. "Anybody for a Krispy Kreme?"

Chapter Eleven

Sam swept branches and leaves from the sidewalk in front of Brilliant's, joining shop owners along Ponce de Leon Avenue clearing the storm's debris from their shop fronts. The chilled air made everything—grass, bare trees, streets, houses, store windows, even the skyline—look sharper, as if overnight the city had moved into a season of definition. Sam peeled up one of the colored leaves the storm had pressed into the sidewalk like a thousand labels. Willy said leaves didn't actually change colors, they already had yellows and reds in them, but you couldn't see them until fall, when the chlorophyll drained away. Absence, he said, brought out true colors.

He dragged a few larger limbs into the gutter, then paused to blow into his cold hands. His head still ached from last night, although some of the hollowness had receded. More had happened in the past twenty-four hours than in six months. His thoughts dovetailed into each other, from Grace to Willy to Kate, from guilt to embarrassment to disbelief. He couldn't shake the feeling that Kate's pregnancy was his punishment for last night with Grace. At the same time, he realized that it was a kind of egotism to think that everything that happened in the world was to instruct him. Besides, Kate was pregnant well before he made love to Grace. Still, in his heart, he felt culpable.

Inside the store, Jessie, Paula, and Carl waited on customers. Afternoon business had been brisk, especially for a weekday. Although the streets were empty, foot traffic

217

was heavy. With businesses and schools closed for the day, people had grown restless in their houses and strolled around, curious to see the damage. Neighbors caught up on gossip over uprooted trees. Teenagers gathered on street corners, smoked cigarettes, and straddled skateboards on the curb, looking less unimpressed than usual. Children boldly steered their bikes down the middle of streets that just yesterday were crowded with rush-hour traffic; others played kickball or tossed Frisbees along the double yellow line. The storm had given the streets to the children for the afternoon. Across the street, the Pub sold beer on the sidewalk. With everybody out and the new coolness, the day took on a festive air. On his way to work, Sam had walked past a busy outdoor cafe whose blackboard advertised a Survivor's Brunch.

He carried the broom back inside the crowded store. Business was always good at the first cold snap. The weather reminded people that the holidays were imminent. Jessie rang up books at the register, and Paula helped a customer in the religion section. A long line had formed at the register. He bagged books for Jessie while she rang up sales.

"Where's Carl?" he asked.

"He went back to the receiving room," she said. "He's too weak to wait on customers."

"Thanks," she said after the line had thinned out. She was pale, and dark circles made her eyes seem sunken. She pinched the bridge of her nose. "I'd close for the afternoon, but business is too good." She patted his shoulder. "I appreciate your coming in."

He hadn't been scheduled to work today, but at about eleven o'clock, three hours after Kate had left with Willy and he'd collapsed onto the living-room sofa, the phone rang. It must've rung for a long time, because it entered his dreams in the form of a fire drill. He awoke with his heart racing. He bounded off the sofa and into the kitchen to pick up the phone. It was Jessie from the bookstore, saying they were really busy. Could he come in? "How can you be busy if the power is off?" She said the power was on there.

After he hung up, he sat at the kitchen table. Kate had come and gone without his asking if he could see her again. Why hadn't he at least *asked*? The only reason she'd come here was because of the storm. It was the closest familiar place, a temporary haven. And even if it was more than that, even if she'd wanted to see him, she didn't want to because of who he was but because of who he wasn't. He wasn't the doctor. He wasn't the father of her baby. He wasn't a lot of things.

The old electric clock on the wall, twelve hours behind, had resumed scratching out the seconds. The light buzzed on overhead, and the refrigerator rattled a couple of times, then began to hum. He pushed himself up from the table with a sense of resignation. Whether he liked it or not, the power was back on.

"After you put the broom up"—Jessie yawned again—"could you run the register for a while? Carl's not up to it."

"I warned him vodka and Kahlúa don't mix." Paula looked up a book on the computer. Her eyes were puffed and her skin was sallow. Even her shocking-pink hair had lost some of its shock. Sam didn't look so hot himself. He'd hardly recognized himself in the bathroom mirror this morning. His face was darkened by two day's worth of stubble, his eyes were bloodshot, and his skin was red and crinkled. His nose, which had always been slightly off center, looked even more crooked; his features had slipped a little last night.

"I made a fresh pot of coffee." Paula blinked vacantly at the computer screen. They'd already gone through two pots.

"We need caffeine IVs." Jessie handed him a huge wad of twenty-dollar bills, checks, and charges. "Do a drop, will you? We've got too much money in this drawer."

Sam hurried back to the office, almost tripping over the Bandanna Man, who was stretched out on the floor in the history section. Vietnam books were scattered all around him. He didn't look up.

Sam slipped the wad of bills into his coat pocket, hoping the Bandanna Man hadn't seen. He couldn't make out the title of his book, but the cover was a black man in combat uniform running through the jungle with a rifle in his arms. The Bandanna Man must've sneaked in while Jessie was busy with a customer or was too tired to chase him out. Either way, he wasn't hurting anybody, even if customers had to step over him. Sam left him alone.

In the office, he poured himself another cup of coffee. He closed the office door, locking the wad of bills in the office safe. When he came out, he found Carl in the receiving room, his head on his desk.

"Can I do anything?" Sam asked.

Carl didn't move.

"Hey, Carl." He touched his shoulder.

Carl gave a little moan.

"Need anything?"

"I've already picked out the coffin." He raised his head, blinking in the light. He was so pale that his face looked bleached. His handlebar mustache had gone limp. "Tell them to skip the embalmment; there's enough alcohol in my veins to preserve me well into the next century." He rubbed his temples. "I saw Kate at the party last night, but then she was gone."

"She didn't stay."

"I thought you might've been too busy to notice." Carl managed a knowing smile. If Carl knew about Grace, so did everyone else.

Business slackened in the late afternoon. Jessie was

in the office going over bills, Paula received books in the receiving room, and Carl had been sent home by Jessie. Sam was still at the register when Ronnie came into the store, muttering to himself. He walked up to the register, the way he always did when he wanted change for the bus.

"How's it going, Ronnie?" Sam opened the register and counted out four quarters, but when he looked up, he stared down the barrel of a gun.

Ronnie didn't say anything, just held the gun on Sam, the same beatific expression on his face, his hand shaking slightly. "Mine had AM *and* FM."

There were no customers in the store. Jessie was back in the office out of view. He could see Paula through the receiving-room window, but her head was bent, probably over some book she'd gotten caught up in. He was alone. Ronnie's gun was small enough to be a toy. He thought of all the stories of robbers holding up banks with squirt guns. Still, he didn't make any sudden moves.

"What do you want, Ronnie?" Sam glanced back at the window to the receiving room and saw Paula still bent over a book, oblivious. "Money?"

"She took it when she left." Ronnie sounded upset. "She had no right to take it. She knew it was the only thing that mattered to me."

"Why don't you put the gun down." He opened the register drawer. There wasn't much money; not that it really mattered. He'd decided a long time ago that he'd hand over the keys to Fort Knox to save his life. He filled a paper sack with the money.

He noticed a movement out of the corner of his eye, back in the history section. The Bandanna Man slowly raised his head. He had an amused look on his face. Then his head disappeared again behind the bookshelves.

Sam finished filling the bag and slid it gently across the counter to Ronnie.

Ronnie didn't even look at it. "She had no right to

take it! She knew how much it meant to me." He seemed to be getting more upset. The hand that held the gun shook.

"Take it easy, Ronnie." Sam's voice quaked. He saw the Bandanna Man tiptoe from the religion section to the psychology section to the sports section, silently moving closer to the register.

"Damn her," Ronnie cried. "What the hell did I ever do to her? She lived with me for two years, then she leaves and takes James Taylor with her."

The radio. That's what he wanted. He unplugged the boom box Jessie kept behind the register and set it on the counter, but Ronnie didn't seem to see it. He kept talking to himself; his muttering became angrier and more incoherent.

"AM! FM! My radio played both!" His face was red and contorted. "And she just took it!" He pounded the gun on the counter.

A cannon had gone off right by his ear. Glass shattered somewhere, and there was a scream. Sam had hunched over, feeling himself, sure he'd been shot. Ronnie blinked at the gun as a singed smell filled the store. When he'd determined he hadn't been hit, Sam turned and saw that the front window had been blasted out.

"What in the hell!" Jessie tore out of the office, Paula behind her. They both froze when they saw Ronnie, who still waved the gun carelessly in his hand.

A small group had gathered outside the store window.

"Get away," Sam yelled to the people outside. "Get back, Jessie!"

"Is a radio too much to ask?" Sweat beaded on Ronnie's forehead as he pointed the gun at Sam.

"Here's your radio." Sam gingerly pushed the boom box toward him.

"That's not my radio." Ronnie's eyes flashed. "You trying to trick me?"

What went through his mind as he stared down the

barrel of Ronnie's gun was that he'd let Kate get away this morning without asking if he could see her again. That he'd die without her knowing his feelings became crystal clear as Ronnie took aim at his heart.

The Bandanna Man leapt out of the fiction section and with one swift kick knocked Ronnie to the floor. He wrenched the gun out of his hand. "You're going to kill somebody."

Ronnie sat on the floor, blinking.

Sam fell back onto the stool behind the register, breathing again. "Oh, man."

"Thank God." Jessie ran up to the register.

The Bandanna Man stroked the gun, weighing it in his hand. He glanced up at the open register and at the bag of money on the counter, then raised the gun at Sam. "Hand it over," he said, "and I don't mean the radio."

Sam pushed the bag of money over to him.

The Bandanna Man waved Jessie and Paula over behind the register with Sam. "Nobody move and nobody gets hurt." He backed out of the store, nearly tripping over Ronnie, who still sat on the floor, mumbling. He ran out the door.

They didn't move for a second after he was gone, afraid he might come back. Then, while Jessie was on the phone to the police, Sam and Paula ran out to the sidewalk, where a crowd had gathered. There was no sign of the Bandanna Man.

Paula put her hand on Sam's shoulder. "I thought you were a goner."

"I'm not sure I'm not." A cold shiver went through him as he realized all he'd just been through.

Someone shoved past them. It was Ronnie, running down the street, the radio cradled in his arms.

"Shouldn't we stop him?" she asked.

Sam shrugged. "Where's he going to go?"

It took Sam several times to explain to the officer

with the notepad that he'd been robbed by a man who'd saved him from a man who was about to kill him because his girlfriend had stolen his radio. He gave a description of the Bandanna Man and Ronnie, feeling traitorous. The Bandanna Man had saved his life, and while Ronnie was about to shoot him, it wasn't anything personal.

After the policemen left, they locked up the store, dimmed all the store lights, and the three of them sat in the office, drinking coffee. They were too stirred up to go home yet.

"Hell, I would've given him more than that for reward money." Jessie propped her legs on her desk.

"That's a shame," Paula said. Sam and she sat on the old couch, squeezed in among the salesmen's review copies and stacks of publishers' catalogs.

From looking at the register tape and counting the money Sam had put in the safe earlier, they'd calculated that the Bandanna Man had gotten away with only forty-three dollars.

"What'll they do with him when they catch him?" Paula asked.

"He was on parole. He'll go back to prison," Jessie said.

"What if we didn't press charges? What if we said it was reward money?" Paula asked.

"The guy might've saved Sam's life, but he also held a gun on him and would've used it. Besides, he robbed the store. I don't reward theft."

"I guess you're right," Paula said. "Hey, Sam, you okay?"

Sam stared off into space, holding the coffee cup between his hands.

"Did that shake you up?" Jessie asked.

"I have to make a phone call."

"Are you sure you're okay?" Paula held his hand.

He jumped up from the couch. "I just need to make a phone call."

"Sure." Jessie got up from her desk and nodded to Paula to follow her. "We'll be double-checking the doors." Jessie pulled the door closed behind them.

He dialed Maggie's first, but when there was no answer, he dialed the hospital, a number he had no trouble remembering even after six months.

"The neonatal unit, please." He waited, his heart pounding more now than when Ronnie held the gun on him. A nurse answered.

"Is Kate Sterling in?"

"Just a minute."

Sam waited an eternity. Through the office window he saw Jessie and Paula move around the dimly lit store, picking up books and reshelving.

"This is Kate Sterling." Her voice was impatient.

"You're with somebody," Sam said.

There was a pause on the other end. He could hear a doctor paged in the background. "Sam," she said. "I shouldn't have come by—"

"Can you see me tonight?"

There was another silence. He could hear a baby cry. "I think I misled you by just showing up."

"We could have a late supper."

She sighed. "I'm with a father," she said. "He just lost his wife and his baby in labor."

"Jesus, I thought that hardly happened anymore."

"The mother had a heart problem they didn't diagnose."

"How's he taking it?" That was an idiotic question. How would anybody take it? "What'd you do?"

"Called his mother."

Sam liked the straightforwardness of the solution. Ordinarily, the father might've been subjected to a barrage of counseling and treatment administered by a whole fleet of M.D.s, Ph.D.s, and M.S.W.s. Sam liked Kate's solution much better: A man loses his wife and child, call his mother.

"Can you see me later tonight?" he asked.

"I don't think so."

"Kate, give me a chance," he pleaded. "I've been thinking—"

"Sam." He heard voices in the background. "I have to get back to the father."

"It could be as late tonight as you want."

"Thanks for calling." There was a pause and a click. She'd hung up.

He slammed down the receiver. The office door opened, and Jessie stuck her head inside.

"Everything okay? Paula's gone home."

"Kate won't see me," he said.

"If Mohammed won't come to the mountain ..." Jessie lifted her coat off the back of the office door and handed Sam his.

"I can't do that. Not if she doesn't want to see me. Anyway, she's at the hospital."

They walked through the dim store. The shelves seemed a little more sinister than usual, as if Ronnie or the Bandanna Man might pop up from behind them. Jessie punched in the code on the store alarm, which changed the little green light to a blinking red. Outside, the wind was blustery and cold. They turned their collars up.

"Besides, my car is in the shop," he said.

"Borrrow mine."

"I won't force myself on her and risk making a fool of myself."

Jessie shrugged. "Just a suggestion." She patted him on the back. "Good night."

They'd walked about half a block away from each other when she called out. "Hey, Sam!"

He turned around. He could see her small figure under the streetlight.

"It's a fool who doesn't risk." She waved, then

turned, having to lean into the wind as she disappeared down the street.

Sam walked home in the dark, cautious of everyone he passed, as leaves scuttled across the sidewalk. When he was within a hundred yards of his house, he saw the shape of a car in his driveway. It wasn't Willy's VW. It was the doctor's car. He was back—the son of a bitch, he thought. What was he doing in his house? But as he got closer, he realized it was his own car. The mechanics had returned it sometime during the day. He climbed in and cranked it, halfway hoping it wouldn't start.

Even after decades, Grady Hospital—a squat sixteen-story yellowish gray monstrosity—still commanded a prominent position along the Atlanta skyline, despite the forest of lithe, gleaming banks, hotels, and office buildings that had grown up around it, as if the old building said, No matter how much time you spend in these other buildings, this is where you'll end up. The expressway had widened so many times that it practically ran through Grady's lobby. You couldn't go anywhere in Atlanta without passing right by it. Drivers would glance up at its thousands of dim, grungy windows (jets of dark steam billowed from various chimneys, the place boiled with maladies) and say a little prayer to themselves, If I am ever gravely ill, please don't let me linger.

Grady looked creepy enough during the day, but as he took the exit ramp and wound around until he faced the hospital, brightly lit in stark relief to the night, he couldn't help thinking of a prison. How could Kate work every day in a building that looked like your chances of ever coming out were slim at best? In fact, she'd grown fond of the huge, old lumbering place because she saw it for what it was, the only hospital in the city where even the poorest people had a chance at decent medical care. For the destitute, the hospital provided a medical loophole. Poor people had such respect for the hospital that whenever they moved, they kept in mind how close they'd be to Grady. Kate said a lot of the older black people still called it "the Gradies," which referred back to a few decades ago when one wing of the hospital was for whites and the other for blacks.

As Sam drove up the street leading to the hospital, he could see why Kate loved the place. It was a toughened, streetwise bully of a building. Its two wings curved outward like powerful arms ready to embrace.

As he pulled into the parking deck, he wondered what he was doing here. What would he say to her that he hadn't said already? What had changed? Something had, he was sure. He'd felt it when Ronnie pointed that gun at him, when he'd thought he'd run out of options. But how would he tell Kate? He parked and turned off the headlights. Last year a nurse had been raped and badly beaten on this deck. He used to worry whenever Kate was late from work. He made her promise to have a security guard walk her to the car, but he knew she was always preoccupied when she left at night, that she charged out here alone.

The hospital lobby might have been furnished by the same people who furnish seedy motels, no two vinyl chairs being quite the same shade of orange. It was a confusion of doctors, nurses, visitors, and patients. If patients weren't in a wheelchair or on crutches, if they didn't wear a cast or a bandage or some other badge of their illness, they were easily identified by their green hospital gowns. Kate said they came down to the lobby to escape their rooms. He'd wondered how their rooms could be much worse until she'd shown him a couple—stark, antiseptic cells that probably encouraged speedy recovery.

He rode the elevator to the fourteenth floor, where the neonatal unit was. He wasn't supposed to be up here, especially at this time of night, but the few times he'd come with Kate she'd said, "Act like you know where you're going and nobody bothers you."

He got a scare when the elevator door opened and he couldn't remember which way the neonatal unit was. A couple of nurses eyed him and seemed on the point of saying something when a doctor came up and started flirting with them. Sam slipped past and hoped he was headed in the right direction.

This floor had a different feel than the other floors. The halls were painted in bright colors. One wall was a big mosaic of jungle animals—lions, tigers, elephants, and monkeys that peered out from behind trees or lurked in bushes. The doctors and nurses walked with a lighter step on this floor. No green-gowned, hollow-eyed patients wandered the hallways. This was the one floor of hope.

He knew he was in the right place after he walked through the double doors and came to a large window that opened onto a roomful of incubators that, according to Kate, controlled everything from temperature to humidity to oxygen—a portable plastic womb. It was a little eerie, all these tiny babies in their climate-controlled boxes and no one else around. He began to feel responsible for this roomful of preemies.

He ducked when a nurse came into the room. She checked the wires taped to the babies and wrote on a clipboard. He heard Kate's voice down the hall. He was around the corner from her office. She'd left the door cracked.

"We can make these arrangements tomorrow," she said. "You need to go home and rest now, Mr. Randall."

"I can't rest till I know it's going to be done right," said a deep voice. He sounded broken, exhausted.

"You heard the lady," an older woman said. "Come on home with me, Bobby. You need sleep."

"I wish I could sleep, Mama," the man said. "I wish I could sleep forever, like Charlene."

There was a long silence. Sam hoped they were hugging. He stared into the sad eyes of an elephant peeking out from behind a bush.

"Come here, Bobby."

"I didn't know what I had, Mama. Is that why I lost them?"

"You shouldn't blame yourself, Mr. Randall." Kate's tone was professional but sympathetic. He'd never heard her sound quite that way. What a tough position she was always in, not being family.

"But how can anything so bad happen, Mama, if I don't deserve it?"

"Nobody deserves it, child. Death just comes. It's not choosy."

Sam felt a hand on his shoulder and found himself faced with a fierce-eyed nurse.

"What are you doing here?" she demanded.

He looked over at the incubators. "I'm a father."

"It's past visiting hours." Her tone mellowed a little.

"I didn't get off work till late."

She squinted at him. "Which one is yours?"

"That's what I was trying to figure out. They all look the same from here." He attempted a smile.

"What's your name?"

Sam read the name taped on the incubator closest to the window. "Williams."

"This one right here is yours?" She pointed to the incubator.

"Oh, right, right. Now I recognize him." He prayed it was a boy.

"This one right here?"

"Yes, ma'am."

She looked at the baby, then back at Sam. "Who the hell are you?"

"The father of that baby." His voice rose with hers. He was mad she didn't believe him.

"If you don't leave this minute, I'm calling security."

Kate came out of her office. "What's going on out here?" Her eyes widened when she saw Sam.

"You know this man?" the nurse asked.

"Yes . . . why, what has he done?"

"He says he's the father of the Williams baby. You want me to call security?"

Kate suppressed a smile. "I'll take care of him."

The nurse hesitated.

"It's all right," Kate said.

The nurse walked on down the hall but glanced back at Sam a couple of times.

"I must not be a very convincing father," he said.

"You're not a very convincing black," she said.

"You're kidding." He looked at the baby in the Williams incubator.

"Black newborns have light skin sometimes." Then she frowned at him. "What are you doing here?"

"Repaying your visit. I know I shouldn't be here. You're in the middle of something."

She put her finger to her lips. "She's about to take him home," she whispered. "Wait here." She went back into her office.

In a few minutes a large black man came out of Kate's office. He wiped his eyes and leaned on a very small, elderly woman who had no difficulty supporting her son. Sam pretended to look at the nursery window.

The man stopped and laid his hand on Sam's shoulder. "Is one of these yours?"

"Yes, sir." He wasn't quite sure why he said it.

"This baby here?" The man pointed to the Williams baby. "He's beautiful. A very beautiful child."

"Thank you."

"How old?"

Kate mouthed, Two weeks.

"Two weeks," Sam said.

The man's mother stepped up and took him by the arm. "Come on now, Bobby."

"Isn't he a beautiful baby, Mama?"

"He is." She peered over her glasses at the baby and then at Sam. She gave Sam a strange look and in that same moment seemed to understand what he'd done. She gave him a dignified nod. "Come on now, Bobby." Kate followed them as the old woman led her son toward the elevator.

When Sam turned around, the nurse stood there shaking her head at him. "What do you think this is? *Mission Impossible?*"

"My man!" Mr. Randall called to him from the other end of the hall.

Sam waved.

"Count your blessings." The big man's voice echoed down the hallway as he and his mother stepped into the elevator.

Sam followed Kate back to her office, where she sat down and straightened her desk, closing a file folder of papers.

"That was decent what you just did." She studied a couple of snapshots she'd laid on her desk. He walked around behind her, put his hands on her shoulders, and leaned over to see. They were bad pictures, taken with a bright flash in a dim room—lots of shadows. The only thing he could make out was a crib.

"It's the nursery Mr. Randall built," she said. "It took him a year and a half, working nights and weekends."

Sam leaned closer to see the pictures. The crib was all that he could really see. He felt a deep grief push against his chest. These were the saddest pictures he'd ever seen.

"Would you rub my shoulders?" Kate sat back in her chair, her eyes closed.

He kneaded her shoulders. "You're tight."

She gave a sigh of pleasure. "Forget this social-work crap. I'd probably do my clients a lot more good if I gave them back rubs." She sighed again. "I'd forgotten how good you were at this." She sat up.

"You're still tight." He didn't want to take his hands away.

She let him pull her back against the chair. She closed her eyes again. "Why are you here?"

"I want us to get back together," he said.

She didn't say anything, but he felt her neck tighten. He rubbed her shoulders a little harder, feeling the muscles warm under his fingers. He rubbed down along the shoulder blades. "I've always liked your shoulder blades."

"I'm pregnant with another man's baby."

He lifted his hands for a moment, but she kept her head bent.

"Please don't stop," she said. "I was just beginning to feel human."

"I think we could work it out." He massaged her neck and then across her shoulders. "I've missed you."

She picked up the snapshot of the crib. "I'm worried something will go wrong."

"Nothing can go wrong."

"You don't know the half of it."

His fingers were tired, but he didn't want to stop, was afraid to stop touching her.

"This might just be too hard." She laid her hands flat on her desk. "I'm not sure how fair it is to bring a baby into the world without a father."

"Are you taking applications?" He kept kneading the back of her neck.

She got up from the chair and walked over to a window that looked out on the expressway and the city. "Maybe I should take him up on that abortion." She sounded so unhappy.

He came over and stood beside her; both of them looked out. Kate's office faced away from downtown. In the dark, the expressway snaked out into the twinkling suburbs.

She kept staring out the window. "What about everything that will go wrong?"

He touched her shoulder. "Let it."

Where do you want to eat?"

"I'm not hungry," she said.

They'd left Kate's car at the hospital and drove around downtown. At night, downtown Atlanta felt so desolate that Sam expected tumbleweed to blow by. Commuters strapped themselves into their cars, double-checked that all the doors were locked, turned up the radio, and pulled onto the clotted expressway. What they left behind was a stunned shell of a city: empty streets, darkened buildings, and storefronts shut up tight. They passed by the Central City Park, which during the day was crowded with well-dressed people on lunch break catching some sun. Now only a few lonely figures loitered under the grim sulfur lights.

He drove along Peachtree Street, which was a little livelier than some of the other streets, with limos and taxis that pulled up to the Hyatt or the Hilton or Peachtree Plaza, skyscraper hotels with fountain-filled lobbies and glass elevators that lifted their guests above the sadness of the streets.

"You know why I came to see you?"

"Why?"

"Because I'm not dead."

They were looking at each other when the car behind them honked. They drove along in silence. Kate was thinking something over. She kept her eyes straight ahead, not saying anything. He pulled up to a stoplight. A couple of street people huddled underneath one of the closed storefronts.

"How about the Varsity?" she said.

"What?"

"Let's eat at the Varsity."

"I thought you said you weren't hungry?"

"I can always make room for onion rings."

The Varsity was a drive-in, the world's largest; at least that's what the sign out front said, and Sam had never heard anyone dispute it. It was less of a drive-in and more of an institution. He knew a lot of people who, if pressed, would argue that the Varsity *was* Atlanta and that the rest of the city was just an excuse for its deep-fried Vidalia onion rings. He didn't feel quite so strongly about the Varsity. Sometimes he felt that all the burgers, the chili dogs, the onion rings, and the fried apple pies were a slight exaggeration, a parody of food.

Kate and Willy would head for the Varsity at the mere mention of a Frosted Orange—a milk shake indigenous to the Varsity. When Kate and Willy were children, their father used to take them and Maggie to the Varsity, and for Kate these childhood excursions were her fondest memories: "To actually eat in the car," she said, "I never felt so free—no table manners, no silverware, no vegetables." She remembered those trips to the Varsity with her father as a time when her family was still intact: "The four of us perfectly contained in my father's '63 Impala, passing warm, greasy food over the seats."

Because it was too cold to eat in the car, they went inside to order at the long stainless-steel counter presided over by a row of fierce, hustling black men and women who shouted out customers' orders in an almost mocking tone. After Sam and Kate got their food, they sat at a table in one of the big TV rooms that always reminded Sam of classrooms—classrooms of people stuffing their faces. For a while they sat there and ate and watched the news.

"I really did care for him," Kate said after a while, eating an onion ring.

"Excuse me?" Sam asked.

"The father." She glanced downward. "I don't want to misrepresent how I felt. I cared for him. I really did."

He tried to take comfort in her use of the past tense, but there was no real solace in semantics. Just because something was history didn't make it any less true.

"And now?"

"When I told him I was pregnant," she said, "he told me he could take care of it." Her voice cracked. "And I said, 'We'll take care of it together,' and he said, 'No, I mean, take care of the problem.'" Her face reddened. "That's when I realized he was offering to abort his own baby."

"Jesus," Sam said. "What did you say?"

"I told him I bet he said that to all the social workers."

He reached across the table and put his hand on hers.

"We kept seeing each other for a while, but last night, after Jessie's party, I told him I didn't want to see him anymore."

He pulled his chair closer to hers and put his arm around her. "I am sorry." There was something tinny about his sorrow. Was he sorry that she had broken up with the doctor? Was he sorry that the doctor didn't want the baby? Was he sorry that the doctor hadn't cared enough to compromise? He wasn't sorry about any of those things because together they spelled another chance. Of course, he would've preferred for her to say that she broke up with the doctor because she cared for Sam instead. But he would take Kate any way he could get her. Love, he began to see, required a mercenary heart.

They watched the family at the table next to them— a mother, a father, two little girls, and between them in a high chair, a baby boy who looked about two and a half and reminded Sam of Joey. The little girls competed for their brother's attention with French fries and pieces of their hamburger buns, while the mother and father, both exhausted looking, kept their eyes trained on the TV. The baby basked in his sisters' attention.

"Shouldn't those children be in bed?" Sam asked.

"Maybe the father works a weird shift and this is the only time they can get out?"

He admired Kate's unwillingness to judge strangers. In fact, he loved her for it. Through her eyes he saw that appearances only obstructed the view.

"Willy!" Kate waved across the room, where Willy stood holding a tray stacked with food.

It wasn't until he started over that Sam saw Grace behind him.

"Kate, you remember Grace," Willy said as they sat down at the table with them.

"It's great to see you, Grace." Kate got up and hugged Grace as she set down her tray.

Grace sat next to Sam, who by this time was extremely confused and embarrassed.

"And you know Sam," Willy said.

Sam felt his face go beet red. He was so shocked to see Grace with Willy and even more shocked that Kate seemed to already know her.

Grace turned to Sam. "Some party last night, huh?" She smiled. "Is your house okay?"

"Fine." Sam was touched and even more embarrassed that she'd remembered why he'd left. Kate watched him.

"When the storm hit last night," Grace said to Kate, "we all ran into Jessie's basement; then the lights went out. When the storm hit, Sam and I held on to each other."

"I bet you did."

"Everybody held on to somebody," Sam explained.

Usually, Willy was more helpful in these situations, but he didn't say anything. He ate his hamburgers and drank his Frosted Orange.

"You weren't at the party, were you?" Grace asked Kate.

"Briefly." Kate's tone was amused.

"How do y'all know each other?" Sam asked Kate.

Kate smiled. "Grace and Willy used to date in high school. How long did y'all go together?"

Willy put down his hamburger. "Three years."

Sam felt a drop of sweat trickle down inside his shirt as he realized he'd made love to Willy's old high-school sweetheart.

"We hadn't seen each other since high school, and we met again at Jessie's party last night," Grace said.

"And how do you and Sam know each other?" Kate asked.

"From the bookstore," Sam said a little too quickly.

"I sure am glad Sam was there last night." Grace rubbed her knee against Sam's under the table. "I never know what to do with myself at parties. He helped me get through last night."

"Sam's always been accommodating," Kate said.

"How 'bout fried pies all around?" Sam got up.

As he stood in line at the counter, he glanced back at their table. Kate and Grace talked while Willy devoured his mound of food. He couldn't get over the fact that he'd made love to Willy's girlfriend. He felt as if he'd made love to his best friend's wife or something.

"Take your order?" A tall woman scowled down at him from the gleaming counter.

"Four fried pies, please."

"Four pies!" she bellowed to the men and women scrambling behind her.

A few minutes later, when he risked another glance back at the table, Kate and Grace talked and laughed. He noticed them nod in his direction a couple of times.

"Mister, your pies." The tall woman handed him his

tray with four warm pies wrapped in wax paper. "Hey, where you going?"

"What?"

"You have to pay." She pointed to her open palm.

When Sam brought back the fried pies, Kate motioned him to hurry and sit down. "Guess what?"

"What?" He was sure she was about to say, We've talked it over and come to the conclusion that you're a real son of a bitch. He handed out the fried pies.

"Willy's moving in with Grace."

Grace beamed.

"I don't see what the big deal is." Willy bit into his fried pie.

"I think it's great," Kate said to Grace. "My brother needs a civilizing influence."

Willy rolled his eyes at Sam, but there was a hint of a smile on his lips.

Grace talked about all the rearranging she'd have to do in her apartment. Willy asked if she'd have room for his rock collection. "I don't go anywhere without my rocks."

Kate watched them with a melancholy smile.

The family at the table next to them had gotten up to leave. The little girls argued over who would help their baby brother put on his coat, an argument they resolved by each helping with a sleeve. The little girls watched with envy as their father picked up the baby, and as they started out the door, one of the girls tugged at her father's coat. "When will we big enough to carry him?"

"When he's too big to carry." Kate slid her half-eaten fried pie over to Willy.

Sam sat in the dark on his steps with his arm around Kate and wondered why happiness seemed a place just off the map. She leaned her head against his shoulder. She'd dug out one of his old flannel shirts and draped it over her blouse. A chilly breeze scattered leaves across the walk and made a soft, hopeless rustle. In the distance they heard the valiant efforts of a small high-school band trying to fill a football stadium with half-time music, a muted confusion of horns and a relentless bass drum. The neighbor's Siamese crept across the yard and froze when he saw Sam and Kate, as if startled to see them together again.

"Come here, kitty." Kate held her hand out.

The cat took a couple of tentative steps toward them.

"Don't encourage him." He'd felt sad ever since the Varsity, ever since he'd seen Willy and Grace together, not that he was jealous or thought they might not be good for each other. What bothered him was Grace's uncanny ability to appear at a crucial moment, making him wonder if love was less a matter of the heart and more a question of timing.

But even that wasn't what really bothered him. He was depressed because of a gesture—a simple, innocent gesture. In the middle of a conversation with Grace, Kate had rested her hand on his knee, in the way she used to when they were out someplace with other people. It was her way of signaling him that even though she was talking to someone else, she was really thinking about him, about getting home and being alone. It had been such a long time since she had rested her hand on his knee, and it made him want to have her home, but in that same instant he realized that they could never be as alone together as they used to be. Conspicuous even in its absence, the baby already intruded.

"What're you thinking?" Kate asked as the cat rubbed against her legs.

Sam shook his head.

"You don't have to want it," she said. "That would be asking too much."

He walked down the steps and out to the edge of

the yard. He stood looking back at his renovated house, at Kate sitting on the steps. Shouldn't this be everything he wanted? He walked back to her and sat down.

"I want to want it," he said.

There was a roar from the football game, a huge wave breaking blocks away.

"Lots of planes tonight." Kate pointed to a row of winking red lights that formed a diagonal line toward Hartsfield. "Look how close together they are. It's a wonder they don't crash."

"They just look close. They're miles apart."

There was another roar, the garbled announcer's voice and the crowd's distant cheer. He remembered how as a small boy he liked autumn evenings when those cheers floated through his open bedroom window.

"You slept with her, didn't you?" Kate asked, but her tone wasn't accusing. She sighed. "Maybe you should take me home now."

"You're leaving because I slept with her? Hell, you did a little more than that!"

There was a silence. The cat butted his head against Sam's hand. He gave in and stroked its back.

Kate pressed his hand. "Grace has nothing to do with it. I just want to go home."

"Then stay."

She sighed. "I haven't told you everything yet."

He sat up. "What's that supposed to mean? Twins?"

"I think we should do this one step at a time." She stood up. "Right now I just want to go home."

He kept Kate's taillights a couple of car lengths in front of him. He hadn't planned this. He'd taken her back to her car at the hospital, followed her out of the parking deck, saw her wave to him in her rearview mirror, and was about to turn on the expressway but didn't. He followed her, through downtown, through the gleaming, deserted business section, and into Reynoldstown, the dingy black section where people, mostly young men, gathered on street corners. Old men sat alone in the shadows of boarded-up buildings.

What was she doing driving through here at this time of night? He told himself it was a good thing he had followed her. What if she'd had a flat or run out of gas? This was no place to get stranded in the middle of the night.

She turned off a main street, taking a back street. There were fallen trees from the storm still on the side of the road, and garbage cans and debris still littered the streets. The city probably cleared these streets last. He wondered if Kate was out of her mind, driving these pitch-black streets in a neighborhood that had more murders per block than about any neighborhood in the country. He locked his doors. He kept some distance between her car and his, but not too much in case she needed him.

She slowed in front of a shabby little house as if to stop, seemed to change her mind, and sped away. He tried to keep up, but she disappeared around a corner and was gone. He drove around the block a couple of times, but there was no sign of her. He pulled over in front of a row of what appeared to be abandoned buildings except that in a couple a yellowish grimy light shone through the windows, indicating that somebody lived there. The sidewalk was strewn with limbs and garbage. He sat in the car, not knowing what to do. He was lost. More lost than he'd ever been in his life. He was in the deepest, darkest heart of where he had never expected to go.

He decided to get out and ask somebody directions. He walked up the sidewalk, picking his way over garbage-can lids and limbs. He stepped around a pair of legs that belonged to an old man who'd passed out against one of the buildings. At first, Sam thought he was dead, but the old man muttered something. He walked quickly on. He could already see the headlines in tomorrow's paper. Hell, his murder wouldn't even make headlines. He'd be buried deep in the paper.

It was very cold. The wind whipped his face. He hadn't dressed warmly enough, not expecting to have to walk anywhere tonight. The smell of woodsmoke settled over the neighborhood, making what lights there were look greasy. He passed by a couple of young men who couldn't have been over twenty. They smoked cigarettes and shifted from leg to leg, waiting on someone. They eyed him as he walked past, and at first he thought he'd just walk on, but then decided he'd have to ask somebody if he didn't intend to walk these streets all night.

"Excuse me."

"Are you Ray?" One of the men asked as the other dug into his pocket and pulled out a package wrapped in string.

Sam shook his head.

The man with the package quickly slid it back into his pocket.

"If you're not Ray, who the fuck are you, Jack?" The first man jabbed Sam's chest with his finger.

"I'm lost."

"Shiiit!" The second man shook his head. "He's probably a cop."

"Who the fuck are you, Jack?"

Sam expected a knife slipped cleanly between his ribs.

"I swear to God I'm lost," Sam said.

The first man turned to his friend. "The white boy is lost."

"Could you tell me how to get out of here?" Sam asked.

The two men looked at each other. "Study." They roared.

"That's right, Jack," said the first man. "Education is the only way out."

Giving up, he walked back toward the car, the men still laughing behind him. He was worried they might follow him, knowing he was lost. He was getting into his car when one of them yelled at him.

"Jack, take a left at the corner, then take the next right!"

"And get your white ass out of our neighborhood!"

They were still laughing at him when he pulled away from the curb. He drove up the street, wondering if they'd given wrong directions. But having nothing left to lose, he followed their directions and felt a tremendous wave of relief when he pulled onto Edgewood. He pulled over into a gas station and sat there wondering what that little nightmare of a detour had been all about. Had she known he followed her and gotten him lost on purpose? Had she tried to teach him a lesson? Or had she gotten lost herself? He reminded himself that Kate had an unshakable sense of direction. He firmly believed that she'd been a cartographer in another life.

Chapter Twelve

The next morning, Sam woke up with a strange sense of mission—to clean house. It was Saturday, his day off. So after a cup of coffee and glancing over the morning's headlines, he started in. All morning he swept, mopped, and scrubbed his way through the house, leaving a pungent trail of Comet, Lysol, and Mr. Clean. He even cleaned over doorways, under the sofa, along baseboards. Kate had always been adamant about cleaning where nobody ever looked. He got momentarily bogged down when he couldn't remember whether she dusted before she vacuumed or vacuumed before she dusted. Whichever way it was, she believed in it ardently.

Upstairs, his bedroom needed a lot of work. Mounds of clothes had to be sorted through, examined, and sniffed to determine their status. He threw dirty clothes into the hamper, then folded the clean clothes and put them away in the dresser drawers. He left a few drawers empty.

He had cleaned every room except one. He paused at the closed door of his study, turned the doorknob, and when he pushed it was greeted by the solemn smell of books. Everything was as he had left it, except deeper in dust. He shoved open a window to let in some air. An island of mold floated in a cup of coffee on his desk. There was a cobweb over the typewriter keys. He rolled up the yellowed piece of paper in the carriage, staring at a paragraph he'd stopped in mid-sentence. He ripped it out of the carriage and balled it up. He felt a rush of exhilaration.

245

He hurried out to the kitchen and came back with a handful of black garbage bags. He slid the stacks of unfinished manuscripts off his desk and into a garbage bag. He emptied all the desk drawers, which were filled with sheets of unfinished stories. He filled another three garbage bags with magazines he'd been meaning to read. He packed away all his books, even those on the bookshelves, and carried them up to the attic. He lifted down his photographs of writers and boxed them up, too. He found the dustcover for the old Underwood and shoved that and the desk into one corner. Then he dusted, scrubbed, and disinfected until there wasn't a surface that wasn't clean enough to eat off.

When he finished, he stood in the middle of the room, feeling giddy with all he'd thrown away.

He ate a quick lunch, then went out to the backyard, leaving the door open so he could hear if the phone rang. He cleared away fallen branches and dragged the limb that had landed on the toolshed out to the curb. He hammered out the dented roof of the toolshed and cleared more limbs that had fallen into the garden. He'd carried an armload out to the curb when Raymond and Bobby rode up on their bikes.

"How's it going, guys?"

"Raymond's Mama needs eggs." Bobby nodded that they were headed down to the convenience store.

"How'd y'all weather the storm?"

"A big tree fell in the backyard," Raymond said.

"Missed their house by that much." Bobby held his hands two feet apart.

Raymond shook his head. "It didn't come close. Mama said it's too bad Daddy's not around to cut it up."

"His daddy's dead." Bobby stuffed his hands into his jacket and leaned back on the seat of his bike.

"He knows," Raymond said impatiently.

Bobby cocked his head at Sam. "Are you and that lady getting back together?"

Raymond smacked Bobby on the shoulder with the back of his hand. "That's none of your business."

"You're the one who saw them sitting out here on the steps last night."

Raymond raked his hand down his face and shook his head.

"Kate was just visiting," Sam said. "She didn't stay."

"Raymond said he wishes y'all would get back together," Bobby said.

"Awww, Bobby!" Raymond rode his bike down the street.

"Now what'd I do?" Bobby yelled at Raymond, who was half a block away. "Hey, wait up." He pedaled after him.

As Sam watched them ride down the street, a deep melancholy stole over him, a sadness he'd put off all morning. Had he actually believed that waxing the kitchen floor would bring her back?

He was halfheartedly raking leaves in the front yard when the phone rang. He sprinted across the yard, leapt up the steps, and tore through the house to the kitchen, picking up the phone. "Hello?"

"Sam?" It was a woman's voice. "Are you okay? Why are you breathing so hard?"

"Rose." His heart sank when he realized it wasn't Kate.

"You're out of breath."

"I was out raking leaves."

Rose and Lamar wanted him to meet them for supper at José's. He thought about it for a minute. What if Kate called while he was away? He could leave his machine on. She might not leave a message. She might interpret his not being there as his having gone on with his life. She might not call at all, and he didn't know if he could stand an evening of sulking around in his clean, empty house.

"Sevenish?" Rose asked.

"That'll be fine."

It was only after he hung up that he began to wonder if Kate hadn't put Rose and Lamar up to it. He hadn't heard from them in weeks; why should they call today? It was too much of a coincidence. Kate had called them. It was her way of signaling she couldn't come back to him.

He didn't finish raking the leaves in the front yard. He just sat out on the steps, getting more depressed. Had he believed that by going to the hospital he'd get her to come back? She'd never come back. She'd called Rose and Lamar, asking that they tell him she couldn't see him anymore.

The afternoon sky had deepened toward evening; a cold breeze cut through the air. Up and down the street his neighbors finished clearing their yards, raking leaves into big piles at the curb. Bobby and Raymond passed by again, riding back up the street. Raymond carried a brown bag, which held the eggs. As he watched the boys turn in at Virginia's, he remembered last night. How afraid he was when he'd found himself lost on the back streets of Reynoldstown and what an ominous feeling he'd gotten when Kate slowed her car in front of that shabby little house.

He arrived at José's a little early. The mother seated him at a corner table, then said in a heavy Cuban accent, "María, she be right with you." She cast a disparaging glance to the other side of the restaurant, where her daughter talked on the pay phone, careful to keep her back to the tables so that no customer could catch her eye. In the kitchen a bell rang and rang as José yelled, "Pick up! Pick up!"

María leaned her forehead against the wall as she twisted the phone cord in her finger.

"María!"

She rolled her eyes toward the kitchen, said a few

more things into the receiver, hung up, then sauntered back, popping her gum.

Sam looked up from the menu every time someone came in. He drummed his fork on the table. When Rose and Lamar walked in, he hardly recognized them. Rose, with her swollen stomach, seemed so enlarged, and Lamar, whose immense presence usually crowded a room, seemed diminished somehow.

"When's it due?" Sam hugged Rose gingerly.

"I won't break." She hugged him hard.

"When's *she* due?" Lamar pulled out a chair for Rose.

"You got tested?" Sam asked her.

"We needed to know what color to paint the nursery." Lamar opened a menu.

"They recommend that women my age have a sonogram." Rose drank from her glass of water. "The baby's due in two weeks, but it could be anytime now."

"Any day we could be joined by this whole other person." Lamar shook his head in amazement. "You'd think that after Joey I'd be used to it."

"Where is Joey?" Sam asked.

"We were going to bring him," Rose said, "but Mama insisted that we let him stay at her house tonight."

"That's a switch." Sam remembered Rose's mother's vow never to baby-sit any grandchildren.

María strolled over to their table, popping gum. "A drink before dinner?"

"No alcohol in her condition." Lamar patted Rose's stomach.

"Coffee or tea?" María asked.

"No caffeine, either," he said. "She'll have apple juice, and I'll have a beer."

María lapsed into Spanish with Rose. "*Madre*" was one of the few words Sam recognized. The bell back in the kitchen rang furiously. "María! Order up!" She glanced over her shoulder and then sauntered back.

Rose reached across the table and put her hand on Sam's. "So how are you? We haven't seen you in a long time."

The last time he'd seen them was one night when they'd had him over to dinner with a work friend of Rose's, a psychologist. She was a willowy, dark-eyed woman who listened attentively, a little too attentively. When she left, she gave him her card and told him to call her, but he wasn't sure if she meant for a date or to set up an appointment.

He told them about Jessie's party, that he'd run into Kate and then found her in his kitchen. He told them about being held up at the bookstore the next day and going to the hospital last night to find Kate. He told them about the Varsity, that Willy was moving in with his old high-school sweetheart. He even told them he'd followed Kate through Reynoldstown and got lost. The events of the past couple of days just tumbled out of his mouth. Several times Rose and Lamar exchanged significant glances. He was sure they'd been sent here on a mission—to break it to him gently.

When he finished, there was an awkward moment when no one said anything. Rose and Lamar kept glancing at each other as if deciding who should tell him. Rose got a pained expression on her face.

"What is it?" Sam asked.

She clutched her stomach. "Whoa . . ."

Lamar leaned over and put his hand on her stomach. "The baby's kicking."

"Field goals." Rose breathed deeply.

A couple at the other table looked over.

"It's okay," Lamar said to them, but then looked at her. "Isn't it?"

Rose continued to breathe deeply, concentrating.

"It's not time, is it?" Lamar asked, a hint of panic in his voice.

The color came back to her face as she breathed more regularly. "No, it's not time." She put her hand over

Lamar's. She smiled at Sam. He guessed he must've had a curious expression on his face. "You can feel it if you want."

"That's okay."

She pressed his hand against her belly.

He felt something move under his hand. "There's something in there."

Lamar laughed. "We take these Lamaze classes for the hell of it."

María came back carrying their drinks on her tray.

"I ordered a beer for myself," Lamar said when she set an apple juice down by his place.

"Not good for the baby." María smiled at Rose.

"Wait a minute."

"Ready to order?" she asked Rose.

"The baby's kicking," Rose said to her.

María knelt down beside Rose and put her hand on her stomach. The women whispered to each other in Spanish. Sam imagined the baby with her ear pressed against her womb, listening to the melodic undulations of a foreign language.

The pay phone in the corner rang, but María's mother beat her to it. "Who?" the mother asked. "María, she is working. Call back next year." She hung up the phone.

María stood beside her mother, a stunned look on her face. "You have no right!" María yelled at her mother in English.

The mother yelled something back in Spanish.

María yelled something else in Spanish.

José appeared at the kitchen doorway, wearing an apron, his face covered with sweat. He pulled the arguing women into the kitchen. His voice joined theirs as bits of their fight flew back into the dining room through the flapping kitchen doors. Pots were thrown. A few more screams. Then silence.

"Either somebody's dead or it's resolved," Lamar said.

Rose was looking at Sam. She leaned over to him. "Kate asked us to meet you."

Lamar drank from his apple juice.

She sighed. "Neither of us feels comfortable doing this."

Lamar took another sip of juice.

"But under the circumstances . . ."

Sam threw up his hands. "I know, I know, I know." He sighed. "I'm just sorry y'all had to be the ones to do it. I know she wants me to stay away from her. I understand that now. I had no business going to the hospital, no business tailing her through Reynoldstown. When it's over, it's over!"

Lamar and Rose frowned at each other.

Lamar patted him on the back. "You've got it all wrong."

Rose sighed. "She wanted us to tell you not to feel obligated . . ."

"Because of her . . . condition." Lamar glanced at Rose's stomach.

"She didn't think it was fair of her to come to your house the other night," Rose said. "She feels she got herself into this and she should get herself out."

"You're kidding." Sam put his hand to his forehead. "I thought she'd asked y'all to be the wrecking crew."

Rose put her hand over his. "She thought it'd be easier if we told you. That way you wouldn't have to see her again."

"She wants you to know that you're off the hook," Lamar said.

"I want to be *on* the hook!"

The couple at the next table looked at him.

"I want to be on the fucking hook. And I don't care

who fucking knows it." He spoke to the couple next to them. They ignored him.

María and her mother came out of the kitchen laughing and patting each other on the back.

"They worked that out," Rose said.

María came up to the table. "Can I get you something else?"

"I'd like a cup of coffee," Lamar said.

María shook her head.

"You're out of coffee? Can't you make some?"

María reached down and patted Lamar's stomach. "Not good for the baby."

After saying good night to Rose and Lamar, Sam walked quickly back up through Little Five Points and down Euclid Avenue, having decided that as soon as he got home, he'd jump into his car and drive over to Maggie's to tell Kate he wanted her to move back in. Of course, the thought had gone through his mind that this had all been a kind of setup. That Kate had asked Rose and Lamar to tell him that she didn't expect him to want to be with her, knowing that he would react the opposite way. Or it might not have even been as deliberate as that, but a kind of subconscious manipulation on her part. He shrugged. What was so awful about that? At least she cared enough to manipulate him.

When he neared his house, he thought for a moment he'd had a little too much sangria. He saw double. Two Tempests parked in his driveway. As he came closer, he saw that while they were identical in shape, one was much shinier than the other, much more polished. He walked around it, saw the medical stickers on the windshield, and felt his whole world take an ominous turn. He saw lights on in the house that he hadn't left on. What was the doctor doing back here, in his house? Maybe he'd come back again with Kate? But then Kate had said she didn't want to have anything else to do with him. Maybe he was jealous? Maybe he wanted to ambush Sam? Why would he have parked in the driveway, making it obvious that he was inside? Sam thought about calling the police. What if Kate was with him? Or what if there was some other explanation? He'd feel foolish with all these blue lights pulling up in front of his house. Kate had never indicated that there was anything dangerous about the doctor. There must be some perfectly rational explanation why the doctor was in his house in the middle of the night. Even so, he unlocked the trunk of his car and lifted out the tire iron.

He crossed his lawn, stooping down in case the doctor watched at the window. He definitely felt someone watching him. He turned around to see Mrs. Smeak out on the sidewalk, squinting at him. She was taking Woofie for a late-night walk.

"It's me, Mrs. Smeak," he whispered across the lawn. "Sam Marshbanks." He waved the tire iron.

She hurried on up the sidewalk, glancing over her shoulder and dragging the snarling dog with her.

He crept around to the back of the house and stumbled over a stack of flowerpots Kate kept by the back door. He waited, and when he heard nothing from inside, picked his way over the shards of clay pots. The kitchen window was halfway open. The doctor must've crawled in there. Sam took out his keys and, as quietly as he could, unlocked the back door and eased it open. He stood in the unlighted kitchen to let his eyes adjust to the dark. He could hear somebody in the living room.

He tiptoed across the kitchen floor and cracked the door. In the living room, he saw a black man in a white coat on his knees in front of the couch, as if in the middle of a prayer. He had his back to Sam, so he couldn't make out his face. He removed the cushions from the couch and ran his hands between the cracks.

Sam stepped into the living room.

The man turned around. It was Horace Franklin, the doctor Kate had worked with, the doctor who'd saved Joey's life. Horace didn't seem all that surprised. He kept feeling in the cracks of the couch. "I lost my wallet," he said. "You haven't run across it, have you?" Then he noticed the tire iron in Sam's hand. He held up his hands. "Oh, hey, listen . . ." He stood up.

"What are you doing in my house?" Sam's voice shook.

Horace rubbed his neck. "I thought I lost my wallet the other night when Kate and I ran in here to get out of the storm. We huddled on this couch. . . ."

"I thought you might be a thief."

Horace nodded at the tire iron. "I figured you weren't changing a flat."

They stood there, just looking at each other.

"I don't appreciate strangers in my house," Sam said.

There was a knock at the front door. Through the front window they saw a police car. Sam opened the door to two policemen, one white and one black. "We had a report of a possible break-in," the white officer said.

"Break-in?" Sam guessed Mrs. Smeak must've mistaken him for a burglar. He paused and looked back at Horace. "There's been no break-in here, Officers."

"And the tire iron?" the black policeman asked.

Sam saw he still had the tire iron in his hand. "I was changing a flat."

The black policeman looked past Sam at Horace. "Friend of yours?"

"Friend of a friend," Sam said.

Both policemen gave Horace a long look, and then the white officer asked if Sam minded if they searched outside. "Sorry to have disturbed you," the black policeman said as they walked off into the yard, shining their flashlights in the shrubs.

"For a minute there I thought you were going to turn me in," Horace said as Sam shut the door.

"For a minute there I was." Sam tossed the tire iron into the corner.

"What for?"

"Stealing." Sam glared at him.

Horace nodded. Then he sighed again and started looking around at his feet. "I was sure I lost it here. I don't care about the money, but it's got my license, credit cards, my Social Security card, even my library card."

As much as Sam hated to admit it, there was something about Horace that he liked—a certain spaceyness. Horace was back down on his hands and knees, feeling for his wallet. He bumped his head on the coffee table. "Shit!" He rubbed his head.

Sam laughed.

Horace eyed him. "That's what you've been wanting to do to me with that tire iron."

"Want a beer?" Sam heard himself ask Horace.

He shook his head. "I'm on call."

"Coffee?" Sam wasn't sure why he was being hospitable, but he couldn't think of anything else to do.

Horace sat back on his heels. "If it's not too much trouble."

Sam headed for the kitchen. "All I have is instant."

Horace's voice echoed from underneath the couch. "Hey, Sam? Easy on the arsenic."

Sam's hand shook as he put the kettle on. Why hadn't she told him about Horace? Really told him? Certainly she wasn't ashamed that he was black. If anything, she'd be proud to be with a black man. She'd be proud that the baby was half-black. In fact, she might've fallen for Horace as a kind of self-imposed challenge. She worked with black people every day—many of them destitute with sick, malnourished babies. She'd always complained that there was only so much she could do. Maybe by having Horace's baby, a black baby, she'd found a new way to share in the responsibility.

On the other hand, what was charitable about having a wealthy doctor's baby? Which led Sam to the other, more painful conclusion that she'd loved Horace, maybe still did.

Sam and Horace sat on the porch steps, where Sam had sat with Kate just last night, and drank coffee. An awkwardness had settled between them.

"How is Joey?" The last time they'd seen one other had been when Joey had fallen.

"He's fine." It had been Horace who'd told Kate that Sam shouldn't feel guilty, that he'd done the right thing by carrying Joey over to Virginia's.

Sam noticed Horace's Tempest parked right behind his. "How many miles?"

"Almost 180,000." Horace sipped from his mug.

"Same engine?"

Horace nodded. "Doesn't even burn oil."

"You've taken good care of yours," Sam said. "Mine breaks down a lot."

"I know," Horace said.

Sam gave him a surprised look.

"I know all about you." He leaned his elbows on the steps. "Everywhere you went, everything you did. I couldn't take her anywhere without hearing about you." He rested his hand on Sam's shoulder. "Your favorite movie is *Never Cry Wolf*; you like your eggs over well. When you were a kid, a copperhead bit you on the leg." He glanced at Sam's chest. "You sleep in your shirt." Horace sipped his coffee. "You work in a bookstore, but you really want to be a writer." He shook his head. "To tell you the truth, I got sick of hearing about you."

There was a long pause as they both drank from their mugs.

"I don't think she should have the baby." Horace was luminescent in his white doctor's coat. He was a handsome man with quick eyes. "And it's not just because I don't want it, although I don't. I already have Letitia. Even if I see her only now and then, she's enough."

Sam remembered the fiery little girl they'd met in the Stone Mountain parking lot. "Why shouldn't she have it?" Sam asked.

"It'll be half black."

"Don't you think she can handle that?"

"Kate can handle anything." He checked his watch. "I've got to get back to the hospital in a minute."

"Why shouldn't she have it?" Sam wanted to know.

"She might be able to handle all the curious stares a white mother and a half-black child attract, but what about the kid? She can't be tough for the baby. The baby's going to be born into trouble. It'll inherit the worst of both worlds." He set his mug on the steps. "Believe me, I know."

The stillness was broken by a loud screech. Horace reached under his coat and turned down his beeper. "Can I use your phone?"

"Sure," Sam said. "It's in—" But he saw that Horace already knew where it was.

When Horace came back outside, he said there was a woman in labor at the hospital. He didn't seem in a particular hurry, though. "Thanks for the coffee," he said. "If you run across my wallet, give me a call."

Sam walked with him across the yard to his car. "Why did you tell me all that stuff about Kate?"

Horace stopped. "You might be able to talk her out of this baby. I could take care of everything. She wouldn't be in any danger." He checked his watch. "I have to go."

Horace got in the car and started to back out of the driveway, but Sam ran after him. "Hey!"

Horace stopped and leaned his head out of the window.

"What makes you think she'll listen to me?" Sam asked.

"She loves you, man." He backed on out of the driveway.

The next morning, when he opened his eyes, in the fleeting millisecond of waking he noticed brilliant yellow maple leaves scattered across his floor, like iridescent footprints left by some extraterrestrial that had tiptoed through his bedroom last night.

He remembered his real visitor. There was nothing otherworldly about Horace. Sam got out of bed and stood by the open window where the leaves had blown in overnight. He wore his button-down shirt from yesterday. He always dressed for bed by taking off his pants and sliding under the sheets.

He could feel the cool breeze on his legs. The maple outside his window had lost its leaves, and so had most of the trees in the neighborhood; their bare limbs looked like stress fractures against a blue sky.

He felt good, and this worried him, because at this point feeling good seemed unearned and out of place. He reminded himself what a humiliating past few days he'd had. He'd sneaked around a lot and fooled no one. As it turned out, he'd been the only one fooled. Not that he believed Kate intentionally deceived him about Horace, but she'd allowed him to fall victim to his own assumptions. But even so, as soon as he saw Horace, saw that he was black, he felt a kind of release. Now that the baby could not even appear to be Sam's, he was free to want it.

He was halfway dressed when he smelled coffee brewing. He thought the smell had wafted from next door; then he heard somebody downstairs. His heart skipped a beat. Hell, maybe Horace never left.

He hurried downstairs and found a half-full pot of coffee on the stove. The back door was open, and Willy sat on the steps, his back to Sam. He had a cup of coffee in his hands. "Willy?"

"Yo." He didn't turn around.

Sam poured himself some coffee and sat down beside him.

"I hope you don't mind company," Willy said in a groggy voice.

Sam thought he should go ahead and hang a Vacancy sign out front: Color TV, No Pool. "You're welcome here anytime. You know that."

"We got locked out of her apartment last night," Willy said, "And I couldn't very well take her back to Maggie's."

"You mean . . ."

"Morning." Grace stretched her arms and yawned through the screen.

Sam cooked a big breakfast. It felt good to cook for somebody again. Willy and Grace were both big eaters, which made it even more gratifying.

"Where'd y'all sleep last night?" He served their plates, then piled his plate full of grits. He felt hungry, too.

"In that back bedroom." Willy buttered a biscuit. "Smelled like Pine-Sol."

"I've been doing a little housecleaning." Sam peppered his grits.

"Who slept there last?" Grace dished a big mound of scrambled eggs onto her plate.

"I can't remember," Sam said.

"Whoever it was makes house calls." Grace got up

from the table and came back with a stethoscope around her neck. She came up behind Willy and slipped it under his shirt.

"That's cold," Willy said.

She listened with a worried look on her face.

"What is it?" Willy asked.

She shook her head, frowning. "A tender heart."

"Give me a break." Willy bit into a biscuit.

"That was in the back room?" Sam stared at the stethoscope. It must've been Horace's, but what were Kate and Horace doing in the bedroom?

"It was in the bed," Grace said.

"*Under* the bed," Willy said emphatically.

Sam picked up the stethoscope and put it to his ears.

"Want a heart to listen to?" Grace slipped it under her blouse, knowing right where her heart was.

He'd never listened through a stethoscope before. He'd had no idea that the heart was such a noisy organ: In the bed, under the bed, in the bed, under the bed. What difference did it make? He was too tired to be jealous.

"What's your diagnosis?" Grace watched Sam. Her hand still held the stethoscope over her heart.

"Nothing to worry about." He knew she'd forgiven him.

After breakfast Grace insisted on washing the dishes. Sam and Willy went out on the front porch and sat on the steps.

"I met Horace last night," Sam said.

"Good guy." Willy sounded relieved to have shifted to another subject. "He lent me his car for a whole week to deliver papers when the VW was in the shop."

They sat there for a while, not saying anything. "What do you think about Kate having Horace's baby?" Sam finally asked.

"It's her baby, too." He sipped from his cup.

Sam hadn't thought of it quite that way. Of course

it was Kate's baby, but on another level, because the baby wasn't Sam's, he'd thought of it as Horace's, as if Kate were nothing more than a vessel carrying somebody else's child.

"But what about the baby itself?" Sam remembered his conversation with Horace. "It won't be black or white."

"Nothing ever is."

The screen door slammed behind them as Grace came out and sat down between them.

"Thanks for doing the dishes," Sam said.

"What are y'all talking about?"

At this point, Sam wasn't sure who knew what. She probably knew about Kate's baby, but he decided to take his cue from Willy.

"Interracial kids," Willy said.

"I used to date a black guy," Grace said.

"Yeah?" Willy yawned and stretched his arms.

"We used to talk about what it'd be like to have kids."

"What'd you decide?" Sam asked.

"It'd be a nightmare," she said.

"Because of the racial stuff?" Sam asked.

"Because neither of us liked kids."

Grace and Sam laughed, but Willy looked concerned. "You don't like kids?"

"That was years ago." She put her arm around his shoulders.

Still, he looked worried. Watching him, Sam realized that Willy would be Kate's baby's uncle, a close blood relative. Without even trying he was closer to the baby than Sam could ever be.

"Say, Sam, what happened to your study?" Willy asked. "There's nothing in there anymore."

"There was nothing in there in the first place. There's just less of it now."

"So have you given up writing?" Grace asked. Sam was surprised she even knew he ever wrote.

"I've given up not writing." Sam petted the Siamese

from next door, which had come up and rubbed against his legs. "I put my typewriter in storage."

"What are you going to do with the room?" Willy asked.

The cat looked up at him, waiting for an answer.

Sam shrugged. "Thought it might make a decent nursery."

At noon Sam went into Brilliant's, having promised Jessie he'd work Sunday afternoon. He was happy to get away from his house before anyone else dropped by to shake him up. Besides, Willy and Grace might like to have the house to themselves.

Carl ran the register, Paula received in the back, and Sam shelved and straightened sections. It was a quiet afternoon at the bookstore for a change. He spent two hours rearranging the fiction section. So much had happened in the last few days. Everything was so momentous, fraught with repercussions, that it was relaxing to do something as inconsequential as alphabetizing. Every now and then the phone would ring at the register, and Carl would ask Sam to look up a book for a customer on the phone.

A couple of times he was tempted to call Kate, but he knew that if he talked to her over the phone, he'd sound funny. He'd end up telling her he'd met Horace, and then they'd have an awful conversation over the phone. If he was going to have an awful conversation, he'd rather have it in person.

It was late afternoon. Macon had come by to talk with Paula in the receiving room. Sam had just finished with the psychology section and was standing up at the register with Carl, who was telling him that he'd been fascinated with funerals ever since he'd watched John Kennedy's when he was a little boy.

"I'd never seen anything like it," he said. "I just planted myself in front of the TV. All those soldiers, all those people. Jackie taking that folded flag from his coffin." His tone was respectful. "Death was the most impressive thing I'd ever seen, and I knew then that somehow I'd make that my life." He sighed. "I can still hear the sad clop of those horses on the pavement."

When the phone rang, it startled them both. "Brilliant's." He paused. "Oh, hello," he said in a casual, friendly tone. "I'm sorry you got away at the party before we had a chance to talk—" But he must've been interrupted, because he nodded quickly. "Sure, sure, he's right here." He quickly handed the phone to Sam.

"Sam, thank God you're there." Kate's voice shook. "I was in a wreck. Not a wreck, really. I hit somebody— not a car but a person, or he ran into me. . . ."

"Kate, slow down." He tried to keep his voice calm. "Are you hurt?"

"No." There was a pause. Sam thought he heard a TV in the background. "I don't think he is, either, not bad, anyway. Sam, he just came out of nowhere. He ran right into the side of my car, and the sound of his body hitting the car . . ." She groaned.

"Where are you?"

"A woman's house. She let me use the phone."

"What street?"

"North Avenue," she said. "Right before you get to the hospital."

He knew exactly where she was. There was a stretch of poor black houses, the remnants of a larger black section that had been gouged out by a new expressway. "I'll be right there."

As Sam sped down North Avenue, he wondered what she was doing in that neighborhood at this time of day. Sometimes on Sundays she went into the hospital to catch up on paperwork. She'd probably been on her way home from the hospital.

He saw Kate's car first, and a small group of onlookers stood next to it. Then he saw Kate, who talked to an old man sitting on a wall, holding his elbow. Several people stood out on their porches, watching.

As he came up to Kate, he felt the eyes of the neighborhood on them. "Are you all right?" He looked her over.

"You beat the ambulance." Her face was pale.

"Ambulance?"

"For Mr. Walker here." She gestured to the old man. "I thought we should get somebody to check him out."

"I don't need an ambulance." The old man hadn't shaved in a couple of days. He wore pajamas, which were torn at the elbow he clutched.

"You don't know what you need." An old woman stood next to him, trying to examine his elbow.

"This is Mrs. Walker." Kate introduced Sam.

"Everything will be all right. Everything will be fine." She turned to her husband, her voice hardening. "Since when do you run out in the street without looking both ways?" Then to Kate and Sam: "Spent his life leaping without looking."

"I looked," the old man said. "She came out of nowhere." He pointed at Kate.

"Just dropped out of the sky," the old woman said facetiously. She turned to Kate and Sam. "Everything's fine."

"I don't want an ambulance," the old man said. "And I wouldn't have to have one if that woman hadn't been speeding."

"This nice lady wasn't speeding," Mrs. Walker said. "I saw what happened with my own eyes. You were talking to Jimmy, who had pulled up across the street in his pickup, and when you finished, you ran right out into the street without looking and ran into the side of her car."

Mr. Walker lowered his head, mumbling. "She speeded."

"One more word like that"—Mrs. Walker shoved her fist in his face—"and one ambulance won't be enough to take back all the pieces."

Sam took Kate by the elbow and guided her over to the car. There was a slight dent in the driver's door, and the glass in the rearview mirror was cracked. He lowered his voice. "What, exactly, happened?"

"Just like she said. I wasn't speeding. He didn't want me to call an ambulance or the police."

"You called the police, too? That's good," he said. "For insurance sake. Did anybody else see what happened?"

"When I first hit him, I got out and asked the man in the pickup if he saw what happened. He stepped down out of his truck and yelled, 'Hell, yeah, I saw what happened. You hit him! Pow, just like that! You hit him!' "

"Son of a bitch," Sam muttered.

"Oh, Sam, it was a sickening sound."

"Anybody else see it?"

"She saw." She nodded toward a woman who sat on her front porch, watching. "She was the one who let me use her phone. She saw him run out in front of my car, but she said she couldn't get involved."

A siren sounded in the distance. More people came out on their porches. Children rode their bikes up and down the sidewalk, looking at Mr. Walker, the dented car, and the two white people.

"Why do they have their sirens on?" Mr. Walker complained as the ambulance pulled up. "Nobody's dying."

The medics hopped out of the ambulance and, after asking Mr. Walker a few questions, examined his elbow, then led him over to the ambulance and sat him down inside.

"I hope he's okay," Kate said.

A police car pulled up behind the ambulance; its

flashing lights warned oncoming cars. The policeman took statements from Kate and Mr. Walker, told Kate she could get a copy of them at the courthouse, and then got back into his car and drove off. By now most people had gone back inside.

One of the medics came over to Kate. "I understand you were the driver. Maybe we should check you over, too."

"Is Mr. Walker all right?"

"Just a bad bruise, but we're going to take him in for X rays."

"Let them check you," Sam said, "especially in your condition."

She gave a big sigh and then allowed the medic to lead her off to the ambulance.

Mrs. Walker came up to Sam. "I'm sorry about all this. Maybe Ralph will learn from this. Maybe he'll look next time. Ralph and I have been through a lot together. I'd hate to lose him for such a silly thing as not looking."

"The medic said his arm is just bruised."

"And his ego." She smiled. "I hope your wife is all right. Don't let her feel bad about something that wasn't her fault."

"I won't." He decided to let the woman's assumption that they were married go by. Now was no time for technicalities.

"Take her home and take good care of her," Mrs. Walker said.

Kate was in the ambulance a long time. He began to worry. What if it had hurt the baby? Cars slowed as drivers craned to see what had happened.

He was relieved when the medics helped her down out of the ambulance. "What took so long?"

"Mr. Walker started talking to me," she said. "He apologized and said he knew I wasn't speeding."

"That sounds more like my Ralph." Mrs. Walker headed over toward the ambulance.

"Mrs. Walker?" the medic called. "We're about to take your husband downtown for X rays. Do you want to ride with us?"

"No, she don't," a voice said from within the ambulance.

Mrs. Walker climbed into the ambulance. As the medics shut the door, they heard her say, "I'm going to get them to X-ray that head of yours, too."

The ambulance pulled away; everyone else had gone back inside, leaving Kate and Sam on the sidewalk alone.

"Thanks for coming." She pressed her hand against his chest. "You were the first person I thought to call. I just found myself dialing your number." She sighed. "I feel bad, though." She sat down on the wall, looking into her hands.

He sat beside her, putting his arm around her shoulders. "But it wasn't your fault."

She looked up at him. "I only call you when I need you."

"At least you call me."

They sat on the wall a little while longer. The children on their bikes circled in the street, waiting for something else to happen.

"I was on my way home from the hospital," she said. "I'd just gone by Rose's room to see how she was doing."

"Rose!"

"She'd started having contractions close together, so Lamar brought her in. The doctor thought it was a false alarm but decided to watch her for a while."

"I just had dinner with them last night."

"I had a lot on my mind when I was driving home. If I'd been more observant . . ."

He lifted her chin with his finger. "A man ran out in front of you. There was nothing you could do."

They looked up at the darkening houses, single- and double-room shacks balanced on bricks. All his life Sam had passed by such houses, simply assuming their presence in the landscape. Only recently had he begun to understand that the lives within those flimsy shelters were not a means to his own edification. There was nothing token about the pain that whipped through those uninsulated walls.

She sighed. "Now what?"

He helped her stand, then walked her over to his car. "Mrs. Walker said I'm supposed to take care of you."

"How do you propose to do that?"

He opened the door and sat her down inside. "Take you someplace."

"Where?"

"We'll know when we get there." He closed the car door. As he walked around to the other side, he looked up at one of the houses. A yellow light shone in the window. A single face, a child's, stared out at him, then disappeared behind a curtain.

In the twilight, traffic was light. The expressway flowed easily through the city, and Sam felt as if he and Kate were riding a smooth river of clean time. When it was uncrowded, he appreciated the expressway, its wideness, its directness, and its singularity of purpose—to get there. He wasn't sure why he'd gotten on the expressway, but the longer he drove Kate around, the longer he would have her company. She didn't seem to mind. She sang along with the radio, an old Jackson Browne song about "seven women on my mind." He liked when she sang along with the radio, that she felt free enough to be mindless with him. It made him feel less obligated. The talent of living together wasn't so much to keep the other person entertained but to entertain oneself in the comfort of the other's company.

"Rose could be having it right now," she said.

"We could run by the hospital."

"We'd be in the way. I'll call when we get somewhere."

At the crest of a hill, he saw the expressway wind ahead of them, as if he looked down into a river valley. The road would disappear behind a skyscraper or a billboard or a bridge, only to reappear again and again, playing hide-and-seek in a too new landscape, until in the far distance it curved to the right and emptied into a pink bloom of nail-polish sky.

"Do you like Atlanta?" He gripped the steering wheel.

She looked over at the skyline. "It's not a bad place to live, but I wouldn't want to visit."

"What if you had a chance to live somewhere else?" He felt her look at him. "Someplace smaller. Someplace that wouldn't be so much work."

"I'd need a reason."

He kept to the middle lane so that cars could enter the expressway on the right and pass on the left. "What kind of reason?"

"Good enough to leave my job."

"Don't most places have at least one neonatal unit?"

"Good enough to leave my family. Good enough to leave everything I know and make someplace else home."

A tractor-trailer pulled up behind them and flashed its lights. Sam pulled over to let it pass. "But if the reason was good enough?"

She looked out the window. "Then I would think about it."

"You'd just think about it?"

"Sam, how can I say what I'd do if I don't even know why I'm supposed to do it?"

"I was speaking hypothetically."

She nodded. "I've made enough hypothetical moves."

Sam and Kate rode for some time without talking. The expressway was empty. They had all four lanes to themselves. It made him feel singled out. He thought about the other night when he sneaked into the nursery and found himself alone with all those babies.

"I talked to Horace last night," he said. "He was in the house when I got back from supper with Rose and Lamar. He said he'd lost his wallet."

She leaned her head against the dashboard. "Shit."

He swerved to miss a peeled retread that flapped like a struck animal in the middle of the expressway. "Don't you have any faith in me?"

Kate stared out the window at a billboard of a TV news team that towered just off the expressway. A white anchorman and a black anchorwoman loomed over outbound traffic. "I planned to tell you."

"Didn't you think I could handle it?"

"I didn't know if I could handle you not handling it," she said quietly.

"You're begging the question."

"That's not what I beg."

As they rode along in silence, he thought how the expressway was in a state of perpetual construction. Overnight it might widen or narrow; a whole exit might disappear and reappear half a mile down, as if it had drifted. "It doesn't matter how I found out." He reached across the seat for her hand. "I would've come to the same decision."

She threw up her hands. "That's why I didn't tell you everything at first. I hoped you'd get so used to the idea of a baby that even when you found out, you'd be too in love with it for Horace to make a difference."

A police car's lights flashed in his rearview mirror. Sam began to pull over, but instead of following him, the police car passed, its lights echoed blue against the intricate scaffolding of an overpass under construction.

"Answer this one question. Do you love Horace?"

"No."

"Did you?"

"You said one question." She paused. "I'm not sure."

"Then why have his baby?"

"It's there to have."

"But isn't it going to be hard to raise a black baby? For you and the baby?"

She nodded to herself. "I expect it to be very hard. But the difference between you and me is that I prefer hard things to nothing at all."

"Have you been talking to Virginia?"

She smiled slightly as she traced "Wash Me" on the dashboard.

They drove along the edge of the airport, which sprang up out of the featureless countryside like a small, sleek city. "After you left," he said, "I used to drive out here sometimes and watch families reunite."

They rode along in silence.

"Are you hungry?" he finally asked.

She shrugged.

"Want to eat someplace?"

"Maybe you should take me home." She sighed. "I think this is too fast. We can't just be apart and then together again. I need a transition."

"We could order appetizers."

She smiled.

"What about the Rainbow?"

"You're driving."

He felt his heart lighten as he looked for an exit where he could turn around.

He sat across from Kate in their usual booth and watched her finger an old tear in the vinyl seat.

Leila hurried past with a trayload of food. "I'll be right with y'all."

"I hope they never fix this place up," Kate said.

"They talk about remodeling," he said.

At night the Rainbow buzzed with families. Mothers and fathers recounted their days to each other, children played under the tables, and babies, locked in their highchairs, squealed with a sense of participation. The Rainbow at night was more festive, more open. There was something unifying about having made it through the day. Even so, Sam preferred the drowsy privacy of early mornings at the Rainbow, when yawning workmen huddled at the counter.

Sam thought about his last breakfast with Kate here, on a morning that seemed years ago. There had been no ill omens. The eggs weren't runny, the biscuits hadn't been burned, and nothing in the newspaper had been especially foreboding, and still, by the next week, he ordered breakfast alone.

"Is it cold out, Sam?" Leila asked.

"It's getting there." He'd gotten to know Leila pretty well. She'd been one of the few constants in Kate's absence. "Leila, this is Kate. Kate, Leila."

"Hi," Kate said.

"I told Sam I don't envy your job," Leila said.

"Leila's daughter was premature," Sam explained, embarrassed to have Kate find out he'd talked about her to someone she didn't know.

"She had a lung infection," Leila said. "For a while they didn't think she'd make it. Every day I visited the nursery knowing it could be the last time I'd see her alive."

"That's hard," Kate said.

"But she pulled through." Leila slid her pad out of her apron. "Now she's sixteen. She just got her license, and every time she walks out the door I say to myself, This is the last time I'll see her alive." She flipped open her pad and slid a pencil from behind her ear. "Why do you suppose we parents are so quick to kill off our kids?" She wrote something on her pad. "What can I get y'all?"

After they ordered, Sam still felt a little embarrassed. "I told her a little about you."

"She's nice." She fingered the tear; her mind was on something else. "Do you have a couple of quarters?"

"Who are you calling?" He dug in his pockets.

"The hospital, to see if I can find out something about Rose and Mr. Walker."

"He just got scratched up. He's okay."

"I *hit* the man. I feel responsible."

"*He* ran into *your* car."

"I want to see how he is." She got up.

From where he sat he could see her talk at the pay phone by the rest rooms. She was probably talking to Lamar at the hospital. He wondered what it would be like when Kate's baby actually came. Who would be there with her? Horace had already balked. Willy would certainly be there as much as he could be anywhere, but even Willy couldn't give her what she'd need.

Leila filled his coffee cup.

He touched the rim of his cup. "I thought you just worked breakfast and lunch?"

"I have a double shift for a couple of weeks," she said. "Nate started football and needs a decent uniform, and Crystal wants to take up the guitar. Have you priced guitars lately?"

"Not lately." He saw Kate was still at the pay phone, dialing another number.

"She might have to settle for a kazoo." Leila headed back to the kitchen.

He knew Leila's children never had to settle for anything. Leila had already done all the compromising.

When Kate came back to the booth, she sat down and took a sip of coffee. She grinned. "Her name is Sarah. She's seven pounds."

Leila brought their food to the table.

"A good friend of ours just had a baby," Sam told Leila.

"No home should be without one." Leila set the tray down. "Who has the vegetable plate?"

After Leila served their food and headed back to the kitchen, Kate said she'd also talked to Mrs. Walker.

"How is Mr. Walker?" He cut into his potato.

"He had a couple of stitches." She peppered her green beans. "When the doctor asked how it happened, he told him Mrs. Walker hit him with a garden rake, and when Mrs. Walker tried to tell the doctor what really happened, Mr. Walker took her aside and said, 'You want him to find out I did this to myself?' "

"Why was he in his pajamas?" The question had just occurred to him.

"Mrs. Walker said he was supposed to be in bed with a cold." She mashed a pat of butter into her potato.

"What was he doing talking to that guy in the pickup?"

"Collecting on a bet," she said. "Mrs. Walker said he'd run across eight lanes of traffic at rush hour if somebody on the other side owed him something."

Sam looked down at his coffee. "You owe me something."

"I thought we were talking about Mr. Walker." She ate a forkful of apple sauce.

"We never talk about what we're talking about."

She wiped her mouth with her napkin. "What do I owe you?"

He leaned across the table. "The benefit of the doubt."

Kate looked beyond him, out the window at a neon sign that feebly flickered Rainbow. "I couldn't stand for you to leave me."

Leila came over to fill their coffee cups. "How's everything?"

"Fine," Sam said. "Real good."

Leila glanced at Kate, who still stared off into space. She turned to Sam. "Let me know if you need anything."

He watched Leila's slender figure maneuver easily between the tables as she filled coffee cups and checked on customers. He reached across the table for Kate's hand.

She gave him a searching look.

"I won't leave you," he said.

"Will we be happy?"

"Maybe we've been through the worst part. What's hard about being happy is figuring out why you're not."

"Don't be clever."

He gripped her hand. "Then marry me."

"Jesus, Sam."

"Marry me."

A little boy in the booth behind Kate stood and looked at Sam.

"Kate, please."

The little boy still stared over Kate's shoulder right at him.

"Will you marry me, Kate?"

The little boy's head vanished. He'd apparently been yanked by his mother, whom they heard say, "Sit straight in your chair, young man, and tend to your own business."

Leila came back to their table. "Could I interest y'all in some peach cobbler?"

Kate smiled at Leila. "I'd love some."

Sam sensed that somehow a chance had gotten away. "I don't care for any." He was crestfallen. He felt like an idiot. Why had he asked her that way, springing it on her as they do in the movies? What a lousy way to propose, to try to humiliate somebody into saying yes.

"Sam?" Kate said.

"I feel like an idiot." By asking her, he'd given up that last piece of himself he'd held back.

"Weren't you just saying how hard it's going to be

to have a black child? It's one thing to be all magnanimous now, but you'll have to live with this for the rest of your life." She slid over to his side of the booth and put her arm around him. "What about in three or four months when I start to show? People will assume you're the father."

"Let them."

"What about when I have it and we go places and people watch us? They'll know you're not the father."

"Or that you're not the mother."

The little boy in the other booth raised his head again and stared at them.

"Hello," Kate said.

But before the little boy had a chance to reply, he was yanked back down by his mother. "You shouldn't stare at people while they eat."

"They're not eating," he whispered.

There was a pause. "What are they doing?" the mother whispered.

Leila brought a steaming bowl of peach cobbler and set it down in front of Kate.

"That looks real good," Sam said.

"You want me to bring you one?" Leila asked.

"You can have some of mine." Kate slid the bowl toward him. "Or do you want one of your own?"

"Someday." He lifted a spoonful of cobbler into her mouth.